FIC
DAV

Davies, Stevie.

Four dreamers and
  Emily.

C1997

$21.95

TEMPLE CITY 628

FOUR DREAMERS AND EMILY

STEVIE DAVIES

FOUR DREAMERS AND EMILY

St. Martin's Press ★ New York

Library of Congress Cataloging-in-Publication Data

Davies, Stevie.
    Four dreamers and Emily / Stevie Davies.
        p.   cm.
    ISBN 0-312-16844-6
    1. Brontë, Emily, 1818–1848—Appreciation—Fiction.
I. Title.
PR6054.A89152F6   1997
823'.914—dc21   97-16648
                                                                CIP

First published in Great Britain by The Women's Press Ltd

First U.S. Edition: September 1997

10   9   8   7   6   5   4   3   2   1

For Ruth Smith,
dear fellow-pilgrim

Where do we find ourselves? In a series, of which we do not know the extremes, and believe that it has none. We wake and find ourselves on a stair: there are stairs below us, many a one, which go upward and out of sight . . . Sleep lingers all our lifetime about our eyes, as night hovers all day in the boughs of the fir-tree. All things swim and glitter. Our life is not so much threatened as our perception . . .

Dream delivers us to dream, and there is no end to illusion.

Ralph Waldo Emerson

FOUR DREAMERS AND EMILY

Prelude

It is as if the glassy brook
Should image still its willows fair,
Though years ago the woodman's stroke
Laid low in dust their gleaming hair.

'My dear girl, you've lost a page. Your book is absolutely falling to pieces. There, look – over there – another page come adrift. Dear, oh dear. Let me buy you another, dear.'

Eileen James' paperback copy of *Wuthering Heights*, which she was about to pack for Brussels, snowed pages. Its spine had broken long ago and she generally held together its disintegrated integrity with a rubber band which however had on this occasion snapped. She restored the scattered pages in their correct order.

'No, mother, don't fuss; really, it's fine. I like this copy.'

'But it's all in bits.'

'Yes, but I'm fond of it – I've always had it – and I couldn't be doing with a new one. It wouldn't be the same at all.'

'Another page over there.' Muriel jabbed with her stick at a stray sheet by the coal scuttle. 'Come on, let me give you the money. How much do books cost these days?' She had not been out of the house for over a decade and a half.

'Mother, I've got money, I can afford a new copy if I want it. But I don't.'

Eileen was sixty-three, her mother ninety-two. The relationship worked because Eileen was loyal and Muriel, though for long seasons resident in another world, loving.

'I think I've left my purse in the freezer, dear. Would you mind just getting it out when you're going past.'

'Yes, of course . . . It's not in the freezer, Mum,' she shouted from the kitchen.

'What isn't, dear?'

'Your purse.'

'Well, I should hope not. What would my purse be doing in the freezer? . . . Excuse me for not getting up to curtsy, ma'am – Eileen, it's the Queen Mother! – my hips are not what they were and I'm considered too antiquated to have them replaced . . . but do sit down, mind the cats . . . how are your dear daughters these days? I hope Elizabeth's over her nasty cold . . .?'

The voice faded as Eileen climbed the stairs and stowed *Wuthering Heights, Jane Eyre* and *Villette* in the case, amongst her dingy cotton underwear. She would no more have gone away without them than she could have left behind her toothbrush and face flannel.

Sharon Mitchell cleared away Marianne Pendlebury's cup. Marianne, whose book lay open on her lap, had not been reading – just staring out of the window in abstraction, tapping her upper lip with her forefinger, the pane reflected in her glasses.

'Hello, Sharon, how are you?'

Amongst the staff, Marianne was unique not only for noticing that Sharon was human but for calling her by her name. Sharon, who had overheard Marianne's colleagues calling her 'a dead loss', had a soft spot for this friendly, dowdy woman. She'd trodden hard on the foot of the geezer who'd said the nettling words and, as there were fourteen stone of her, he'd felt the weight of her protest.

'I'm okay.' She dawdled, to prolong the contact. 'What you reading?'

'Oh—' Marianne coloured up. It was like being caught narcissistically smirking at your own face in a mirror. 'It's actually a book I wrote, years ago, on Emily Brontë — I'd not looked at it for ages, and opening it brought back all sorts of memories — but look how yellow all the pages have gone round the edges. Gave me quite a turn. You wouldn't think it was published just nine years ago.'

'Can't of been very good paper, can it, if it went mouldy like that so soon,' said Sharon practically.

'I think you're right, Sharon — that must be it. Cheap paper.' Some hint of condescension in the tone of 'I think you're right' (as if it came as a surprise that a nineteen-year-old waitress could hit on the obvious) faintly irked Sharon but she did not show it. Instead she said, 'It must be great to of written a book.'

'Yes . . . it was. Once.'

Sharon had read *Jane Eyre* and seen the film of *Wuthering Heights*. She thought of mentioning this but for some reason shied away.

'Well, back to work,' she said. A queue had formed at the counter. Marianne watched her plod away. She was a huge girl, a moving mountain.

Marianne had been reflecting upon the person she had been when she wrote her Emily book: a questing, burning intelligence searching for a way to know her self and her world through reading. So dreamy that she'd once banged into a plate-glass bookshop door and given herself a black eye and bruised nose. She'd roamed the moor above Haworth looking for Emily in a high wind; convinced herself she heard the swish of vanished skirts above the song of the wind through striding electricity pylons. Charged home and wrote it all down: the mystery, the tonic air, the purple horizons of her infatuation.

Where had that spirit gone? She was visited by the ghost of her young self rising from its interment in a prematurely musty book. Three young children, a mortgaged income, a querulous child-minder and an increasingly resentful husband chased the spirit into the past.

She looked up now and saw the eyes of Sharon Mitchell far across the common room staring out from behind the counter. Marianne waved but Sharon was not looking at her; rather beyond and through her.

Timothy Whitty dozed off, his book open in his lap. The book was a Folio Society volume of Emily's poetry, which he couldn't afford on his pension but he treated himself by budgeting because he loved Emily and, having been a printer in his time, prized beautifully bound books on fine, grainy paper with antiquarian print which accorded to each word its fullest value and meaning. Tatty second-hand Penguins and Everymans he owned but did not cherish. To him a book was more than the sum of its words, for he tended to idolatry.

He had sent a copy of this Folio volume to his unseen friend, Marianne Pendlebury, having ascertained that she did not already possess the edition. Her letters had kept him alive, so it seemed, throughout the winter of his widowhood. Now, when he read his familiar Folio *Poems*, it gave him an achingly sweet sensation because he knew that Marianne would read them in exactly the same text. Her eye would dwell on the identical page as it took in to her mind the same lines. The poems would be the space where their spirits met and mingled. He would become Marianne and she Timothy as their minds were inhabited by the one spirit.

The only obstacle to this ideal meeting seemed to be timing. He might be reading while she peeled a carrot. But he brushed aside this impediment as unworthy. He read on.

But he kept falling asleep by day because he couldn't sleep at night, and when he awoke, the poem on the page was drained of all significance. As if to intimate impending blindness, dusk was beginning to fall and had greyed the paper. Failing light threw his holy objects – his Venus figurines, ankhs and his dead wife's oil paintings of streets in starlight, trees in moonlight – into shadow. Marianne fled away like a perished daydream as he struggled up to switch on the light, and only his present state of physical decay and the fearful emptiness of the interior, void of Joanna, carried any reality.

The expensive book slid to the floor and lay there, splayed and dishevelled.

Chapter 1

Sleep brings no rest to me;
The shadows of the dead
My waking eyes may never see
Surround my bed.

There she was again. The figure of a woman. Emily Brontë by the bookcase.

It had taken so long to achieve sleep. Head and shoulders raised on pillows at one end because of lung-congestion and legs propped up because of the swelling at the other end, sleep was inevitably hard-come-by. Timothy tried to be philosophical. He said a mantra . . . imagined a candle-flame . . . a fit of coughing seized him. When it subsided, he tried again with the candle-flame.

The candle-flame began to list and curl; as it tilted left-wards, he allowed himself to capsize with the leaning flame, his mind curving sideways: the flame dilated, then dimmed. Joanna was his last thought. Jojo who was not here. Would never be here again. He let her go; the flame went out; he slept.

Convulsions of coughing awoke him from some deep crimson dream. Hoisting himself on his elbows, he fought for air. Timothy stood aside from Timothy's body and coolly

7

pondered whether this was finally the end. For perhaps twenty minutes the coughing persisted.

Sipping water and squinting at the clock, he registered with disappointment that it was only three in the morning. Only two hours' sleep, and that might be it for the night. His dentures grinned in their beaker. The cabinet was covered with medication, methodically arranged by his sister Margaret. She gave practical help but no sustenance. It was understood between them that she would drive over from Altrincham twice a week and perform whatever tasks he had not succeeded in doing – cleaning, bringing in coal, shopping. But that it went no further than that and he wasn't to ask for more. He understood this. She had her life to lead; and had always been a private, matter-of-fact person. Her manner was brisk, cheery. Margaret never complained of her arthritis but he always made sure to enquire. She would sit down after her labours and frown out of the cottage windows over her teacup at the stern beauty of the landscape; then shoot him a querying look, and, though she never spoke the accompanying thought, the thought was this:

'Were you and Joanna stark staring mad, or what, to sell up and come and live up here in this howling draught at the end of your days?'

They had retired to Hayfield for the walking and the views, the brilliant air that shone with cold and iced their eyes with light; the breasts of the hills intimating the gentleness of a mother-country. And still this sense of blessedness returned to haunt him on good days when he might shamble out with his stick round towards Little Hayfield, but the beauty was all coloured by his mourning; or rather, it coloured his mourning. His bereavement was tender-green as the valley pastures and purple and scarlet as the heather and bilberry. For Joanna had begun to die almost as soon as they'd installed themselves in the terrace. In the full vigour of her sixty-sixth year.

With so much go in her.

Died singing and told him to marry again. (Nothing, she believed, and bracingly told him, was as pathetic as a widower.)

Now the village seemed a trap. It was all steep hills and cobbles; the cold in the stone-flagged cottage could be perishing, the neighbours surly. Margaret once mentioned an old people's home.

'I know of one where there's ever such an artistic matron,' she said. 'She knows whole chunks of *Antony and Cleopatra* off by heart. And you'd be allowed to smoke your pipe in the billiard room. There's a billiard room, you see, for the gentlemen.'

Margaret had evidently thought this mixture of culture, individual liberty and concern to foster virility would be a speaking inducement to Timothy to abandon his eyrie. She had always previously slighted his literary interests as effeminate: 'feet-off-the-ground, my brother'. Timothy wheezed that, no, he could manage fine where he was, and if it was too much for her coming in, he'd be glad to pay someone. Margaret raised her eyebrows and said no more.

When she'd gone, he was invaded by images of a kinky nursing home whose matron greeted her old men from the billiard room with 'O infinite virtue, com'st thou smiling from/The world's great snare uncaught'; confided 'Eternity was in our lips and eyes' as she changed the catheter bag, and held an asp to her bared breast over breakfast.

Over his dead body would he be put away in a home, however arty-farty. He'd rather die on the mountainside of frostbite. These rebellious thoughts put spirit in him.

He'd lost his voice when Jojo died. A very odd symptom.

Now he was permanently hoarse and when he spoke a kind of rasping whisper came out. The doctor said he'd overstrained his heart, lugging his wife about in her final illness. That accounted for the fluid in his lungs and ankles. He didn't regret all the effort he'd put into caring for Jojo, not for a minute, but he did wish someone had warned him in time that you could strain your heart; for now it was a damned nuisance. He wanted to get out and about. He wanted to live. Prospects did not seem wonderful but he'd always possessed a reserve of optimism, initiative, and the fund was not entirely drained.

Books lined the walls; books stood in dusty piles against the shelves. Books crammed a wardrobe and sometimes pitched out when you opened it. The house would not hold all the books they'd owned, so he'd had to sell off a job lot to a second-hand bookseller, bringing in a thousand pounds. Much of their capital had now gone, for they only had his state pension to live on, and illness, they found, was an expensive business: a luxury, Joanna said. An extra we can't afford.

She had lived without a left breast for thirteen years. She had been strong, and brave, and proud.

He wasn't strong, or brave, or proud. He was sorry for himself in a way she'd never have permitted. He longed for her to come and hector him back to health. He sat in the silence of his loneliness at the front window with cold hands.

Sleep would have helped him make progress – uninterrupted sleep. But almost as soon as he nodded off, he'd cough himself to consciousness, awakening several times a night to the concussive shock of Jojo's desertion. It was as if a voice awaited him with the news, 'By the way, your wife does not exist.'

But the mind . . . or the body . . . played strange tricks. For there she was again . . . Emily Brontë, by the bookcase.

He'd coughed till he thought he'd burst a blood vessel. Sagging back on the pillow, he became aware of a breathing that was not his breathing. It soughed all around as if the walls respired. At first he'd not located her. The streetlamp outside his window cast a question mark of reflected light against the curved brass stem and glass bowl of the simulation oil lamp. It streaked the obscure wall with a line of coded patternings. Blurs of shadow deepened to skeins of darker shade and areas of pitch black, the shadows of shadows. Then revelatory car-lights rushed up like twin suns and raked the room like something bursting through from the outside to the interior. For a long moment Jojo's cello became luminous, with a pale spiritual gleam upon the generous curves of its body. He had manhandled it out of the case earlier that day and held that lifeless chamber in his arms, between his legs, wetting its cool wood with tears, but lacked strength to replace it. The case lay gaping open like a coffin.

The disturbing lights roared off up the road, leaving a tremor, a vibration in the penetrated room, an unease in his being, that caused the walls to tilt inwards, the light-hanging to quiver. But she stood still in the rocking room, leaning slightly backwards, her hands clasped in front of her, apparently studying the favourite books he kept on the top shelf of his desk bookcase: the Folio Society volumes of her own works and those of her sisters.

'Emily,' he croaked. '*Emily.*'

The person turned in his direction. The floor slid aslant but she stood firm. Neither smiling nor greeting him, Emily looked at a point several inches to the left of him with such alert attention that his eyes involuntarily swivelled sideways to catch what she saw. Blank wall. When he turned back, he had the impression that she had used his distraction to snatch a look at him. She seemed to have moved a step forward; and frozen.

So thin. She was horribly thin, he saw: as thin almost as he was himself.

But memo: she had a bosom. He tried to notice other details to remember – the full, leg-o'-mutton sleeves of her dress stood out against the orange light of the streetlamp outside his bedroom windows. Her skirts were neither stiff nor full but hung limp from her waist. There was an impression of dowdiness, a homespun person who patched her own clothes when she could be bothered . . . for there was a hole, he perceived, in the black shawl draped round her shoulders. A scruffy ghost; a tall ghost. Her hair . . . not tied into a prim Victorian bun, but cropped short. It gave her an urchin look.

Most important: has bosom.

Jojo had worn a 36C-cup brassière from Marks and Spencer. This fact flashed upon him.

Not mutilated. Both halves of bosom intact.

But she was looking at him now with grave, reserved eyes. 'Hello, Emily . . . I'm glad you've come back.'

His voice came out as a whisper; without body. He did not feel afraid, only consoled and agonisingly curious. What would her voice be like, supposing he could coax it out? But Emily did not speak to order. She now turned back to the books on the desk and, stooping slightly as if to scan the titles, put out a hand, allowing it to rest on the casebound set of Charlotte's works. And it was as if she indicated that she had had her say. Make what you like of it. See if I care.

Her attitude now had an edge of contempt. He recognised the look. She would soon go if he didn't find some way of preventing her. Panicking . . . hoisting himself to sitting with a fresh outbreak of sweat . . . half-fainting, he lunged forwards. But as he did so a car rumbled past on the steep cobbled road outside. She lost concentration, glanced keenly from the window to himself, from himself to the window, and faded.

By that time Timothy was sitting on the edge of his bed, within three feet of where she had been standing. He might have reached out and touched . . . what? . . . air? the hem of her garment, the hem of the garment of the dead?

He ate a boiled egg and several slices of soft toast. Though his ankles were not really much less swollen than usual, it was somehow clear that the physical burdens of his bad heart and circulation were not in themselves as disabling as the heavy swelling in his mind which crippled his spirit. He'd certainly go out today. For his was a health-giving ghost, a comfortable demon. Like sex or sea-bathing, she had a tonic effect.

He did wonder what Marianne Pendlebury would say if he revealed Emily's visits.

'I wish you to know' (grandly) 'that I am the subject of supernatural visitations.'

'By the way' (casually) 'I see the ghost of Emily Brontë every fortnight or three weeks.'

'Naturally I put it down' (rationalistically) 'to oxygen starvation combined with the psychological effects of bereavement.'

'And yet' (hesitantly) 'I can't help but wonder . . .'

'And indeed it's true to say' (defensively) 'that Jesus Christ, St Teresa and Emily Brontë all saw visions and no one calls them nutters. Blake conferred with souls on a frequent basis and the poet Yeats, I believe, practised automatic writing.'

13

It would help his credibility if he could write poems or paint pictures of the Other World. He could do neither.

Marianne he saw as a suavely eminent academic, to whom he had a horror of presenting himself as a common crank. She occasionally wrote comic accounts of such characters, describing them as plentiful in Brontë circles; and he had been at some pains to dissociate himself from their ranks by toning down for her consumption the more eccentric aspects of his experience. He feared that the Tarot and rituals to welcome in the new moon were even less respectable in intellectual circles now than heretofore.

More deeply, his Emily was private; she gave herself in confidence, to him alone. To gossip or brag about her would be transgressive. She might slip away and leave him, never returning – an unendurable prospect. He would not publish Emily.

Perhaps later on he'd do some spinning or knitting. The spinning-wheel lay idle in the corner of the tiny sitting-room, a half-spun fleece in the shoe-box beside it. Fleeces were expensive for his narrow means and the flying particles from the wool did his lungs no good, so he hadn't persevered. All the old crafts fascinated him; his dextrous fingers picked up the skills easily. A local farmer supplied fleeces. The lanolin roughness of the wool straight from the sheep's body chafed his hands pleasurably and, as he spun, carded, knitted his way through the immemorial process from fleece to cardigan, he felt a complex fellowship with the sheep. He'd probably passed the very creature, bleating as it ran before the farmer's dog. Nature had to be taken apart to fill our requirements. Witness the sheepskin coat he now buttoned on against the cold, topped with the fur-lined deerstalker with earflaps Jojo had always said made him look like Sherlock Holmes.

The turquoise day stung Timothy's eye with sharp excess of light. He propelled himself on two sticks up towards the Kinder Road and the next-door children hunkering down on the pavement went quiet before they broke out, 'Weirdie Beardie! Weirdie Beardie!' He felt Hayfield's eyes on his back, laughing him off, squeezing him out. It was natural, Jojo had said, that the Hayfielders resented the middle-class cranks, pie-in-the-sky academics and fell-walkers who had invaded their village. In time they'd make friends. Jojo attracted many friends. Timothy had called them 'our friends', but with her death they had melted away. 'Weirdie Beardie!' was at present the limit of his human contact.

Past the quarry cliffs, the empty car-park and the bridge across the rushing stream he laboured, rowans rustling all along the way. It was worth the struggle. He propped himself against the river wall to enjoy the embrace of the ridge on the left, like an arm of stone crooked round the curving path, and on the right the smooth green pasture of the valley falling steeply away. The early sun cast generous shadows from thistle and dock; from still sheep and running lambs. The ridge lay entirely in shadow. His own shadow, cloven by the wall, reappeared in the pasture beyond, immensely elongated, its head resting against the body of a black-faced sheep. Her slantwise shadow carried them both into the space of her twin lambs, a black and a white. And so on down the valleys, patterns of oblique shadow gestured like a complex of signs pointing all one way. At the base of the valley, beyond the river, stood the grey farmhouse where he bought the fleeces and beyond this the Peaks surged monumentally upwards. The farmhouse cast the shadow of a farmhouse and the mountains rested their shadows upon one another's shoulders.

An auburn girl on a pony clopped by, erect in the saddle,

her breath and the pony's breath hanging on the air. She smiled down as she passed. A file of riders appeared round the curve in the path: one after another horses materialised, chestnut, grey, dappled, white, and each rider in turn greeted him as they passed downhill at walking pace. The clap of hoofbeats echoed in the valley and faded, restoring the silence. As they passed a sense of wonder stole over him. Such beautiful, warm, weighty creatures; one after another appearing round that bend, until you wondered however many there were to come in the procession; then, suddenly, they had all come, and all had passed away.

On the ridge, beech and oak trees rustled faintly; rustled, it seemed, the very light on their leaves, as he stood looking up. Beauty was all around him, and he longed to show it to Jojo, who had an eye for such things.

Vetch, he saw vetch; and clover; harebells. *Look, Jojo.* In his mind's eye she crouched down even now, just here at the road's edge, her Ordnance Survey map tied upside-down round her neck with string, a small backpack on her shoulders; and she'd finger out the vetch, with its delicate flowers, yellow and purple, and tendrils like the curlicues of an Elizabethan signature. *And over there*, he pleaded. *Just look at those harebells, Jojo.* They quivered in breaths of air from thread-thin stems and could survive impossibly in crannies amongst the rocks or in dry-stone walls. And Jojo, who believed that all that lives is holy, bent in her own absence to examine all this when he pleaded *Look, Jojo.* The wraith of Jojo, the sleeves of her maroon blouson rolled up to reveal her muscular forearms, knelt to view this blue beauty at eye level.

For Jojo had adored it all; literally, worshipped it, never caring a fiddle what people thought of her. She'd march along singing at the top of her voice her impromptu hymns of praise. Climbing over the stile to Kinder the day she got the death sentence, she burst into song. She warbled to the Great Mother. A group of woolly-hatted climbers paused to grin and clap.

A roar of blood in his head was the only warning before he fainted, keeling sideways on to the turf.

'You all right, mate?' A cyclist leaned over; chafed his face with gloved hands; heaved him upright.

'If you'd . . . just be so good . . . as to pass over my stick,' Timothy whispered hoarsely. 'I've some medicine in it.' He'd made and carved the collapsible walking-stick himself, hollowing out the interior at one end so that he would carry a flask of brandy at all times. 'My own design. Never go anywhere without it.'

They sat and drank coffee laced with brandy. The stranger did most of the talking while Timothy got his breath, telling his life story, which led from Ashton to Heaton Moor, where he owned a bike shop, and round and round the Peaks, the Lakes and the Dales in long-winded weekend dashes measured to the nearest mile.

'So what's your line of business?'

'Oh I'm retired now,' said Timothy. 'I never settled long to anything. Jack of all trades. I've been a printer – had my own firm for sixteen years, then it folded during the seventies, due to labour costs – since then I've been a driving instructor, a yoga teacher . . . all sorts. My wife and I . . . we . . . Anyhow I live down there in the village now. Been a great walker in my time. Not now though. Bad heart, do you see,' and he patted his chest with his gloved fist.

'Bad luck. Still, it's a grand place to live.'

'Certainly,' agreed Timothy. 'But cold.'

The cyclist saw him to his door, feigning not to notice the elderly man's rasping breaths and spasms of coughing;

but the expression on his face said clearly enough, *Poor old chap, what's he doing out here, this slippers-and-cocoa case?* With a pang of envy, Timothy watched him vault on to his mountain bike and freewheel downhill, leaning his helmeted head into the bend with one hand raised in farewell. Once he too had inhabited that careless country of youth and health, where a night's sleep restores vigour. It was hard to accept that you'd never get back again. You never thought of it, or valued it, when you had it. He'd never imagined for a moment he'd grow old, or past it; and could scarcely believe it even now. It was as if a shambling shadow-self impersonated him while his real body had gone missing. He turned the key in the lock. Two letters on the doormat: the electricity bill and an envelope with the graceful, serene handwriting of Marianne Pendlebury.

Marianne could not bear it a moment longer. She couldn't and she wouldn't. The uproar and the nuisance. And Thomas banging out in that bloody selfish way, saying *he* had work to do. So did she have work to do. Why did he assume privileges she couldn't have? She slammed her books down on the desk. The bulb fell out of the reading lamp and a cascade of papers slid to the floor.

From upstairs a tempest of howling from Charlotte at being dumped in her cot and told to shut up for Christ's sake had diminished to moans of ritualised despair.

Andrew was playing with his Lego in his room quite quietly. That might last half an hour, barring the emergence of architectural design faults. Then violent acts of demolition would be initiated, with shrieks, the kicking of his teddy bear and threats to batter his sister. But just now he was engrossed, breathing deeply.

Emlyn, thank Heaven, was at school, and Marianne prayed

that he wouldn't pick up any germs to get in the way of the Haworth conference. The conference was her baby. It was a once-in-a-lifetime event which she *must* bring off. And now the child-minder claimed to have an earache. Well, she had an earache. So what? Marianne often had an earache or the equivalent and *she* had to soldier on – no retiring to bed with a hot-water bottle when you had three screaming brats in the house. You just bloody well got on with it.

Christ, she could scream. *Scream.*

She did scream.

Then she walked out of her study into the hall and hollered up the stairs, 'Charlie, shut up! Shut bloody up! *Now!* Go to sleep. *Now!*'

A big mistake, and an elementary one, which set Charlie off again, far worse. The child had been jolted out of her terminal despair into a condition of recovered hope. Up on her feet she leapt and rattled the bars of her cage, roaring. Face flushed and hot, her nappy probably off and flung into the abyss beyond the cot as a protest message. It was hopeless. Hopeless.

'Andrew, will you just sit in with Charlie while I get one or two things done?' she appealed to the turned back of her son. This was risky, since interruption might make him lose interest in his construction and bring him into the kitchen with a view to rolling pastry. Andrew did not turn round. He just shook his head, slowly and definitely, hunched his square shoulders and carried on building his spaceship.

'Please, Charlie, be a good girl for Mummy, will you?' Marianne besought the cherub in her arms. 'Do now. Do, love.'

'Not go bed,' Charlie insisted. 'No. Not go bed,' on a rising cadence.

'Watch television, Charlie. Then we'll have some biscuits.'

'Biscuits!' The toddler scudded along in her wake and stood shaking the bars of the safety barrier, bawling 'Biscuits!' and 'Bena!'

Having provided a handful of biscuits and a mug of Ribena, Marianne escaped again to the study, leaving the door ajar. She bolted in and snatched a pen, gazing glazed at the distraught memos attached to the pinboard.

'Conference: Guest speakers – shopping – what wear? – rail-booking – Neil Thorniley Tom Lassiter Kerry *Timothy Whitty, can he make it?* – check accom. Rewrite lecture –'

Her lecture was utter drivel. On three hours' sleep a night, what else could be expected? And there was no time to do anything about it now. She crossed off 'Rewrite lecture' and scored through 'shopping' in angry red: Thomas could damned well do the shopping for when she was away, why shouldn't he? And if he couldn't be bothered, they'd just have to starve.

Instead she wrote out another memo, in large, calm capitals, using a felt-tip pen: MARIANNE: MAKE YOURSELF A CUP OF COFFEE, SIT DOWN AND DRINK IT. This she pinned to the board and obeyed its directive, cross-legged by the gas fire. Then she scored through the instruction in red. That felt better already.

'Dear Timothy,' she scrawled in her fine, distinguished italic hand. 'I do so hope you can make it to Haworth. I often think of you up there in the Peak, reading Emily's poetry and communing with the natural world. It would be wonderful if you could tear yourself away from the peace and quiet' (what wouldn't she give for about a month in Hayfield, or preferably half-way up Kinder Scout, where nobody could get at her with cries of 'Mummy!' or 'Dr Pendlebury, would you mind . . .?') 'of your hermitage' (she envied him) 'and give us your company at the conference. I think I can promise you an interesting and indeed stimulating list of speakers – and, of course, we shall have the leisure to get to know one another properly. It seems odd that we have never met in the flesh, doesn't it? I feel I've known you for a long time. In fact I've formed rather a definite visual image of you, Timothy, and shall be intrigued to see if it in any way corresponds to the reality.' (In her imagination, he was a tall, thick-set man, in late middle age, his dark hair flecked with grey. This correspondence had been far more pleasurable than any with fellow academics; since he cared, really cared, for poetry, for itself and not for how many learned articles could be wrung from it. Also it was nice to be revered as an expert. Impossible to deny that a worshipper or disciple filled a need when your nearest and dearest were occupied in throwing up all over you or slamming the door in your face and calling you 'Woman'.) 'Anyway, I'll end here and hope so much to see you soon. Your friend – Marianne.'

'Your friend – Marianne,' Timothy read. He could hardly contain his almost painful excitement. 'Your friend – Marianne'.

She had such beautiful handwriting. You could tell much from people's handwriting. This young woman, for instance, in an age of impersonal word processors, still bothered to use a fountain pen for personal correspondence. Her words were inscribed with vigour and decision, in black ink, and with a kind of flourish so that the end of one word was tied by a light trail of ink to the beginning of the next. She lived amongst an élite. But there was no 'side' to her, no affectation.

He had written to her on impulse, in response to her slim book on the Brontës, picked up for a pound in a second-hand bookshop, little expecting to receive an answer but so touched by her treatment of the sisters' motherless condition that he could not resist. Then he had been delighted and flattered by her response, almost scraping the writing off the page by scouring it with his eye-beams. However many times had he read that letter? Joanna had been dead several weeks; he was struggling back to life, struggling and failing, struggling and falling. The contact gave him more than a boost: it gave something to live for.

He was careful not to allow Marianne much idea of his actual state of physical and moral decrepitude. He tried to make up a character and way of life that would be interesting to such a person as he imagined her to be – attractive, intense, eloquent and deep. He even took up calligraphy again. Although his hand was shaky these days, he persevered.

Ruined drafts crammed the waste-paper basket. The impression of spontaneity was striven for tirelessly.

He suppressed most of what dominated his life – his remaining teeth all having to come out and the misery of his dentures which didn't fit; the harrowing nights of coughing and pain; the all-embracing loneliness; and the foul weather. For he knew all too bitterly how friends fall away if you put too much pressure on them. He represented himself in a poetical way, as a recluse, pondering the mysteries of nature; and this was indeed not so very far from the truth – ideally. Indeed, as he composed these letters, he felt that the letters somehow composed him. He shifted from the rather pathetic and blighted old man he'd become into someone ardent and committed. And the magical reward for these endeavours was 'Your friend – Marianne'. The very word 'friend' in her dashing handwriting carried a glow; a promise. He allowed himself occasionally to dream. Marianne came to visit him at Hayfield. They strolled out into the woods together, hand in hand (he being miraculously cured). He

taught her to spin . . . they became soul mates. 'Your friend
– Marianne' became 'Your lover – Marianne'; age no
impediment. Breath-soft kisses . . . silken limbs . . . his face
buried in swathes of rich, dark hair . . . potency restored . . .

But Timothy was wise enough to constrain all this to the
sphere of occasional fantasy. He was grateful for friendship,
which he knew how to value. The fortnightly letters lay in
his hands like tokens of the existence of a world of human
concern and communion which had not turned its back on
him.

That night he enquired of the Tarot whether he should
go to Haworth or not. The Tarot replied, unequivocally, yes.

He stood at his bedroom window, looking out at the black
ridge silhouetted against the blue-black sky, the moon being
nearly full and the sky clear of clouds. On nights like this
you could almost see the astral influences pouring to earth.
They'd devoutly felt there was meaning everywhere, if only
we had eyes to see it. They'd tried to purify their eyesight,
using skills unrevealed to earthly opticians. The murmur of
a mantra still had a calming effect, and beauty could still
impress him with a sense of a hidden message waiting to be
decoded. Yet one part of his mind was cynical, blackened by
Jojo's cancer. It gave short shrift to the superstitions of the
other half.

Still, he'd go to Haworth, if it killed him.

It probably would kill him, come to that. Shivering, he
climbed into bed and pulled up the duvet. It took a while
for the warmth of the electric blanket to suffuse his bones.
Too skinny, that was the problem. What would Dr Marianne
Pendlebury think when she clapped eyes on the actuality of
him?

Perhaps he wouldn't go after all. How would he even get
there, when the simplest functions of life drained all his

strength; when for days on end he never put his nose out of doors? And what a fool he'd sound at a conference. You didn't go to a conference if you'd lost your voice. How could you meaningfully confer?

And then again, there was the problem of reclusiveness. In another incarnation he'd been the chatty, outward-going type, always interested in people. Loneliness somehow made you flinch from others, especially encountered in groups. Just chatting to that young chap this morning had taken it out of him. And talking to women made him painfully aware of his dentures, the slight whistle on some of his 's' sounds.

Should your dentures be allowed to dominate your whole life? *Did* a person come down to the sum of his false teeth?

No: but the dentures seemed to clinch the argument. With a sigh of relief, he extracted them from his mouth and dropped them into the glass. His face caved in and was comfortable.

Would Emily Brontë come again tonight, he wondered in the wakeful near-dark, a frisson of excitement stirring. She'd never yet come two nights in succession but seemed to wait until he'd forgotten to expect her; and then she manifested, almost in mockery. He wished she'd explain herself. He longed to ask her, 'Are you dead, Emily? Are you a ghost? Are you real?' Then he would (if he could summon courage) enquire, 'Have you seen Joanna?' He clasped the woollen-coated hot-water bottle to his middle. No amount of heat was enough heat.

Her silence was in character. In life she'd flayed strangers with dumb insolence . . . Was he then a stranger? He felt not. He was sure not. He sensed he'd known her for ever, twinned to him from before birth. So much so that, as he read her poems and *Wuthering Heights*, or recited them inwardly from memory, the thought had sometimes flashed upon him: 'I *am* Emily Brontë.' He had never told that to anyone, including Jojo. She would have given him a funny look.

And indeed, it would have put her in a somewhat anomalous relationship with him, he reflected, swirling on the mirthlessly witty edge of sleep. Jojo would have been Emily Brontë's wife.

He slept for six hours almost. Woke himself with a choking cough; expectorated; did a brief survey for ghosts (none); fell fast asleep for a further two hours and came to consciousness singularly refreshed. You could not pick up a phone to call the dead and book a time for interview. Their timeless diaries left them free of commitment; and once again he envied them their dispassion.

The nib of his home-made quill scratched slightly on the home-made parchment:

'My dear Marianne, I so much appreciate your thoughtful reminder about Haworth. My health, as you may have guessed, remains somewhat frail – but I have completed the booking form and hope' (he paused) 'and expect to be there. Do not be too' (he discarded 'shocked') 'surprised at my physical appearance, which, I am sorry to say, reflects the infirmity which came upon me when my wife passed away. I am told I am somewhat' (he flicked at his chin with the quill, delving around in his mind) 'gaunt' (yes, 'gaunt' was preferable to 'wasted' or 'emaciated') 'and breathless.' He reached for his pocket flask and took a sip of brandy. Thus fortified, Timothy advanced across the page with a swagger of loops and slides which gave body to the hollow subject matter of his spectral self. 'You and I know better than to judge by material appearances,' he affirmed confidently. 'But I thought it right to warn you. Meanwhile, my dear, take care of yourself, and I trust the arrangements are all going as smoothly as may be.'

Thomas had refused to take the day off so that Marianne could get into the Institute. He had pointed out that the Bursar's Department depended on him to continue functioning. Without the presence of Thomas Pendlebury all computers would fail; secretaries' fingers stall in mid-air; meetings abort; the entire administrative block undergo subsidence.

'Are you telling me that if *you* take one day off to look after *your* children . . .?'

'Well, really, you know, I am . . . it's just not possible.'

'*One* day?'

'Honestly, Marianne, I can't miss today. I can't be *seen* to miss it. I've got the big meeting with the Grants people at two . . .' He enumerated the reasons for his indispensability. There were at least seven complex and distinct reasons for each day, stretching well into the following week.

'Oh, I see,' said Marianne, jabbing the bottle into Charlotte's mouth. '*I* see. You can't take a day off because you're *necessary*. But *I'm* not. *I'm* unnecessary. Is that it? Have I grasped your meaning correctly? Stop it, Emlyn. Put it down. Tom, get that knife off him.'

'Put it down, Emlyn. Immediately.' Tom disarmed his son.

'And don't you *ever* play with knives again,' said Marianne. 'Tom, I'm telling you, you'll have to take the day off. I've *got* to go in today. I've five seminars and the lecture.'

'Look here, Marianne, you're the mother.'

'And you're the father.'

'Well, it's different.'

'No it's not different, how is it different, tell me that? We always agreed: equality. We *always* said we'd share the responsibilities. It's sexist . . . underneath all that simpering liberalism you're a . . .'

'Marianne, I . . .'

'Sexist.' Tears of resentment sparked. Her face was hot and red. 'Bloody sexist.' They shouted above the routine din of the three children's breakfasting. Andrew and Emlyn struggled over a Sugar Puffs free offer while Charlie, lolling over the arm of the high chair, snorted with laughter as she dripped milk from her bottle on to her doll's head.

'I didn't mean it that way. Calm down, do.'

'I warn you, Thomas, I warn you now, if I miss another day I'll lose my bloody job and if I lose my bloody job, how the bloody hell are we going to pay the mortgage? Tell me that.'

'We ought to be better organised. There ought to be a system of back-ups,' Thomas said. 'Go on then. I'll phone in and say I've got a virus. But I can't keep on doing this, Marianne. I absolutely can't.'

'Neither can I.' She started stuffing papers in her briefcase. There was milky dribble down the sleeve of her sweater and a crucial folder of unmarked essays seemed to be missing. She sponged, swearing, at the sleeve.

'It's okay − slow down. You've got time.' Now that he had acquiesced in his martyrdom, Thomas dropped his hostility. 'Take it easy. No panic. Now . . . have you got everything? What about this?'

A grey essay-folder, speckled with orange juice, was retrieved from under Andrew's bricks. Thomas helped her on with her jacket. As she lurched out into the rain, he handed her the post and gave her a small kiss on the cheek.

'Thanks, Tom. *Sorry*,' she placated.

'Mummy NOT GO!' Charlie let out a foghorn-blast of grief

which pursued Marianne as she thudded down the street, coat flying wide, briefcase snapped open.

The tram was bliss. She called in the scattered pieces of herself as it slid on smooth tracks past staccato traffic and furiously pedalling cyclists. She would just sit . . . get her breath . . . not mark these essays until her free period, then just skim them . . . the lecture would be okay. Marianne was a dull lecturer who got little more than 50 per cent attendance. Hugh Brenner, who bounded up and down the platform, forged into the audience, sang, leapt, cracked jokes, played all the parts in the play, scored 95 per cent. Unnerved by large crowds, Marianne was better with smaller groups, though latterly even that had seemed to slip. Now that the Institute was seeking university status, the staff were being endlessly appraised. Appraisers sat in on her classes, saying, 'Now just pretend I'm not here, carry on as normal, I shan't obtrude', and occasionally scribbled in a notebook, looking up with a bland air like a doctor who has diagnosed a terminal case. Afterwards you got ordeal by 'friendly and positive criticism'. At the end of every module, the students filled in questionnaires exhorting them to give a candid opinion of the quality of the intellectual wares on offer. 'Dr Pendlebury knows a lot but keeps it to herself' had stuck in her mind from last term. 'Communication skills' were mentioned by Professor Price over a cordial cup of tea as due for inspection and polish.

She'd always thought things would be different; that she'd achieve something greater; have some fresher or profounder insights to offer. In her twenties enthusiasm had been abundant: intense chats with students in corridors, her little book on Emily Brontë, reading with racing heart deep into the night, she had thought of herself as a strong, questing person. Now in her thirties freshness had drained away. She rarely read a book for its own sake. Reading was forbidden in her house. 'My love for Linton is like the foliage in the woods . . .' you read, and some roughneck sped in and grappled the book out of your hands. 'Whatever souls are made of, his and mine are the same,' you read, and a fight broke out on the stairs. Were all children as villainous and barbaric, or were hers specially gifted? The mums at the school gates, exuding doughy virtue, rocked their neat babies in prams. Their talk was of rashes, rattles, sausages and the whiteness of nappies. *Why, then, did you have babies?* they silently demanded. *How did you not know they'd turn into children?*

She had been pregnant with dreams. They had filled her inner space with premonition. Then their reality burst out and you fell painfully in love with them while they trampled your personal desires to pulp.

Anyway . . . let Thomas cope today. She glanced through the mail in her lap. Something from Timothy, bless him. He never complained, though she was sure he didn't enjoy first-rate health; but he'd never burden her. The sight of his envelope brought a little glow. She kissed the letter and placed it in her pocket, to look forward to.

But this one . . . she recognised the writing . . . it was that Passion Woman, wasn't it? The tweedy lady from Ludlow who haunted all the Brontë do's and sat through the talks like a pent storm, then, the moment the speaker was through, leapt up and harangued the company on the Passion of the Brontës. Claimed descent from the Nussey family. She could see her now, poised on the front row ready to spring: middle-aged, stocky, genteel, with a grey dome of lacquered hair. Didn't look fiery at all. Looked the last person to rant of Passion.

'Dear Dr Pendlebury,' she read. 'I trust I am not too late to enrol for the conference, of which I have just obtained notice, having returned from Brussels only yesterday *with some most interesting and possibly significant information concerning the Pensionnat Heger* and Charlotte's relationship with M. Heger. I look forward to . . .'

Of course, the Brontë lot mostly had bees in their bonnets and went round buzzing mildly or wildly. Whenever two or three were gathered together, it was a hive in uproar. Some, who seemed at first quite normal, turned out to be obsessives transfixed by a punctuation mark whose placement had become a life's work. Code-breakers and sleuths had unearthed an Irish peasant who was acclaimed as the original for Heathcliff or a local curate the alleged boyfriend of Anne.

One was obsessed with Charlotte's footwear.

Another claimed to be a Charlotte lookalike.

Certain of the scholars were viciously envious of their fellows; they fought over their darlings like jealous husbands.

Of course, there were some good eggs in the basket of enthusiasts: feminists, scholars from the Brontë Society, ordinary readers with considerable knowledge and sensitivity. And there was Dr Marianne Pendlebury. *She* wasn't a crank. But she'd announced a New Theory and would have to think one up before Friday week.

Chapter 2

And when the world despises,
When heaven repels my prayer,
Will not mine angel comfort,
Mine idol hear?

Eileen Nussey James, exhausted but excited, sat back in her train seat with her trophy held against her breast with reverencing fingers. She examined with satisfaction her work-roughened hands. Alone, it seemed, amongst her generation, she had no interest in cuticles. Proudly concerned with internals rather than externals, Eileen had listened with disdain to contemporaries deploring the contours of their own nails and enviously or hypocritically admiring those of their neighbours, pursuing an apparently endless battle to push back the encroaching cuticle so as to expose the desirable white moon. Care of fingernails was taken to be a test of respectable character.

Yet Eileen made sure to be neat in appearance and was careful about her hair – her 'busby', as her mother called it.

'Mother, I am not a grenadier.'

Muriel, wisely and tactfully, had not replied.

Perhaps she was somewhat regimental in her dealings with her mother. She did not mean to be. It was her instinctive reaction to the boundaryless rovings of Muriel's dementia; and perhaps a symptom of her own suppressed rage for freedom. Getting away was almost frighteningly loosening to her spirit. She felt she might leap out of control, in a world of many avenues. A sensuality persistently denied beckoned in every taste and colour beyond the drab routines of Ludlow. Brussels had been especially powerful in allure.

The whole journey, her first outside Britain, had been a pilgrimage; and with something of a pilgrim's awe she had followed in the footsteps of Charlotte and Emily at the Heger school, down the '*allée défendue*', to the Opéra, the Cathedral. And at every point it seemed the skirts of the two girls had only just vanished round the next corner; the curious illusion had waylaid her that if she just put her skates on, she'd catch up with them. And she was ambushed by the conviction that they called to her to hurry up and follow. They led her by strange alleyways to the antique shop in the rue Albert.

There she had come upon the ink and watercolour sketch of a tree beside a diamond-paned window, the window being open, and a kind of face peering out from behind it. At least it could be a face. Nobody could prove that it absolutely was not.

There could not be any real doubt about the attribution: Emily for sure. It was in her characteristic style. The antique shop owner had not the least idea of what lay in his hands. He assured Madame that the charming picture dated back to the period of the First World War. Eileen knew better. Her hands trembled as they touched the priceless article; tears quivered in her eyes. She sat there in the gloomy interior between a bronze Cupid and an inlaid table with spindling legs and thought, as the Cupid smirked and chandelier-light winked on mirrors and porcelain, how unfathomable life was. That the Emily picture should have come to her – to *her*, Eileen Nussey James (for the Nussey name she had claimed by deed poll) – in the context of all this Belgian junk, it showed . . . it showed there was a pattern to things. Her Baptist upbringing had prepared her to intuit leadings and providences. *This*, she thought, *was meant to be.*

However, she was not too destabilised by rapture to fail in haggling the salesman down a few francs. Bargains could also be providential, driven by shrewd cooperation between human and divine will.

Bruxelles, she thought, *Bruxelles*. French words and names intoxicated her. She entered fully into Charlotte's passion for them. Somehow the foreign language glorified and glamorised mundane things. She reread snatches of *Villette* with its undulating rhythm between French and English. Tall shadows fell from poplars across whole fields where even the cows in their transfigured status as *des vaches* were lustrous in the dying sun. *Un cheval blanc* was a cantering dream of pure power, next of kin rather to the unicorn than the horse.

The ticket collector was a most handsome man.

She yielded up her ticket.

She had never married.

Multitudinous cats swarmed all over Eileen as she sat and told her mother of her adventures, excluding the purchase of the picture.

'And how have you been?' she asked, dumping the animals from her lap and shooing them from the chair-back and arm. 'Go off, you blighters, I want to drink my tea.'

'Oh I've been lovely. I *couldn't* have had better care . . . except yours of course, dear,' Muriel added quickly, lest her daughter feel unneeded.

'You've always got me,' said Eileen from the centre of a complicated knot.

'No need to shout, dear.'

'I wasn't shouting.'

'Well, but it *was* loud. Betty, my helper, has such a gentle voice and she enters into things so well. We had some parties while you were away. Kaiser Bill came to one . . . but before you get alarmed, I must say in his favour that he is most charming on the personal level. I could not fault him on manners. Betty agrees. Of course, he was Victoria's nephew and well brought up. The Prussians were always polite . . . if nasty. He didn't seem nasty. But in any case he may come again; you can judge for yourself. You may have a chance to talk to him in person.'

'I don't doubt.'

'You know,' said Muriel, and she stroked the curled-up cat purring in her lap, 'I'd rather you'd stayed away longer if you were enjoying yourself. I tie you down. Betty and I . . .'

Hot jealousy of the adorable Betty flooded Eileen, catching her unawares. Muriel was a ball and chain, dragging at her whichever way she moved. But Muriel was also a rock. She occasionally wondered who was the more dependent and well-orientated party.

'I don't know what I'd do if you weren't here,' she blurted; and immediately regretting it, took refuge in snapping, 'Oh, do take that tea-cosy off your head. It's a tea-cosy, not a hat.'

'Oh, what a shame. It feels so nice and warm on my head.'

Eileen knelt beside the top left-hand drawer of her dressing-table. Laid out on tissue paper was a locket containing, she believed, a tress of Anne Brontë's hair. She had purchased this from a dealer in Keighley over a decade ago. He had several such lockets in stock, all early Victorian, but something about the pale colour of this lock (matching the one preserved in the Parsonage Museum) convinced Eileen that this was the real thing. All he could tell her about its history was its acquisition in a job lot in Thornton, from an old lady's attic. Later she had added a broken pen and inkwell, various old photographs and three lace collars. She now placed Emily's picture beside these precious objects.

Ludlow overflowed with tourists. They thronged Castle Street and nosed around the book shops searching out remainders. They drank morning coffee at De Greys, still wearing their cameras round their necks, and were served buttered scones by elderly waitresses whose shoe leather squeaked over polished floorboards in the respectable quiet beneath the low roof-timbers and slumbrous light, where nothing had changed materially since pre-war days. Eileen sipped her China tea and remembered herself as a giddy teenager in 1944, larking with the sixth-form boys evacuated from Birmingham. They had sat round that same circular table where now a party of elderly Australians was unfurling napkins and ordering teacakes.

One boy in particular revisited her mind's eye. There was an empty place amongst the Australians; she sat him there, his back to her. People's heads were very vulnerable, seen from the back.

He turned his head, arm crooked over the back of his chair, and grinned. Such a sweet smile. One noted that his front teeth were discoloured, for people didn't bother with dental hygiene to the same extent in those days; and then one forgot. A decent, well-read, kindly boy. All those lads had received marching orders and been shipped off in khaki to the Pacific. She could have married the diffident boy with the crinkly hair. (The bad teeth could have been remedied.)

But she'd always been waiting for something more . . . powerful . . . thrilling. Love should throb through you like an electric shock, a kinesis which charged you with emotion.

You would know for sure that this was your person. Frank hadn't kindled her in that way. She had greatly liked him but he was no Mr Rochester.

'I'll write,' he'd promised. But he hadn't written.

She wished he'd written.

Fifty years on, Eileen strode out of De Greys into Broad Street and left, it seemed, something of herself haunting the round table with the red and white check table-cloth, slightly soiled from generations of teacups.

Mother had been elevated to the peerage during the brief period of Eileen's absence. As Eileen hung up her raincoat in the hall, she heard her modestly disclaiming greatness whilst advising an invisible enquirer to look up her name in Debrett's if he wished to learn more of her lineage.

'So tasty,' she then announced in a confidential undertone. 'Never had such good flapjacks since I was a girl, staying with dear Alexandra at the Balmoral estate. Do you know Crathay, Your Reverence?'

'Hello, mother, I'm back.' Eileen put her head round the door and boomed. Although Muriel was not deaf, her daughter sometimes found it necessary to raise her voice in order to make herself known through the clusters of imaginary or remembered persons whose company Muriel kept. 'I say. I'm back.'

'No, I won't have a scone,' Muriel insisted.

'Mother. It's me. Eileen.'

'No, dear, really,' emphasised Muriel, politely but firmly. 'Offer one to the cardinal. Now, Cardinal, you'll have a nice scone, won't you?' She handed an airy plate to the ginger tom basking in the nearest armchair. The cardinal having accepted the scone without dispute, Muriel swivelled in the general direction of her daughter.

'Mother.'

'I heard you, dear. You're back.' She covered up for her daughter's bad manners for the benefit of the high-born guests. 'She's an intellectual, you see. Lived with her head in a book since the age of four and a half. Say hello to everyone, Eileen . . . *nicely*,' she added in an undertone.

Half a dozen cats stole from settees and hearthrug, to sleek their pelts around Eileen's legs.

Eileen greeted the Duchess of York, the Empress of Russia and her daughter Anastasia, Lady Helen Windsor and several Church dignitaries.

'Dear Rasputin could not be with us,' explained Muriel. 'He is out distributing loaves and fishes amongst the poor of St Petersburg.'

'Very nice, mother. Would you like a cup of tea?'

'Ah, now, Helen, don't go just because Eileen's come home . . . Fergie . . . Cardinal . . . Well, if they must go, help them on with their coats, Eileen. I'd get up myself, only once I'm up, there's all the bother of getting down again. I need one of those technological chairs you read about. . . .'

'Well, goodbye all,' said Eileen. 'Nice to have seen you. Come again.' Cooperating in the fantasy was often the best way to control the improvised amateur theatricals of their day-to-day life. Rather than allowing herself to give way to irritation and insisting on her version of the real world, Eileen would try to play along, cuing the action in to the necessary routines. 'Cup of tea, mother?'

'Oh *no*, dear. I couldn't possibly. I've already had *three*.'

She hadn't, of course. Her lips were parched. But she looked blissfully content, stimulated and comforted by the attentions of such a varied company of thin-air people. She undoubtedly led a fuller and more interesting life now that her mind could invent it as she went along, than ever in the past.

'Drink that up,' Eileen ordered.

'Well, if you insist. Just to please you. You're a very bossy girl, Eileen,' she added, in mild reproof.

'Good thing I am, with you to keep in order.'

Muriel drank, with relish. 'Anyway, you make an excellent cup of tea,' she said. 'And what have you been doing today, dear?'

Eileen detailed her day's shopping itinerary. Muriel's face wore an expression of controlled incredulity, as if the world of Ludlow market and De Greys Café had a merely theoretical or fabricated reality.

At seven thirty she retired to bed. She invariably began to nod in her chair during the seven o'clock news. And invariably, when Eileen woke her to say it was bedtime, Muriel's eyebrows went up. She complied only to humour Eileen, for in her mind it might be mid-morning, and the year 1952, or 1922. She rarely contradicted Eileen directly, except in the scruple of an eyebrow's scepticism. She caught her daughter's reality by glimpses. It was her faith that you could disagree, even over fundamental issues, such as the Year of Our Lord, and still get on; still accept one another. So, though convinced that dawn had just broken, Muriel permitted her daughter to conduct her to her bedroom and settle her for sleep.

'Have you been to Wem, dear?'

'Wem? Do you mean today, or ever?'

'Wem. I thought you said you were going to Wem.'

'No, I never said anything about Wem.'

'Ah.' Muriel, her thin white hair down over the pillow, lay and pondered for a while. 'Are you sure?'

'Of course I'm sure. I'd know if I'd been to Wem, wouldn't I?' Eileen tucked in the bedclothes securely.

'Well, if you haven't been to Wem, who has?'

'Never mind about Wem, mother. Nobody's been to Wem.'

Muriel was silent, brooding upon the emptiness of Wem, as Eileen closed the gap in the curtains.

'If it wasn't Wem,' she heard Muriel deliberating, 'it must have been Much Wenlock.'

Evening was a poignant time for Eileen. For although she looked forward to the relief from her mother's needs and fantasies, there was a hollowness to these hours. Longing might seize her; craving even, for something as yet denied. Occasionally she hired a babysitter and went to a classic film: *Howard's End* for instance, with the lovely photography, or the new *Wuthering Heights*, about whose disgraceful deviations from the text Eileen had kept up an audible commentary and was shushed by her neighbours. But how could one be expected to tolerate in silence this pouty-mouthed Cathy with the French accent, the sexy scamperings from box bed to mystical tree?

Oh, no, this was not how it was; this was nothing like the truth. 'You've been conned! Go home and read the book!' she wanted to exhort the audience. 'Demand your money back!'

Now, looking out of the sitting-room window into the rainy garden, a quirk of the rapidly dying light disclosed the likeness of a dark figure between the hedge and the iron gate. She had seen this effect before and knew that it was the gatepost, dark with wet. But she thought of Heathcliff . . . Heathcliff waiting out in the grounds, rain having fallen all night on his bare head . . . stock-still beneath the ash trees, from whose buds the sticky sap distilled . . . at his feet the mated thrushes passing, carrying twigs to build their nest . . . his dark head black with wet . . . oblivious to the cold. This was what it was all about, this need and affinity and absolute hunger.

She believed each person had a Heathcliff.

He was meant but had never come. So she had waited; and still was in a posture of waiting. Part of Eileen was still twenty-one; yearning, and breathless, and ardent. Her elderly reflection in the mirror seemed wrong for this ardour, like a decaying outfit you had no means to change.

It was not Heathcliff but a gatepost.

Yet a gatepost could stand as a memorial of the deepest truths she knew.

She closed the curtains and took out her battered old *Wuthering Heights*, its chaos of adrift pages secured with a rubber band.

' "Nelly, I *am* Heathcliff – He's always, always in my mind – not as a pleasure, any more than I am always a pleasure to myself – but as my own being – so . . ." '

And as always the skin on Eileen's back prickled with a light fluey sensation and something in her said, *Yes*, with a sigh of recognition, as if she were reading words she herself had composed and put away to keep.

These professors of this and doctors of that possessed very little idea of Emily Brontë's true meaning. She attended all the Brontë events in the hope of hearing one voice, just one, which could put words to what she, deep within her, knew. But as soon as they began their lectures, she knew they had let her down. If they were distinguished, they were rarely ardent; and if they had fire, they were almost invariably crackpots. Impelled by indignation, she'd be moved to jump up and denounce them, the moment they'd discharged their message. 'Cowards!' she wanted to shout. 'Frauds!' For they claimed to be professionals; experts in the field. Perhaps cognisance of the secrets they professed was only granted to amateurs, who read for love.

Yet she had not the words at her disposal. She felt she had the knowledge but lacked a language. They, who possessed so many words, and such exceedingly long ones, trailing tails like 'ology' and 'ography', had not the heart's understanding. Red and hot, she would hear herself compulsively spluttering about 'Passion' to a tittering multitude.

Nevertheless, she would attend Dr Pendlebury's conference.

It was not with an intent to deceive that she extracted the Victorian pen, loaded it with black ink and scratched the words 'Emily Jane Brontë 1842' in costive print just above the topmost branch of the tree in the Brussels picture. So authentic was the effect that it was as if her hand had been guided in its signature by an unseen presence.

She let out the tense breath she had been holding while she wrote. T. J. Wise had been a criminal. He'd forged Charlotte's signature on Branwell's stories, to make money out of them, and fame. These were not Eileen's motives. She knew a secret truth and was supplying other people with evidence so that they too could see it.

Nevertheless, her face burned and she rapidly returned the picture to the drawer.

She looked in on her mother, in a businesslike way. Her mother was wide awake, lying obediently with a certain wistful puzzlement, as if curious to know why she had been put to bed at the wrong end of the day.

'Oh, mother. Do go to sleep.' The daughter's voice was raw and grating.

'But it's nine o'clock in the morning,' Muriel complained.

'No . . . it's nine in the *evening*.'

'The morning.'

'No, mother. Night. Look, it's dark.'

'So it is. Haven't they turned the clocks back yet?'

'Oh dear.' Eileen let fall the heavy curtain. 'Couldn't you just accept . . . do you think . . . if I say so . . . that it's the time it is? I wouldn't make up the time, would I?'

'But you might not know it, you see. You've so much to think about. Whereas I can keep my eye on the sun.'

Eileen sat heavily down on the bed with a little unaffected laugh and took her mother's hand in both of hers.

'Emily Brontë preferred night to day,' she said. 'Perhaps your body-clock's like hers.'

Muriel screwed her eyes tight shut. Once Eileen was off on her hobby-horse there was no knowing where the conversation might go. She feigned a yawn.

'I think I do feel sleepy after all,' she confided.

Chapter 3

Woods, you need not frown on me;
Spectral trees that so dolefully
Shake your heads in the dreary sky.
You need not mock so bitterly.

At first Marianne, seated behind a pillar in the common room marking essays, took it that her colleagues were discussing forestry.

'Dead wood,' they were saying. 'Dead wood.'

She had nearly finished the marking. Then she would read Timothy's dear letter, as a reward.

'Drastic pruning . . .' said Hugh Brenner. 'So Idris says the committee says.'

Sherwood Forest swam into her mental eye: skeletons of dead trees still standing amongst the living oaks.

'The cuts . . . the cuts . . . Oh damn. Look at the time,' said Danny Lesser, and then he abruptly pushed his chair back and left the room.

'What's all this about cuts?' asked Kate Sanderson, taking his place.

Marianne carefully wrote up the hasty guesswork of her marks in a column of her register book. Here you could be private and quiet if the right table was free. Lined with green carpet and punctuated by round pillars, the room had the air of a stately ship's saloon. A black grand piano stood at the door to the newspaper and magazine room, where the most antique of the academics would be found comatose, sunk in shabby armchairs where they seemed to have spent decades. If you went in, they might all ignore you, or all elect to grunt at you in chorus; or one might detain you in a monologue of dire longevity. Latterly they had become fewer, dying off or being elbowed into retirement. The magazines had also become fewer.

'Dead wood,' said Hugh Brenner. 'So Danny says Idris says.'

'Christ,' groaned Kate Sanderson. 'Did he name anyone in particular?'

'Not *you* Katy – don't worry about *that*,' said Hugh protectively. 'You're too young and bright and sassy, and in any case you're cheap to pay.'

Sassy, thought Marianne with disgust. Imagine being called *sassy* in that condescending way. Hugh had been on an exchange to South Carolina last year and brought back *sassy*. He'd have his arm on the back of Kate's chair, his stubby fingers prowling. Hugh pawed everything female, or tried to. *Except me*, thought Marianne with a complex feeling of gratification and insult.

'Well, that's a relief . . . but who then?'

'Who do you think?'

'Haven't a clue.'

'Well, it's obvious, isn't it?'

'Not to me,' Kate fenced.

'Oh, come on.'

Marianne suddenly saw who the 'dead wood' must be; and that it was indeed 'obvious'; must have been obvious for several years. But at the same time this was an impossible thought which she could not entertain.

'Two categories, Idris says. The older generation who are coming up for retirement anyway, like Denis and Mike and so on – and then people like David Villiers and Marianne and poor Charles, who just don't pull their weight. "Failure to make an adequate contribution to the Institute as a centre of excellence", he calls it. He's got hold of all the latest lingo. Makes you sick to hear him. He calls himself a *manager*, you know – have you heard it? Yes, honestly, a *manager*. Damned charlatan.'

'Oh,' said Kate. 'It's too bad. It really is.'

'What's too bad?' asked Charlie Braine, bearing two coffees and trailing a beautiful Brazilian student he'd 'befriended', as he put it. All Charlie's waifs were ripe and voluptuous. Meagre exiles escaped his patronage.

Marianne came trembling round the pillar.

'Oh *Hugh*,' she said quietly. 'Did he honestly say me?'

Hugh stumbled up, wincing with embarrassment.

'Christ, Marianne . . . I had no idea . . . Look here, it's probably just gossip . . . nothing in it . . . look here, I'm so sorry.'

'Doesn't it make any difference . . . about the conference . . . and my book?'

'Oh yes, I'm sure – Look here, take no notice, there's probably nothing in it but Idris sounding off.' He shepherded her, to hide her tears from public view, holding her arm, and they stood together at the window, looking down into the concourse. 'It's just . . . you've been off sick so much . . . he notices that kind of thing these days, whereas before we could go off for a week at a time and nobody would notice. And those student complaints . . . about your being inaudible. Bad PR.'

'Yes, but I had laryngitis.'

Afterwards she cradled herself in her own arms, as if she herself were the child she had to carry. Fixing her eyes on the pillar, she complained inwardly to it. *I'm up all night but still I function. I've always got a cold but I still turn up and lecture. I've got three children under six and no reliable child-care but I'm organising a conference.*

'She couldn't organise a bus trip to Bradford swimming pool,' snorted Idris Price. 'Not meaning to be unkind *but*. . . . The woman is spinning on the spot.'

'Antsy,' said Hugh. They were propping up the bar.

'I beg your pardon?'

'Ants in her pants. American expression.'

'Not up to the job. Too many family commitments.'

'Well – I don't know. She may surprise us yet.'

'I hope for her sake she does.' Idris smiled cordially, showing his perfect dental endowments. He himself was an ageing young man, making ever more desperate efforts to scale the greasy pole of office. The high-flyers looped the loop in the zenith that was forever above and beyond him. Younger and more pushy specimens scrambled below him. He kicked them down whenever he spotted a head bobbing up. Idris suffered gastric disorders on a chronic basis; the nagging pain did not soothe his dyspepsia with those colleagues who let the side down.

'And,' said Hugh, penitent for the distress he had inadvertently caused earlier, 'she's quite well known amongst the Brontë bunch. Has contacts everywhere. An asset in some ways. This conference of hers. . . .'

'Just wipe down the tables, would you, Sharon,' Dot asked the youngster. 'I'm going behind for a fag.'

'Sure.' Sharon was always willing; a good worker. Dot vanished illegally into the storeroom behind the servery, to rest her legs and light up. Sharon went round with a wet rag, conscientiously wiping up spilt coffee and ash. She cleaned all round a bald, stout man who was writing in an exercise book. She lifted his cup and wiped under it, saying 'Excuse me', and he didn't even look up. They generally acted as if she didn't have any real existence, looking through rather than at her. That suited Sharon fine.

Sharon returned to the servery, wrung out her cloth and plodded back into the common room. She liked her work. It gave her satisfaction to do it properly, and the companionship of the other girls was good. They all got together round the table in the refectory after they'd served the lunches, and had a good laugh. They laughed at the men who sat round another large table; and the men laughed back. Dot and Annie had voices on them like foghorns and they didn't mind what they said. Sometimes they teased Sharon for her quietness. But not unkindly. They had a standing joke that she had a crush on Andy, the equally quiet man who looked after the heating system. He was small and wiry, hardly more than five foot two; she large, outwards and upwards. That was why they made the joke. And her size was why she kept so quiet. Sharon did not like to draw more attention to her bulk than it already attracted.

But they only meant it in fun.

Of course they did.

Dot flirted with the customers. She knew them all by name and their taste in teacakes and malt bread; and whether they liked their coffee strong or weak. She gossiped to Sharon about what they got up to. The number who had it away with their girl students, according to Dot, was fantastic. It was difficult to believe that the girls could be attracted to

47

such dreary old men; to Sharon at nineteen, they mostly seemed old and dried-up and dull. The really ancient ones smelt of mothballs – mothballs that had failed in their job, for their tweedy jackets looked moth-eaten; one or two seemed hardly able to walk. The medium-old ones were leftover hippies from the sixties, shaggy and shabby in faded corduroys or jeans, or respectable-looking gents in suits.

Lately a tide of young men and women had swept upon the scene. These were understood to be 'new blood'. They were always dashing to and fro, with hardly time to swallow their coffee. Some were 'hunks', as Dot and Annie agreed, and deserving of swift promotion.

And talk . . . they could talk like nobody's business. Never had she heard so much argument. They knew so many long words; words she had never heard before – words with tails which they used to spank their opponents. When she hoovered round them, they just turned up the volume. Sharon did not dislike the long words, though she knew what Dot meant when she said that these people farted in Latin. At school she had done well at English, and often wished she had stayed on to make something of herself. But no one in her large family had stayed on after sixteen. They lived in a tower block. The boys wagged off school, were excluded and left without any qualifications; her two sisters, Sammy and Lisa, both had babies by the time they were seventeen. Sharon, with her one GCSE, was her mum's pride and joy, the high-achiever of the family.

Sharon cruised round with the hoover and caught snatches of conversation bawled over the roar of the machine.

'But as I have consistently argued,' bellowed a bumptious character Sharon had often heard laying down the law, 'my research shows that the tribal customs of the Mandinga are . . . Can't hear yourself speak in here, it's like a railway station.'

He glared reproof at the hoover but avoided Sharon's eyes.

A small man wearing a red pompom hat and bicycle clips arrived, a schoolboy satchel under his arm. He did a Scottish dance with the vacuum lead before going off to fetch his coffee.

Sharon moved on from Social Anthropology to English Literature.

'Vaginal orgasm, huh!' a woman was shrilly saying. Sharon tried not to stare as she plugged the cleaner into a new socket. That wasn't the kind of thing she expected to hear shrieked at the top of your voice in a public room. But the woman didn't seem to mind at all. 'The prick,' the heated young woman went on, 'always the prick. The prick was God to Lawrence. Narcissism, you see – closet homosexuality.'

'I can't have that – can't let you get away with that, much as I love you, Margot,' said the man beside her, and he clapped her on the back with a hearty hand which the woman seemed strongly to resent. 'A great teacher . . .' he went on, but Sharon lost the rest as the hoover took her in the direction of the grand piano no one ever played. Sometimes when the room was empty, she raised the lid and fingered the keys. She'd have loved to learn an instrument.

When she was sent out to wipe the tables again, the place was nearly empty, save for a few browsing solitaries.

'Oh,' she said, when she came upon the woman weeping behind the pillar. For a moment she had no idea what to do. So she stood there with her cloth and perplexedly wiped the pillar. Then she retreated to the other side.

It was Mrs Pendlebury, who was constantly bustling round in a harassed way, looking over her shoulder as if someone were after her. But she was one of the few to treat you as a fellow human being; she would pause with her coffee (and her hand trembled so that it slopped in her saucer) to say hello and ask how you were. Sharon used to offer her a tray to hold her coffee, seeing as her hands were so nervy.

Once she had brought her children in; and they were so *tiny*. There was a baby, and a toddler, and another boy. The boy bombarded all round the common room, clambering over chairs and tables, throwing a magazine; and Mrs Pendlebury kept calling him in a furious whisper. Finally she dragged him away by force; and the baby howled; and all the frosty old men looked up in disgust at the invasion. Sharon didn't really think it right, to go out to work when you had such a young family.

She went back round the pillar. Marianne was blowing her nose and had taken off her glasses to wipe her eyes. She looked up without being able to focus.

'Excuse me, miss, but are you all right?'

'Oh how nice of you to ask, Sharon. Yes, I suppose I'm all right. It all gets on top of me. Can you see my specs? I'm blind as a bat without them.'

Sharon handed her the glasses. She wiped at the table, trying to think of what to say.

'Shall I get you some more coffee?'

'Oh no . . . no thanks. Anyway, how are you?'

'I'm okay. Just normal really. I'm going on a diet. Next week, like, I'm going to start.'

'Well, take it easy. You have to do these things gradually, so I'm told. I've never tried.' It must be grim, thought Marianne, to be so huge. Sharon really was obese. The thought took her mind off her own woes, just as the sight of Marianne's tears took Sharon's mind off her own mass.

'*You* don't need to,' said Sharon enviously. '*You*'re all right.'

She didn't normally speak to anyone about her weight. It seemed to advance before her, announcing itself in a giant wobble wherever she went.

'I don't *feel* very all right,' said Marianne. 'I've got this Brontë conference to organise and I haven't even prepared my lecture.'

'My English teacher at school, she were lovely. She lent me ever so many books. I loved *Jane Eyre*. "Do you think, Mr Rochester, because I am poor and plain and little, that I have no heart. Well, you think WRONG!" ' Sharon declaimed; and then flushed up scarlet. She'd never been able to read aloud in class, though she would go home and perform Mark Antony's Oration in the bathroom, from memory. She'd never seen an actual play in a real theatre.

'But that's wonderful, Sharon. You're a real reader and I never knew. Can't you sit down a minute?'

'Better not,' said Sharon. 'I might get done.'

But a dreamy look had come into her eyes. Thinking of *Jane Eyre* brought back feelings she hadn't connected with for years . . . knowing exactly how Jane felt when that foul boy threw the book, and shouting back over the banisters at the old bag of an aunt, and how she was on her own in the world, not the right shape and size, with no money, and standing up to Mr Rochester . . . Being too small, though, was a lot less freakish than being overweight. 'I wish . . .' she said.

'What?'

'Oh, nothing. I just wish I'd kept up more with books and that. Telly's not the same.'

'Sharon!' called Dot.

'Better go,' said Sharon. 'I hope you feel better soon. I hope the meeting goes well.'

'Why don't you come along?'

'Me? Oh no, I don't know a thing . . .' She looked, and was, horrified. She'd be a figure of fun.

'Oh, you wouldn't have to,' Marianne assured her. 'Preferably what we want is *real* readers – people who are interested in the books for themselves. Not academics. People who care about books and want to know more.'

'*Sharon!*' called Dot. A queue was forming at the servery.

'Well,' said Sharon, awkwardly withdrawing, 'I'll think about it.'

'Do. Now do. I really and truly mean it.'

Sharon, having ladled twenty spoonfuls of tea into twenty small teapots, began to serve the old geezers their afternoon tea. The boiling water from the urn spurted into the teapots, scalding her hands and wrists with drops. It was hot in the servery and she sweated in the green and white check polyester uniform which, being a size too small, cut in under the arms; her bosom and hips bulged beneath it. Normally she wore loose, flowing garments to disguise the full extent of her girth. It was her glands, her doctor said, her metabolism. It was true that she ate too many chips and chocolate; but all her family were well built. Magazines told her you could have liposuction or stomach clamps, but she didn't fancy that.

'Pot of tea for two with extra hot water and two scones,' demanded a voice. No 'please'. Followed by no 'thank you'.

She laid out the tray.

'Apparently Idris has given Charlie and Marianne an official warning. "Achieve or Go",' confided the rude orderer to his companion, in a low voice. Sharon glanced up, pausing as she poured milk from bottle to jug.

'*Really?*'

'Cut-throat world now, isn't it, though? Sink or swim according to how much waste paper you generate. Of course,

Marianne is notoriously unreliable – and she's the kind of wreck who can't hide the fact that she's a wreck.'

'I have some sympathy for Marianne. Thin end of the wedge. She wouldn't do the evening teaching, you see; that's what really began to needle Idris. Family commitments. He says we're carrying her and boozers like Charlie. Dead wood. He's all for these new ideas, such as teach-yourself packs. Give out tapes at the beginning of term and the students report progress every month. Interpersonal contact rendered anachronistic.'

Sharon bumped the cups and saucers down on the tray. She picked out the two stalest and smallest scones with the tongs.

That evening she sat at the breakfast bar eating sausage, beans and chips, with *Jane Eyre* open beside her.

As she chewed, she glanced at the surface of the text without taking anything in, for she was imagining a slimmed-down version of herself poncing around amongst the know-alls, spouting brilliant witticisms in a posh accent that would make them all sit up and stare. Sometimes she had to serve them at their cheese and wine parties. Standing behind a buffet covered in wine glasses, she would ask them if they wanted red or white. Then one fogey addressed all the other fogeys on some incomprehensible topic, and some of them sidled round for a fill-up. They were all supposed to know so much. On degree days they sailed around in black gowns like bats or red gowns like Santa Claus.

Her brother Jason was kicking a basketball round the sitting-room, the telly up full-blast.

'Shut it, Jason. Mum's trying to sleep, isn't she.'

'Sod off, widcy,' said Jason. He was off school again; had been suspended for smoking draw behind the bog. It wasn't known yet whether he'd be allowed back. The heavy basketball slammed into the television screen and ricocheted into a lamp.

On the way to work she had seen a dead rat floating in the pond. It had been so big, she'd taken it for a small terrier. 'It's a rat, that,' a child had said. On her way home she had turned her head away so as to avoid seeing if it was still there.

Tomato sauce bloodied the opening page of *Jane Eyre*.

They thought they knew so much, those geezers at the Institute, but they didn't know they was born. They didn't know nothing.

'So how was your day? asked Marianne tentatively.

'Hell.'

'Oh dear.'

Thomas did not ask how hers had been and so she did not tell him. First thing the following morning when she reminded him about the conference at the weekend, he exploded.

She exploded back.

Charlotte was sick over the wall and half her cot.

Andrew ran off into the back garden with Emlyn's dinkies, which he threw one by one over the wall into next-door's garden.

Emlyn lashed out at Andrew, who keeled over, hitting his head on a rock. He came in howling and bleeding, and Marianne had to race him to the Infirmary, where his head was X-rayed.

By the time she got back, Thomas had left for work, Brenda had arrived, Charlie had been sick again into a bucket and Emyln had gone to school.

Brenda complained that her ear was still not better, she had only come because Thomas had more or less begged, and she might have to go home again if the pain came on badly. It was clear that she was none too keen on a day with a toddler puking up and a child with possible concussion who must be watched in case he should either go into a coma or also start puking up.

She didn't much care for people vomiting, Brenda confided.

Marianne agreed that it wasn't her favourite thing either, but that if it was your profession to look after children, she supposed you took it in your stride.

Her blood boiled. She could have struck her. She had had to cancel her first lecture and she would be late for her seminar if she didn't get out now.

She remained polite.

Her mouth smiled.

As she bolted from the house, she could hear Charlie retching in her bedroom.

Idris Price was reading Marianne's 'Lecture postponed' notice as Marianne dashed up to her office. Hands behind his back, he nodded and sauntered off down the corridor.

'Sorry I'm late,' he heard her distraught voice say to those students who had bothered to wait. 'Unavoidably detained. Now . . . oh . . . what book are we meant to be on?'

Brenda made it clear that Andrew (who had been crying for his mum) had been brought through his trauma solely by her unflagging ministrations; that Charlotte, who had been badly ill all morning, had likewise been suffering from terminal separation anxiety, but that Brenda (whose ear was hurting almost unbearably) had kept reassuring her that Mum would be back soon. Emlyn was a naughty boy and she had had to send him to bed without his tea. She was now going back to the doctor's to get her antibiotics changed, and would ring up to say if she'd be well enough to come in tomorrow.

Thomas hurled a soup dish at the wall. He was damned if he'd babysit the whole weekend while she swanned off to a conference.

'But you promised, Tom! You promised!' she wailed.

She sat down and cried. Thomas said they couldn't go on like this. His nerves couldn't stand it. He had an exacting job. He was the chief earner in the household.

'So what do you want me to do? Me give in my notice, is that it? Stay at home and mind your children and lose my independence? — we'd have to sell the house you know — and move to a smaller one. That wasn't the life we wanted.'

Thomas said yes, yes, it was the only way.

Marianne stamped round the room. It wasn't fair, it wasn't fair. She slammed the doors and screamed. The children were silent, in a huddle on the landing. Thomas also stamped. He opened the doors she had slammed; and slammed them himself, harder.

Marianne found that she had thrown, amongst other items, a carton of eggs across the kitchen. They oozed down the wall in a mess of slime.

'She's thrown eggs at the wall,' Emlyn reported to Andrew. Andrew put his hand over his mouth. He stared out through the bars of his cot, a plaster over his cut forehead, his eyes wide.

'Splat,' said Andrew.

After midnight, Thomas got into bed beside Marianne. He took her stiff body in his arms and promised to cope over the weekend, provided, he said, *provided* we reassess the whole arrangement afterwards.

'I'm probably going to get the sack anyway,' said Marianne bitterly. 'So that should solve all your problems.'

Sleep was not possible: she was too tired and wrought, though Thomas slept soundly, sprawled on his back, and she held that against him. Now that he had fallen asleep and was no longer accessible, she longed for the embrace she had formerly refused.

Charlie was sitting up in her cot; just sitting there holding her woolly comfort-cloth in one hand and sucking her thumb. Her forehead resting on the bars of the cot, she was pondering her night-light, an object of intense reverence to the child, for in the orange tabernacle of its china interior a family of mouse-people lived, invisible by daylight.

'Mama,' said Charlie, without taking her thumb out of her mouth, or her eyes off the lamp. 'Mouses in there,' she added.

A pang of tenderness, mingled with remorse, quivered through Marianne. She had gone off and left Charlie to be sick all day in a stranger's keeping. She hadn't really cared at all, except about the nuisance.

'Charlie, I'm so sorry,' she whispered, and gathered the heavy girl up into her arms. 'Are you feeling all right, love?'

'Been sick,' said Charlie.

'What, now?'

Charlie nestled her face in against Marianne's neck. She shook her head as she nuzzled in.

'Better now, Charlie.'

Marianne kissed over and over again the irrepressible pale curls that clustered on Charlie's head. The downy baby hair was soft and springy as she rhythmically brushed her cheek and lips against it. The beautiful firm weight of the baby's bottom in her hands, the body against her body, reassured and substantiated her.

'Mouses in the light,' Charlie reminded her.

'Yes, that's where they live, isn't it? They watch over you while you sleep.'

'Lady in the garden,' mentioned Charlie, as an additional piece of information.

Marianne drew the curtain and together they looked down on the moonlit garden. Around the old apple tree, whose upper branches glimmered in the silver light, lay swathes of shadow, and the rocking boughs cast grids of criss-cross shadow over the lawn.

'Nobody out there, Charlie,' said Marianne. She held the child's plump left hand in her right hand. 'Just the moon and the apple tree.'

'Is a lady there, Charlie seed her,' said Charlie with conviction.

'Not there now.'

'*Is* there. Lady *is* there. Look.' She leant forward and pointed towards the triangular wedge of shadow at the base of the tree. Her finger traced an erratic arc as it designated an array of spaces inhabited by the alleged lady.

'That's just shadows, Charlie. *I* can't see a lady.' She pushed the child's hair back from her brow with tender fingers, and each time the challenged curls sprang back.

'*Not* shadows!' exclaimed Charlie rebelliously. Her freedom-fighter's jaw jutted forward.

Why deny the child's perception? Why say there's no friend out there if she dreams one up? After all, Charlie didn't seem frightened or distressed by the phantom. As far as she was concerned, it was just a matter of fact.

Together they said good night to the outsider.

Marianne had derived comfort standing here, lulled by her daughter's uncritical embrace; as if she had been the child and Charlie the parent. They changed places . . . she was gathered into safekeeping at high altitude . . . she swayed

58

where she stood, half asleep . . . and Charlie's breathing was deepening too, she was letting go. Marianne drew the curtain and laid Charlie back in her cot on her side.

'Sleep tight,' she said. Charlie was an imaginative child who often awoke with nightmares. 'No bad dreams.'

Perhaps she'd give it all up: retreat from the working world and be with the children. No more baleful-eyed Price snooping at her office door. No more rushing from one botched job to another. No more baby-minders with earache. Yet at the very same time as she was thinking these things, up had popped the ghost of an idea for the lecture. And it was something to do with Charlie's lady under the apple tree . . . something to do with seeing things . . .

Thomas not only helped her to pack, he ironed her trousers. Emlyn sat on the case so that she could pull the straps tight. Charlie slept in and refrained from being sick; Brenda's earache had improved and she arrived on time. Marianne put the finishing touches to her lecture.

Chapter 4

And I can tell by thine altered cheek
And by thy kindled gaze
And by the words thou scarce dost speak
How wildly fancy plays.

It stirred Eileen inexpressibly to be standing here at the Parsonage gate, looking out across the sloping graveyard. It was like a city of tombstones, their weather-worn slabs all tilted at discrepant angles to one another as if paving over some obscure underground disagreement. A wash of sunlight slanted on lichenous stones and trunks; rooks called; a scatter of winged sycamore seeds littered the graves. Emily too had stood here; seen along this eye-line. Eileen exhaled a sigh of qualified bliss, sharing space if not time with Emily.

If only the people would go away. People who had no real business here: garish, loud-mouthed people who got in the way and stopped Eileen from communing. She had come to commune; they had come to gawp and loiter.

A group of visitors was perched on a raised table-like tombstone, using it as a picnic area. They ate pizzas and sandwiches out of greaseproof paper and shared cans of Coca-Cola. Eileen didn't like that. It was irreverent. So many of the old values and codes of behaviour had passed away.

She stalked towards the family with fierce intent, mouth pursed. A lad in jeans and big boots sat astraddle the gravestone. He had very little hair, and a stud in one ear. Stuffing a handful of crisps in his mouth, he chewed insolently at Eileen, staring her in the eye. She marched up to him and said . . . nothing.

Nothing came out.

'What's up with her?' enquired the youth, and threw his crisp bag on the ground.

Eileen gave the crisp bag a scandalised stare. It bowled away in the breeze around several headstones and lodged at the base of the tree.

'Litter louts,' stated Eileen. 'Disgraceful. In a graveyard too.'

She glowered at the mother.

'You got some sort of head problem?' enquired the mother, glowering back.

'Don't you know this is a churchyard? Have you no regard or respect for the dead?'

'Oh bugger off,' advised the mother.

The hairless boy inserted his index finger into his right nostril and screwed it round vigorously.

His sister mentioned that it was a free country.

The libertarian boy lay back on the tombstone and, folding his arms across his chest and wagging one black-booted foot in the air, took up the strains of 'Rule, Britannia'.

'Hey, watch out Damien, I said watch out, you've put your elbow in the . . . God, get up, you slob, look now you've knocked it over . . . Damien, I said sit *up*. Now look at you, it's all over your coat, wipe it off. Get up.'

'I got nowt to wipe it off with.'

The mother scrubbed furiously at his jacket.

'It were *her* fault,' he said, jabbing a forefinger in Eileen's direction. 'Bloody interfering old cow. . . .'

A spillage of something that might have been yoghurt oozed across the gravestone and dripped off the edge.

'*Well*,' said Eileen. '*Well*. Now I've heard everything.' She was quivering with a complex of anger and embarrassment. 'Defiling the graves. Disturbing the well-earned rest of the departed. For your information, young man, this is hallowed ground, you are committing sacrilege, I could make a citizen's arrest.'

'Just you try it,' said the mother.

'Yeah, go on, just you try.' The son thrust forward towards Eileen, who took a step back. But she continued in a strong voice to advocate the rights of the dead.

'The dead don't give a sod. Because,' said the youth, 'they're *dead*. Get it?'

The mother, having gathered together the detritus, shot Eileen a withering look but indicated an intention of retreat.

'Come on Damien, come on Sean, Caroline, we're going. I'm not staying around *here*.' Her injured look seemed to demand if there were any better use that Eileen could think of for a mouldy old tombstone than for healthy outdoor family recreation?

Eileen was incensed that vulgar people should spoil her pilgrimage with their rubbishy way of life. She deplored their blue T-shirts bearing the motto 'Exterminator'; their Liverpool accents; their pepperoni pizzas and their smelly burgers.

A dog burst into the churchyard, a giant of a dog. It bounded past its owner and tore through the gravestones.

'Kipper! Heel!' the young woman called. But Kipper was away. A massive creature, Eileen saw, a cross between bulldog and mastiff. People got out of its way rather fast. It snarled and snuffied amongst the chip papers, licking up the grease. Then it turned a great dolorous face towards Eileen. She was aware of its heavy panting; smelt its animal presence.

'Kipper!'

The dog butted its head against Eileen's skirt, then wetly and familiarly slobbered at her hand, sniffing with its chill black snout. She took courage to pat its solid flanks.

She had come over quite faint; teetered back towards a tombstone and sat down heavily, closing her eyes. When she opened them again, Kipper had been retrieved by the young woman, who had him on a chain and was leading him out of the gate on to the moorland path. The graveyard was now empty, apart from an infirm old man slowly and wheezingly threading his way amongst the tombstones, leaning on a stick. She wiped her hand on a tissue. Odour of dog was still about her, which, being a catty person, she found disagreeable.

Lemon-coloured cool light lay over the graveyard. It was at once peaceful and melancholy; just right. She had come for this, exactly this, and was not to be disappointed.

The sky was silver-grey with a thin film of cloud that veiled the sunlight so that it touched all surfaces of tree and stone with gentleness.

She began to dream.

'Never', said the dark man, '*never* was anything at once so frail and so indomitable.'

'I am a free human being with an independent will,' replied Eileen with a voice that shook with emotion but remained strong and definite, 'which I now exert to leave you.'

But he mastered her . . . he pinioned her . . . she shook free, or rather his hands fell away. 'Whatever I do with its cage, I cannot get at it — the savage, beautiful creature! If I tear, if I rend the slight prison, my outrage will only let the captive loose,' he went on.

'Do you mind,' wheezed the old man, 'if I join you?' He waited for her to nod before perching on the tombstone at a respectful distance.

Eileen, blushfully plucking imaginary specks from her jacket, inspected the old man out of the corner of her eye. The old chap was clearly in a bad way, getting his difficult breath as he gazed studiously towards the Parsonage.

'Grand weather,' croaked Timothy. The old dear was sitting up erect as a ramrod; yet there was a touchingly little-girl look about her, for her legs were so short that her feet did not quite reach the ground. And she seemed to be coming adrift from herself in some indefinable way; her hair in its sheath looked not quite right; her jacket askew.

'It is indeed. Most pleasant.' The ghost had thinned away to nothing and fled, leaving as always that feeling of disrelish, like the sour taste in the mouth on waking, which has to be flushed away with a brisk mouthful of water.

'Come far?' he enquired. Loneliness exuded from her.

'From Ludlow.'

'Oh – Ludlow. A most historic place. My wife and I stayed there – on several occasions. Have you been round the Parsonage?'

'*Many* times,' replied Eileen frostily. She bristled. It irritated her beyond words when casual visitors assumed you were a fellow tourist, whereas in fact you were practically related to the Brontës; well, at least, to the Nusseys, which was the next-best thing.

'Ah,' he said. 'You're the same as me. An *aficionado*.'

'I beg your pardon? A what?'

A fit of coughing bent Timothy double. Hoping it wasn't

catching, Eileen squirmed nearer to her end of the gravestone.

'Heart condition,' he wheezed, purple in the face.

'Oh dear. Do you wish me to summon assistance?'

He shook his head. The seizure was abating. 'Quite normal,' he spluttered. 'Passes off.'

Eileen was queasily aware of a strong resistance to exercising her caring skills. She was after all supposed to be off duty. Gathering her handbag and raincoat together, she slid down from the tomb, murmured a goodbye and scuttled away up the path to the turnstile leading to the moors. There she reproached herself for her lack of charity, imagining a prostrate form beside the tomb, and retraced her steps to see the old man shambling back towards the church.

Somehow the sight of his decrepitude inspired in Eileen a heady sense of her own vigour. She strode along the path, past the chicken coops, along rustling hawthorn hedges, scanning out over the valley to the grey-green ridge with its windfarm. The blades of the white windmills busily sliced the gusty air. As she scaled the steep tree-lined path to the moors, past the farm where the alsatians barked, the wind quickened, her excitement rose, and as she reached the top of the path and the shelter of walls and trees was withdrawn, the wind rushed up to meet her with a shout. Over the road were the dark, wintry foothills of Emily's moor. Buoyant, billowing, Eileen sailed across, her carefully built hairstyle flying asunder, and began to climb the path like an eighteen-year-old.

Timothy toiled downhill, grumbling to himself. It was just as bad as Hayfield but far more imbecilic. The village was in the hands of madmen, and overrun by visiting lunatics. He could scarcely move for the press of tourists, who crammed the streets and butted one another for access to trinket shops. The Land of Gondal – the Villette Coffee House – Wuthering This and Blithering That. Children with helium balloons squirmed through the crush, grizzling. Other children demanded ice cream and genuine Yorkshire fudge. They must have it, they screamed. They would die without their genuine Yorkshire fudge. The arms of parents were yanked. The parents retaliated by minor acts of violence. The affronted offspring called for justice at the tops of their voices. Potbellied men drifted downhill with gormless expressions, turning their heads as if looking for something, but unsure what exactly they were seeking. The wind spanked them all and the cloud frowned. Militant persons heading uphill battled against the army on its downward manoeuvre. Some seemed to hover, as if speculating as to which side was the more likely to prevail.

Wedged against a shop advertising Brontë Buns, Timothy laboured for breath.

'Oh,' said the woman who had poked him with the spike of her umbrella. 'Excuse *me*. It's such a crush.'

A space opened. Launching himself into it, Timothy was carried downhill by the thrust of a band of leather-clad youngsters who barged forward confidently, their whole lives ahead of them.

Then he saw the fire-eaters.

A family of fire-eaters had set up on the steps of the church, taking turns to perform their acts. A young man with a ponytail, dressed in leathers, shoved a burning gas torch into his mouth and blew out flame. He did this in a matter-of-fact way and then retired to sit on the steps in a condition of apparently terminal boredom as his swarthy father heaved himself from his torpor and undertook to juggle three burning torches. His expression was one of resignation. The moronic throwing of fire-brands into the air for a thankless public was, his world-weary face implied, a calling which he would gladly abandon for any other profession which suggested itself – but none did. The mother, who did not actively participate either in juggling or eating the fire, kept an eye on the cap into which the crowd threw occasional coins.

Above her head a notice prophesied a pious coffee morning; to her left a guide-post directed pilgrims to a shrine selling Miss Eliza Branwell's home-made teddy bears and assorted superior cuddlies.

Past the Black Bull, Timothy went with the crowd. The smell of chips wafted on the air in waves of aroma at once appetising and nauseous. The clink of glasses in the pub was attractive but he knew his lungs would never stand the fug of smoke. However, he absolutely must sit down before he fell down.

The young woman seated opposite him in the café morosely consumed an eclair.

She then started on a doughnut.

She was a hefty size, he reflected, eyeing the immensity of her bosom with some pleasure, for he had no objection to a bit of flesh on a woman; none in the slightest. Jojo had been (he called it) well made – ample. And such lovely breasts. Full, beautiful, generous breasts. So soft in his hands, and somehow flowing, overflowing. She was proud of them – as well she might be.

And then to have one sawn off – thrown into the fire like a piece of diseased meat. He could not think of a woman's breasts without that physical pang of dark recall. Jojo going into the hospital in all her superb womanliness, and coming out one-breasted. An Amazon, she said. She'd taken it in her own style; cried a few times (but not on his shoulder);

consulted the goddess. The goddess fortified her with iron strength. There was no point in lamenting, Jojo told him severely; she had her life. She was going to live it to the full, breast or no breast, though she admitted she did feel lopsided. But she wouldn't wear a prosthesis; that wasn't her way. Songs to Mother Nature increased in volume and frequency. Humbly, Timothy tried to join in. Some days he came upon her sitting at the window, sombre and separate. But mostly she sang.

Oh my courageous Jojo, he thought to himself now. And the tears sprang in his eyes.

He started to lever himself up, pulling on the bench and the table, puffing hard; but could make no progress and had to let himself capsize ignominiously back. The young woman put down her doughnut and stared. A blob of cream moustached her upper lip. She would fetch him a cup of coffee, she said, and advised him to put his feet up.

'Go on – no one'll mind,' she chivvied. 'And if they do, too bad.'

He rested his pulsating feet on the bench. The water pills had been helping but could not cope with the pounding he'd given himself today. He accepted the coffee gratefully, and added a tot of brandy from his flask.

'You'll have a drop?'

'Go on then.' She giggled. There was a pretty face peeping out through that mass of flesh. When she thrust her chin forward, the drowned face surfaced from the flab. 'I'll need this, for the conference,' she said. 'I've not been to one before.'

They exchanged names and a bit about their backgrounds.

'Mrs Pendlebury invited me, like. She said I were a real reader. I weren't going to come, I mean, I thought it were ridiculous . . . and then I thought, why not? It might be a laugh. I've read *Jane Eyre* and that.'

'So you . . . *know* Marianne Pendlebury. I mean, personally.' He could not say the name without a shiver of veneration. 'What's she like? I've only corresponded.'

'Oh . . . decent,' said Sharon, consideringly. 'No side. A bit of a wreck though.'

Decent . . . a bit of a wreck. This was nothing like the Marianne Timothy had divined from the wonderful sequence of letters. The girl's words offended him; and yet they aroused his curiosity.

'How do you mean?'

'Well – decent. You know. Not everyone's decent, are they? Some of them old blokes she works with . . . a right shower.' She ladled two spoonfuls of brown sugar into her coffee. 'They don't think we see nothing from behind the counter, but what we couldn't tell their wives is nobody's business. . . . Well, at least she treats you like a human.'

'But you said, a bit of a . . . wreck?'

A black-haired man in a paper cap and an apron clapped his hands authoritatively. He had issued from behind the bakery counter, where he had been serving a non-stop queue of customers Yorkshire curd tarts and lemon flans, Parkin cake, vast scones, Brontë biscuits and Norfolk fruit loaves.

'Now – ladies! ladies! – your attention please!'

Guffaws from male clients greeted this address but the café became perceptibly quieter and accorded its attention to the speaker, whose ringing tenor enunciated with a southern accent, not without affectation. Timothy expected a lecture on the social history of the area at the very least.

'Ladies! The moment you've all been waiting for – late-afternoon bargains galore! Four cream cakes for the price of one . . . four curdies for the price of two . . . five custards for the price of three. . . . You, madam, will have four cream cakes? Excellent, how discriminating . . . you won't regret it, I promise you . . . now who'll have the custards . . . all fresh, home-baked. . . .'

An expression came over Sharon, needy, raw, voracious. She made a wobbling dash for the tray. She couldn't resist. Returning, red in the face, she rested on the table two carrier bags.

'What did you get?'

Timothy listened with awe as she enumerated her buys. He restrained himself from asking whether and, if so, how, she intended to eat all those herself. Her face, tinged with embarrassment, was also vague and far away, like someone stuck half-way in and half-way out of a dream.

'Sounds good,' he said.

'I shouldn't really.'

'Well . . . if you enjoy it.'

'Excuse my asking,' she said, as they got up to go. 'But how long've you had that beard?'

'Let's see, oh, thirty years at least. It covers a mass of defects.' He fingered it tenderly. 'I hunker down behind it,' he confided. 'Wouldn't feel dressed without it. And too lazy to shave.'

It was a notable beard, long and thick but carefully trimmed in a curious wedge shape, and varying in colour, chiefly pale grey but with flecks of black, like a badger. He *was* a queer old stick, Sharon thought, but friendlier than most and a bit unusual. She helped him down the hill to his guest house.

'See you this evening then.'

She wandered the streets, liking the place very much. She loved the shops with the horse brasses, the statuettes, Victorian dolls, books, pictures and china shepherdesses; all things

70

she didn't normally see, novelties to put on your sideboard to show you'd been. She bought a mug decorated with the pictures of the three Brontë sisters. She'd meant it as a present for Dot, but when she'd gone back into the street and taken it out of its tissue paper to examine it, she decided to keep it for herself instead.

The fire-eaters had attracted quite a crowd. Sharon stood on the fringe, sucking a lolly. In this kind of place there was always something going on that you wouldn't normally get the chance to see. It was as good as Blackpool but more tasteful. She began to forget herself as she eyed a good-looking boy who was standing smirking at the front of the circle. A powerfully built lad, he had on a sleeveless T-shirt and you could see his muscles bulging under the tattoos. His hair was long and fair, and there was a stud in his left ear. That was the kind of lad she could really fancy. He was well fit. He looked brutal and callous but as if somehow there was a soft side to him. She'd like him to. . . .

'That's it now, folks. Show's over.' The fire-eaters abruptly switched off their implements and began to pack them away. A jingle of final coins was cast in the cap, which the woman emptied into a drawstring purse. The good-looking male caught Sharon's stare. He winked. She flushed. Did he? Would he?

Fatty Mitchell, they had called her at school. *Gross*, they labelled her. Or *Widey, Wide-arse*. You never got used to the sting, although, clenching your teeth, you smiled.

And so she had retreated into solitary apartness; stood as an observer to life.

'If you've got it,' said the fair-haired lad, 'flaunt it.' He stood over her, taller by a head because the pavement shelved so steeply. 'Gorgeous, aren't you?'

Was he kidding? Taunting her? His ginger-haired mate

stood behind him looking on, chewing gum, with a Walkman clamped over his ears.

'Don't,' said Sharon, half-grinning, coming over all hot.

'Come on darling.'

'What?'

'Come round behind the car-park for ten minutes. Come on. You're too gorgeous, you. Isn't she gorgeous, Jason?' The ginger mate seemed to sneeze into his cupped palm; looked up with eyes of scorching mirth.

Sharon saw the trap; stepped back; half turned away.

'No, I mean it. Not kidding you, pet. You're the best thing since. . . .'

'Enough for two of us there, Dave . . .'

Sharon plunged through the crowd away from those vile mouths. She ought to have socked them one. She heard the word 'whale'. She did not look back. They ought to be locked up; they were animals.

Back in her room in the guest house, she avoided her reflection in the wardrobe mirror. Her heavy body always seemed separate from herself; she'd never have chosen it if she'd been given a chance. Obviously she'd have been a slender light girl with skin that wasn't greasy. Yet her body was her. She had to be it.

Anyway that lad had rotten skin, when you looked at him close to. Acne. The thought of his defects consoled her. She put away her underclothes in the drawer that smelt of mothballs. Her own skin might be greasy but at least it wasn't spotty. And the ginger one was a right weedy specimen. She should have socked him one – floored him.

In her mind's eye she saw Ginger laid out on the church steps with a black eye; herself marching off, punching the air in triumph. Applause. A better Blond Lad with a kinder nature following her to the guest house, coming up here and lying in her arms on the bed. The beating of Ginger was somehow easier to visualise than this bedding of Blondie. For one thing the bed was so narrow. And . . . the hurt would keep breaking up the picture.

How cruel he'd been, cruel, in leading her on like that. Sexy people could be cruel. They could afford to be. Excitedly you switched on the light and instead of brightness got an electric shock.

She automatically searched for comfort in the usual place. Opening the bag of cream cakes, she drew out a cardboard box which, when opened, revealed ruin. The custard slices had been squashed and their contents impacted with the wreckage of two fragile eclairs. It all looked as if it had been sat on by a large bottom: unappetising.

They provided tea-making equipment in these places now. Under a list of 'Do Not's' was a small round tray containing kettle, cups, teabags and cartons of milk. She was pleased by this and immediately put the kettle on to boil.

Do not spill Beverages on Carpet or Furniture, she read. *Do not Smoke in Bed. Leave Room as you would Wish to find it.* The proprietors wished their tidy guests a pleasant stay. There was quite a view down over the grey rooftops to the hills. Standing at the window, she took in the vista of pearl-grey sky and the charcoal-grey shoulder of the distant hill. Her mind calmed. It amused her that the ornaments had been glued to the windowsill in case you made off with them. She tried to lever one up but it must have been stuck down with Araldite.

The cakes tasted fine despite being smashed. She ate the cream with a teaspoon and washed them down with tea. She hadn't come here for the lads anyway, she'd come . . . she wasn't sure why . . . but it was a change and something to talk about to Dot and the girls when she got home. She'd wear her black two-piece to the Dinner and Introductory Meeting. It was actually a maternity evening gown she'd bought in Mothercare, wide and floppy. Black seemed to shrink her. Sharon brushed back her shiny brown hair and caught it at the side with a silver slide. Round her neck she placed a silver cross on a fine chain.

She should have slugged him one in the eye with her fist and kicked him in the balls.

She put her paperback *Jane Eyre* in her coat pocket and let herself out.

That is, if he had any balls.

'Good evening,' she replied to an elderly woman in a herringbone coat who was scrabbling her key in the lock of the adjacent room.

She should have said something dignified at the top of her voice such as, 'How dare you speak to me like that?' as soon as he propositioned her. That was her mistake.

'I'm frightfully late,' said the woman. 'Supposed to be at a conference,' she added with a certain magnificence, 'in ten minutes.'

'Oh,' said Sharon. 'I'm going there.'

The woman shot into her room. The door clicked shut. Sharon arranged her scarf and buttoned up her coat as she went downstairs. *A right pair of wankers*, she thought derisively, and, booting Ginger and that lad who thought so much of himself one final time in their respective groins, shoved them to the back of her mind.

Eileen surveyed the wreckage of her expensive hairstyle with a groan. She had asked Kathleen to apply a double squirt of lacquer yesterday, to make sure it stayed in place all weekend. The top part was supposed to be bouffante; the rest was pinned up at the back in a sort of French roll. The idea was that it should be at once elegant and built to last. This meant you didn't actually comb it except superficially between sessions. Interventions could be disastrous. Now the top part was standing up like a crest, and several strands had completely escaped the pins. She plumped down in front of the dressing-table mirror, panting. Her face was red and she felt frazzled. Her only real desire was to burrow under the quilt and have a nap; but then she'd miss the opening and it was important to get your oar in from the outset, otherwise advantage was lost. She had it in mind just to mention the existence of her new-found original watercolour by Emily this evening – to whet expectation. Then to produce it from her handbag at some suitable time.

The wind up there on the moors had rushed her into roaming the heather in a delirium of ecstasy, murmuring fragments of Emily's poetry, thinking 'You were here – exactly where I am now – Emily – I'm walking in your footsteps', and she had roved across the zigzag tracks to Penistone Hill, with its view over the reservoir. Lapwings rose and rode the air currents, skimming and diving; she caught their frail calls through the roar of air. She looked out over the wind-ruffled surface of the silver reservoir and the lush green of the lowlands to the blackness of the hills and wondered when she had been so happy.

Then all of a sudden the exaltation died. The slamming wind caused her ears to ache; she felt fagged and chilled, and reeled back along the lower path, stumbling in her unsuitable shoes. When she realised the time, she was exasperated with herself.

'Stupid woman,' she ticked off her mirror reflection. 'You really should organise yourself better.'

Eileen powdered her face so that it appeared less florid, and mended the beehive as best she could. That was what came of giving way to Instinct and Passion. Yet without Instinct and Passion, life was a poor, pale thing.

> 'Riches I hold in light esteem,
> And love I laugh to scorn,'

she informed the dressing-table mirror. No doubt people sniggered at her. She knew they did. They thought of her as an odd bod. She *was* an odd bod.

So was Emily Brontë an odd bod. And no one laughed at her. She stood out for the value of peculiarity.

Yet at the same time there was a dismay, rather difficult to bear, at the thought of not fitting. It sang in her ears, the loneliness, and the shyness she had to break through in order to signal her presence to others. Sometimes she'd listen in to her own voice, apprehensively wondering what she was destined to hear herself say next.

If there were only some one person to love her. If she had only had the good fortune to walk accompanied through life.

She shut the door upon the single bed and made her way vigorously downstairs; handed in her key; ventured into the street. A sprinkling of strollers still drifted around but most visitors had roared off down the motorway to Manchester, Halifax and Bradford, leaving the village quiet in twilight. Eileen navigated downhill over the cobbles, behind a couple in late middle age walking hand in hand, the woman leaning inwards towards her husband.

Eileen focused with a pang on the linked hands; looked away; stared again.

The husband, wearing a check cloth cap and carrying a stick, looked large, nondescript, dependable. If you had one of those, you need never feel out on a limb. You would be equipped, protected. A profound longing welled up for a husband. Any husband. That husband there.

She plucked the wife away and sent her spinning into space. Eileen slipped in and, taking the woman's place, clung to his arm, coupled herself up. She was safe and secure, out of the force of the wind which his robust mackintoshed person broke for her. How comforting to rest under the shelter of such a rock. She snuggled in under his arm. He'd open the door and usher her through ahead of him. He'd methodically lock up at night and make sure all the bills were paid, relieving you of all practical worries.

'And so I said to him, you've not done a good job on those gaskets, I'm not satisfied, mate, that's not what I call a proper service, I'll take my custom elsewhere, that's what I said to him, I told him straight out,' was the message the husband was imparting to the wife as Eileen passed by them. He was wagging his walking-stick in front of him to emphasise his points, which Eileen felt must be a very aggravating habit.

And she bet he snored too.

The trouble was, if you acquired a husband, you had to make do with what you'd got; and you could never be quite sure what you'd landed yourself with until it was too late. This was the wisdom on which she had acted as a young woman, waiting for the special, the providentially indicated person to appear round the corner. Hence she had remained a virgin.

Well, there was still time.

Not much though. If only that young lad in De Greys had kept in touch. Crinkly hair and a diffident but thrillingly beautiful smile when it came. Loved Beethoven. Poor teeth. Lost his mother when he was seven. Gentle as a lamb.

She hadn't wanted a lamb.

She'd been awaiting a lion. But the lion never came. And the teeth could have been seen to. His love of music was most touching. And he'd told her music took his mother's place. Where his mother had been, there was first nothing, a gap, a hole; some religious feelings; then music. He'd stood at the graveside, so he said, with a roaring in his ears, and his mother in a box was lowered into the earth, and he looked up and saw his father crying behind his hand; and remorse had come over him for he wanted to but couldn't help his father; and they all had to throw earth – earth on his mother. 'But I was all right – quite all right,' he'd reassured her brightly and kindly. Then he went to Burma. No word came.

'And anyway the cylinder head wants cleaning, I told him that, and the batteries want looking at and there's a squeak in the back, I told you about that squeak, but the squeak's still there . . .'

How did women put up with men who went on and on about gaskets and squeaks? The wife's eyes were glazed; she was in her own world, and as they in turn overtook Eileen she heard her say 'Yes dear'. Then she said 'Braised beef, I think', as if in answer to a phantom question. And the husband replied, 'Well, I'll not go back *there* in a hurry.'

The lamb was probably lamb chops. Died in some POW camp. Or else came home and became a music teacher and married . . . or never married . . . Eileen stopped in her tracks.

He might still be alive. Her Frank might never have married. Illumination poured from a streetlamp by the Railway Museum. She might be able to trace him, even now. A reunion at De Greys, where nothing had changed. They'd talk about old times and exchange life stories. She would show him her memorabilia of Anne and Emily Brontë. She would shyly admit, 'I always liked you'; and there in the murky light, with a lorry clattering past, fifty years too late, it was clear she had made a mistake.

For it was nowhere stated that Heathcliff had to be six foot tall. Built like a prizefighter. Thews and brawn. Bull-necked. Muscle-bound. The eternal rocks beneath must be stable and securing.

An avenue seemed to open into the past.

The beeches outside Timothy's mullioned windows surged and soughed in a breeze that could find no entrance to become a draught. Marianne had done him proud, lodging him in the best hotel in the area, plush and comfortable, and wonderfully warm. It made him aware of how draughty the Hayfield cottage was. Downstairs was an immense log fire in an original dog-grate, throwing out vital heat into a wide semicircle, within which two golden Labradors basked. A copper scuttle gleamed in the red, flamy light. It was as if Marianne, discerning his need for warmth, had laid it all on for his benefit; to show how truly special he was to her. He curbed his rising excitement.

'You are a lovely woman,' he would say to Marianne. 'A beautiful woman.'

Nonsense. Nonsense. And as if to punish his folly and self-deception, a fit of coughing tore at his lungs. Afterwards he lay feeble and spent, incapable of moving, though he was desperate to pee.

What a room, though. It was a place to study and marvel over, being genuinely ancient, with walls part wood-panelled, hand-carved furniture and a four-poster bed with bevelled and fluted posts, and red velvet hangings within which you could sequester yourself if you chose. Around the walls hung original oil paintings, no more than moderately competent but certainly the real thing – amateurish portraits of local mill owners' wives and views of Heptonstall under snow and Stanbury by moonlight. Upon the sumptuous array of the crimson bed, his nervous, narrow body lay like a sad little private irony, appreciated only by himself.

There was scarcely any time to make himself presentable to attend the introductory do. Perhaps he wouldn't bother. Perhaps he'd lie here and nap and watch Sky TV, try to assemble his strength for tomorrow.

But then he wouldn't see Marianne, beautiful special Marianne, until tomorrow. Marianne who had singled him out and made his failing life lustrous with her regard. With tremulous hands, he knotted his tie. The devil of a job to tie his laces. A nip of brandy for courage. He hung the quincunx round his neck as a talisman.

Chapter 5

Vain are the thousand creeds
That move men's hearts, unutterably vain,
Worthless as withered weeds
Or idlest froth amid the boundless main

'And now,' announced Neil Thorniley, 'Dr Marianne Pendlebury will deliver the introductory address.'

Vigorous clapping ensued from a hall packed with expectant enthusiasts, of diverse shapes, persuasions and nationalities. A cluster of orientals beamed in the front row; a scattering of elegant and distinguished scholars sat with their knees crossed amongst scholars just as distinguished but more rumpled and homespun. The Reverend Ron Hebblewhite, the authority on the Reverend Patrick Brontë's *Cottage Poems*, sat in his dog collar, sandwiched between two militant feminists from opposing schools of thought, Gillie Deneuve of Princeton, who believed Charlotte wrote the perfect ('uterine') female sentence, and Laurie Morgan of the New University of Chichester, who had deconstructed *Wuthering Heights* in a manner so brilliant that few could understand it and even fewer could fault it with conviction, though many burned to do so. Laurie, in a silk blouse of violent green, wore earrings which were great loops of gold. They caught the light quiveringly and entirely unnerved Marianne, who had hoped Laurie would not attend. Laurie smiled dazzlingly up at Marianne.

Stan Smedley from Hull sat with his associates Tom Lassiter and Alexander Mulryne from Glasgow. They collaborated over learned articles on Anne Brontë's use of the semicolon and the dash, and how far the excess and defect of these might be attributable to Compositor A, B or C. At intervals of a decade they collected their bibliographical findings and published them as books which they regarded as daring and sensational. They were decent, gentlemanly academics of the old school, who dressed in shabby corduroy jackets, possessed a fund of courtesy and tedious anecdote, and voted Liberal Democrat.

Kerry Richards was there, Marianne's friend from undergraduate days. Gentle and compassionate, she could never hold her own in argument but would tend to agree effusively with whatever was put to her; and now nodded affirmatively at Marianne as if to endorse in advance any and every opinion she might emit. Yet Kerry had written a swingeing book shredding most of the Big Names in what she denounced as 'the Brontë Industry'. Next to her sat a large-framed man with a frizzy white beard, resembling a Cumberland Shepherd; beside him another bearded old man, thin and coughing; and beside him, Marianne recognised the girl from the canteen, Sharon. So she had come then. Whatever would she make of it all? And – oh dear – Mrs Passion had come – sitting bolt upright, looking roused, red-faced – and that extraordinary individual with the sonorous voice who would rant on about the Magnetic Vision and the Electric Genius of Emily Brontë, and might be moved to burst into song. They all looked, from where Marianne was sitting, pent, buoyant, infinitely disputatious.

'So . . . Marianne – ' Neil Thorniley stood aside.

The room wobbled, teetered, under the stress of her fright. Gripping the lectern, Marianne sucked in a deep breath. Her notes swam. When she looked up, she saw there were identical twins, identically dressed, in the front row. This pair of doubles increased the sense of vertigo. Her voice came out high and girlish.

'Ladies and . . .'

She dropped it.

'. . . gentlemen. I'm so happy to welcome you all to our conference.'

(And please be nice to me; and like me; and agree with all my words of wisdom, however gormless they may superficially appear.)

'Very happy,' she added miserably.

(She'd lost her place in the script.)

'I'm sure it will be a most exciting and stimulating occasion, with so many diverse minds . . . and . . . after all, we have so much to share, so much in common, a common love which makes us one . . .'

(Laurie's earrings trembled as she shook her head very decisively. Dissident light spangled from them. No way were we one, her earrings asserted. As Marianne would soon see.)

(But, riposted Marianne desperately, these are just my polite opening remarks. You can't in all conscience disparage my opening remarks.)

'. . . although,' she faltered, placating the earrings, 'we can't expect to agree completely, we shall have our differences, even passionate differences, and air them . . . perhaps vehemently . . .'

(Mrs Passion, smiled, or so it seemed, keen encouragement. This was what she liked to hear. Kerry sat forward in her chair and nodded. Marianne began to feel better. She sketched in the programme for the next two days, together with the walk to Top Withens, which was punctuated by racking fits of coughing from an aged person who seemed to be dying of lung disease in the middle of the room.)

'And now,' she went on. 'My talk today. I have entitled it "The Real Emily Brontë".'

That man's cough was truly dreadful. Impossible to speak through. She paused for a moment; then passed her water to someone in the front row, gesturing for it to be relayed back. The cougher was doused and quenched.

' "The Real Emily Brontë",' she repeated.

(Tom Lassiter raised his eyebrows humorously at Stan Smedley, lounging back in his seat with folded arms. But the Cumberland Shepherd sat up expectantly. And the twins at the front both began to scribble.)

'I expect you think it's a tall order,' Marianne confided intimately. 'After all, I've only got an hour. The subject needs a year at least. A lifetime. Several lifetimes. We all feel that.'

(Murmurs of assent. Marianne smiled.)

'For there are thousands of Emilies. We each carry one about with us. She belongs to us. We are bonded to her and she is made of the raw material of our dreams, in deep communion with the text of *Wuthering Heights* and the poems. If I tell you about my personal Emily Brontë, therefore, I cannot be telling you about the *real* Emily Brontë; and neither is it practicable for me to go around collecting the thousands of Emilies at large and put them together in one great compound. So what am I to do?'

('Waffle,' said the closed expression of Gillie Deneuve. 'Wake me up when you have something to say.')

('Nice woman though,' mused Alex Mulryne. 'If terribly vague.' He scratched an itch between his sock and trouser leg.)

('*My* Emily *is* the real Emily,' protested individuals who knew in their bones that nobody but themselves possessed the key.)

'Well,' Marianne proceeded, and turned over the page. 'What I propose is this . . .'

The lectern was quite inadequate for its purpose. Two sheets of paper slid off and wafted on the wings of a draught down into the audience.

'There, just by your foot,' whispered Kerry Richards to the Japanese woman next to her. They scrabbled together for the second sheet, which was passed back up to the dais.

'There ought to be another one,' said Marianne. 'There, just by your bag . . . Sorry about this,' she apologised to the audience, which squirmed on her account. 'What I propose . . .'

(Hot with embarrassment, she gave up pretending to speak extempore and just read the thing aloud. She'd like to die. She was hopeless. She'd be better working in a supermarket. Could not be natural. Could not confront people. Was a failure. A joke.)

She came to the end. The applause was thunderous. Probably corporate relief that it was over.

'Absolutely splendid,' said Alex Mulryne, pumping her hand. 'You've certainly got us off to a good start. Given us something to think about.' He sipped his sherry.

'Really?' She could scarcely recall what she'd said. Was still shaking with nerves. She took a stiff swig of sweet sherry.

'That was so lovely,' Kerry said. 'I was terribly moved.'

'Were you?' said Marianne. 'I felt a bit . . . uncertain, to tell the truth.'

'Well, it didn't show.'

'It was awful when my notes fell down.'

'Broke the ice,' Kerry reassured her.

'Honestly?'

'Oh sure. Something like that happened to me at the MLA in '89,' said Ellen Rooney Herzog. She told the tale, to polite laughter. 'Never again,' said Ellen. 'I staple my notes together now and glue them to the desk.'

'Off to a cracking start,' said Stan Smedley.

'Quite fascinating,' gushed Mrs Passion. 'Food for thought.'

Marianne began to float. It was all right then. She had not made a complete ass of herself. She was a success. Stan topped up her glass. He was imparting his latest thoughts on Anne Brontë's misspellings in *The Tenant of Wildfell Hall*. His theory was that a boy read the manuscript to the compositor, thus occasioning errors.

'Oh yes?' said Marianne.

'Bit of a daring hypothesis. Still. You have to shake 'em up occasionally.'

'Oh you do. Absolutely.'

The crowds eddied around Marianne. Polite flattery had gone to her head and, from believing herself to be a sickening failure, she now celebrated inwardly a resonant success. She floated off to the loo and locked herself in a cubicle.

Wonderful. Brilliant. A brilliant woman – and a natural speaker, commented inward voices. *Knows all there is to know about Emily Brontë,* said an authoritative male voice, a voice coming from someone in a dark suit who had been looking round for years for someone to label Grade A. *And so easy with people – sensitive, thoughtful,* purred another voice.

She reached for the toilet paper.

Almost a genius, said a voice of treacle.

Yes, but modest. Wears her learning so lightly.

She pulled her pants up. She sucked at the teat of fantasy

all the while; and the generous teat came pouring out sweet nourishment.

Oh, yes, when she speaks in a large room, you feel as if she's addressing you personally.

Oh, we all feel that.

Marianne looked at her tired face in the cloakroom mirror: the fluorescent lighting betrayed the sallowness of her skin, the lacklustre brown hair whose short crop somehow failed to give the urchin look to which she aspired. Washing her hands, she flashed a bright, public smile to discountenance the depressing insight the real face threatened.

'Charlatan,' the face told Marianne bleakly. 'Humbug.'

She turned away to dry her hands. This gave the adulating voices fresh access.

Marianne is very sincere. Genuineness and intellectual acumen: these are a rare combination of gifts in our profession: a helping of syrup.

Such a powerful mind: wildly whipped cream.

Beautiful speaking voice: brown sugar, melting on the tongue.

Eloquently lovely face: oozing caramel.

'Christ,' she thought. 'Better get back.'

She mingled. An ancient man, thin and intense-looking, manoeuvred into the corner of her eye. He was vainly attempting to make contact through signalling round the bulk of a garrulous person who was telling an anecdote about Branwell Brontë in Bradford which he seemed to be making up as he went along.

'Kerry, for pity's sake,' said Marianne, 'save me from that Ancient Mariner.'

'Who?'

'That poor old crock. I *don't* want to be unkind, but I don't feel I could face a long tirade.'

'See what you mean. Come and speak to Viv and Val Passmore. They're twins – identicals – longing to meet you. They're from Truro.'

'We *loved* your talk,' said Viv and Val almost in unison.

Marianne smiled, modestly.

He hadn't at first believed that that insignificant-looking little woman shabbily dressed and with a pronounced nervous tic, perched up there at the table so ill at ease, could be Dr Pendlebury, *his* Dr Pendlebury. He conceived the woman to be a secretary or administrator who would take notes in shorthand, or someone's wife; and had kept craning round to ascertain whether Dr Pendlebury had arrived yet.

'That's her,' said Sharon. 'Mrs Pendlebury.'

'Doctor,' he corrected her, concerned for his idol's dignity. 'She's Doctor not Mrs.'

Sharon shrugged, much as to comment that if it were demonstrable that Mrs Pendlebury could splint a broken leg, she'd start calling her Doctor.

'Anyway, that's her,' she concluded. 'Have a cough drop.' She held out a packet of Tunes.

'That wouldn't help,' wheezed Timothy. 'But thanks, I'll have one anyway.'

As he sucked the sweet, he tried to adjust his glamorous preconception to the shock of her commonplaceness. Marianne entirely lacked the air of distinction manifest in her handwriting, that slight frisson of the formidable (but feminine) implied in the bold italic script. He'd thought she would be tall and striding and strapping; she was mousy and of middle height. She could boast no bosom, as far as he could see. So striking was the contrast that Timothy still mentally projected on to the dais his own version of Marianne Pendlebury. This woman was not quite an impostor, but a stray.

Jojo would have snorted. Jojo would have derided him: *What are you after, a beauty queen?* Looks didn't count for her. It was what you were that counted, under the skin.

And after all, he reminded himself, as Marianne, blotchily red, grabbed up her briefcase and rummaged in it – after all, the Brontës had been nothing to look at either. Plain girls, pathologically shy. You could be a genius, or eminent, without being a great beauty; and when she got up to talk, the glow and power of what she had to say would probably transfigure her ordinariness. The light would beacon out; the light he had come all this way to find.

He interrupted the opening of her address with his coughing fit; that was most distressing, and could not have improved her confidence.

But the poor woman – she couldn't talk at all. Had no idea, apparently, of voice projection, and he had to sit at the alert, to catch her breathless mutterings. Some of the audience seemed to give up rather early in the proceedings, slumping back in their chairs, reading their programme notes or taking a nap. Out of loyalty to his prior conception he glowered at these. But why hadn't someone taken her to one side and had a quiet word with her? It was so frustrating. He caught snatches, which seemed quite nice. But it was like throwing peanuts to hungry monkeys, aimed just short of their reach. Out came the spray of peanuts; out shot his simian paw; missed.

Furthermore, the canvas seat and steel frame of his chair were exactly wrong for his back. However he positioned himself, some bar dug into his spine; and his sore feet pulsated, swollen out against the ridge of his shoes. The experience to which he had looked forward as something almost holy was just irritating.

'So how did you find it?' he asked Sharon, when Marianne, stuffing her papers gracelessly in her pocket with an air of ill-concealed relief, had sat down and the applause had subsided.

'It were okay,' said Sharon. 'Over my head a bit.'

She had devoured the entire packet of cough sweets. 'Couldn't hear some of it. Could you?'

'The acoustics are not that good in here,' Timothy said, looking round the raftered ceiling with a critical air. He found himself wanting to defend Marianne, who had once more become *his* Marianne, but in a different way, now that she had lost face before all these people. He turned to his neighbour on the other side, with the aim of promoting Marianne's interest. 'Acoustics aren't at all good in here,' he stated in his loudest whisper, leaning over to the towering fellow with a voluptuous beard that made his own seem the merest wisp.

'Speak up,' said the giant, bending. 'I can't hear you.'

'The acoustics . . . not that good,' panted Timothy.

'Oh . . . aye . . . aye.' He had evidently not caught what Timothy was saying. *Probably a poet*, thought Timothy. He had the air of a poet – Walt Whitman, for instance, or that Scottish fellow. He wondered if he, with his own eccentric beard and hand-knitted sweater, also looked like a poet to the other guests. It was this thought that gave him courage to try to approach and introduce himself to Marianne.

But she had sheered off through the crush, and he had been elbowed and shouldered out of her orbit by the press of people. Straining for a view of her, he could only make out one hand gesturing nervously, for she had been engulfed behind a heavy, jowled person who stood impenetrably with his arms folded as a terribly intense woman aimed at him a story of devastating length.

'Got you a glass of sherry,' said Sharon. 'Two actually. In case it runs out. They're knocking it back, this lot.'

Timothy, who had been on the look-out for greatness and had seemed to be drowning in his discouragement, was suddenly and sharply touched by this unpretending face.

'Is this your calling then,' he asked, 'bringing succour to doddering old duffers?'

'It's my job,' she said, simply. 'I'm a waitress. Thought I told you. Don't know about sucker. Pot of tea for two, coffee, hot chocolate, teacakes.'

'That is succour,' said Timothy. 'Thank you, my dear.'

'You know what Mrs Pendlebury says about me?'

'No. What?'

'She says I'm a *real person*. "Oh Sharon," she says, "you're such a *real person*." I'm still puzzling it out . . . I think she means I'm lower class. And,' she laughed artificially, 'solid.'

Timothy scanned her face: there was a complexity and a sadness. Again he was haunted by the impression that from within the house of clay someone peeped out: a slender person, tender-spirited, buried in that porcine mass.

'Oh,' he said consideringly. 'No. She would mean . . . honest . . . kindly – wouldn't she?'

Sharon shrugged. Her black-clad bosom rose and fell. He wished she would do it again. It wobbled so beautifully.

'Just blah really,' she said. 'Here. Have your second glass.' She exchanged his empty glass for a full one, and took a swig from her own. She was comforted by the old geezer, who had kind eyes and seemed to feel as out of place as she did, and hence could afford a haven in these tossing seas of blah. She felt she could tell him things but could not at present summon words for them.

'I mean to say,' came a rich contralto voice, 'what I mean to say is that we *cannot* talk about Emily Brontë . . . we cannot *do* it . . . I mean it cannot be *done* . . . I mean, who *is* she? Where is she?' The voice waxed jocular; a slender hand rose in the air, palm uppermost; a shot-silk green sleeve flashed and earrings trembled as a face searched round in irony. 'Come on Neil, show her to me – lead me to her. She doesn't actually exist. So we must put this figment, this candy floss, this hallucination, out of our minds.'

'Death of the Author, RIP,' said an equally ironic male voice.

'Well,' said the green-silk woman, 'take up the challenge. Where is she? You tell me, Tom, I'd dearly love to know. Let me see, she'd be – what – 175 years old by now. Quite a geriatric.'

'Oh,' said the middle-aged man, stepping back, 'don't you start deconstructing *me*, Laurie. I'm a simple fellow. But not that simple. I'm not going to be drawn into that trap.'

'Well, can you tell me?' Green Silk turned to the group immediately around her. 'Can anyone tell me – Marianne, how about you? – we are all *looking for* Emily Brontë. We want her to *explain* her book to us. But where in God's name *is* she?'

Green Silk had a carrying voice.

'What's she on about?' asked Sharon.

'Well, there's some dispute, I don't really follow it, about whether the author should have any control over a text. Or whether the text can mean anything we can read into it. Something like that.'

'Oh.'

'Well,' put in an American voice. 'We can say one thing at least. She *was* a woman. She was not a man. She wrote *as* a woman. Not as a man. The text is female. It is not male. That, I think, is indisputable.'

'As far as it goes,' said Green Silk.

'Well, Laurie, that is very, very far. That is − like − a *journey* to the *centre* of the *earth*.'

The semicolons men had drawn discreetly off and were lighting up their pipes with private murmurings and small snortings by the drinks tray.

'I must say,' said an earnest young woman acting as decoy, 'the Brontë Society has been jolly generous in letting a rival group set up in their very midst.'

'Come on, Marianne, everybody, I still want to know, where is she − your "real" Emily Brontë?' Green Silk was not to be distracted from her quest. 'Shall we go and dig her up from under the church floor and interrogate her remains?'

'Codswallop,' observed Sharon.

'*I* know where she is,' faltered Timothy huskily, but no one heard.

'Who *is* this woman?' the Poet wanted to know, and was not enlightened.

Marianne, turning red-faced from her conversation, at last confronted Laurie Morgan.

'Oh Laurie, how lovely to see you. I haven't had a chance to say hello,' she said with gushing insincerity. The two women kissed lightly on either cheek, a ceremony which was repeated with the Americans, Gillie Deneuve and Ellen Rooney Herzog. Everybody watched. 'So glad you could both come. I thought you'd be too busy.'

'Marianne, settle this for us. Where *is* Emily Brontë? The "real" Emily Brontë. You seem to think there is one. Now for me, you see, she doesn't exist.'

Timothy cleared his throat and said with a tremendous effort, 'She's in the book.'

'I think not. The book is paper, covered with inky marks.'

'Her testament,' managed Timothy.

'*A* testament. But to what?'

'To Emily Brontë.'

'Again I think not. A testament to language; to plurality of meaning; to the polyphonous dialectic of intertexuality . . . and *that* is the whole fascination . . .'

Sharon blew her nose trumpetingly. But Green Silk spoke above this nose-blowing. She spoke of matters lofty beyond the highest reach of Timothy's comprehension. She spoke authoritatively. She spoke with conviction. She made it seem as if her words must carry absolute weight. Timothy, labouring, felt he knew her to be wrong and yet how could she be wrong? Her arguments all fitted together like a Rubik's cube that is systematically brought into alignment. How could you prove someone wrong if what they were saying was beyond you? You could just say, as Sharon did, *Cobblers*, but *Cobblers* was an unsatisfactory and too concise retort, unlikely to persuade the uninitiated.

'Yes but . . .' he began, and Green Silk courteously gave way for him to speak. 'Yes but . . .' and could not pursue his own drift, which led home to Hayfield, to the person he recognised as Emily who stood over his bookcase in the night. It led to one's own kind of illumination, which might after all be the madness of a mind skewed by bereavement and susceptible to illusion. A trick of the light merely.

Marianne shot the Ancient Mariner a grateful look. She had once unwisely engaged in a public debate with Laurie Morgan's ex-husband and had been thrown all the way round the packed lecture theatre. That had not impressed Idris Price one little bit. For despite the demonstrable fact that he had even less clue about postmodernism than she did, it enabled him to label her 'an intellectual lightweight'. The

Ancient Mariner's 'Yes but' was like a frail buffer between her lecture and the siege of rocks with which Laurie was demolishing its foundations: quite useless in practice but a comfort nevertheless. She felt remorse at having so obviously given him the slip earlier on.

'For many people,' she said carefully, taking over from the Mariner, 'Emily Brontë is a very real presence. A person they are in touch with when they read.'

'But, you know, that's a delusion.'

'Well, but, if so many people feel it – and care about her – and hear her speaking to them – '

'A million housewives every day
Pick up a tin of beans and say
Beanz meanz Heinz.'

Laurie sang the jingle *con brio*. She was wonderfully good-humoured when she carved you up. Her students adored her. Although they knew theoretically that she was in her late forties, Laurie's following felt her to be a member of their own generation. She made you laugh, hammered the Establishment, and wore her hair spiked and hennaed.

Eileen could stand it no longer. She hadn't spent all that money to attend a meeting where the Principal Speaker seemed to have no idea of what anything meant and a crazy woman held forth that nothing meant anything, and, because she spoke in polysyllables, was listened to with reverent attention.

'Young woman, have you got the cheek to tell me that because *you* come from Oxford – '

'Chichester,' corrected Laurie equably.

'And I'm just an ordinary person – '

'Oh, I'm ordinary too,' insisted Laurie, more uneasily.

'From Ludlow – '

'Well, I'm from Liverpool originally, working class – '

'Working class!' Eileen shrieked.

'Certainly,' said Laurie, rattled. 'My father was a docker; we had no – '

'Well, *you*'re no docker, that's for sure.'

'Well, no, I – '

'Exactly. Don't you go telling me you're a docker when you're nothing of the sort.'

'But I wasn't – '

'Now you look here, just because you've some high-and-mighty job at Cambridge – '

Laurie did not see fit to contradict her.

'*Which*, no doubt, is a meal-ticket for life – it does not follow that I and my ilk . . . don't know how to read a book. We may not have had the privilege of a university training but we have attended the College of Life. And if you ask me how I know there's an Emily Brontë – is that what you're asking me, young woman?'

'Certainly,' said Laurie, recovering herself. 'I'd be most interested to learn.'

'I know it *here* and *here*,' replied Eileen. And with each *here*, she bunched her hand into a fist and smote her heart and her temple, with such vigour that Timothy thought that, if she carried on, she'd do herself an injury. He had at once recognised the woman whose acquaintance he had made on the tombstone.

'There's no answer to that,' Laurie conceded. 'That's true for you.'

'Pre-cisely.'

The dialogue shuddered to a halt on that 'Pre-cisely', and there was a silence while people tried to think of things to say. Eileen's sensation of triumph curdled into embarrassment. She cringed and had an impulse to bring out her compact and powder her nose, which she resisted. Well, it was right, it was proper, they had to be trounced occasionally, these self-declared dockers who would not know a wharf from a loading-bay, and denied the existence of the Immortal Soul. She especially objected to the woman's hair, which was dyed bright red, like those Mohican Indians who sometimes invaded Ludlow on motorbikes; and to her nose, which had a stud in it.

Her own hair-do, she recalled, left something to be desired after the blasting it had taken on the moor. She patted it experimentally to test whether the top portion (always the danger zone) was staying down. It was.

'Can I get you a drink?' asked an imposing person with an immense white beard and half-moon spectacles.

'Thank you. A medium sherry would be most acceptable.'

Such a beard. And not much hair on top, so that his head had a curiously ill-conceived topsy-turvy character, as though it had been stuck on upside-down. She rarely drank, and the sherry exercised an instantaneous and rather vertiginous effect.

'You certainly gave her what for,' said the Beard admiringly.

'Well, honestly, what can one *say* to these people?' asked Laurie of her companion, a young man in his mid-twenties, eager, hook-nosed, good-looking and with a bending, willowy tallness. He stood over her like a falcon on his perch awaiting commands.

'Not a lot.'

'It's hopeless – quite hopeless,' said Laurie, looking discomposed. Her class origins were sacred to her. That woman had touched a very raw nerve; and ridiculously she had let her get away with it. She sighed. Duncan brushed the inside of her wrist with a delicate finger.

'So what's next on the circus circuit?' he asked. 'The Grand Tour of the Graveyard? Visit to the Museum to view Charlotte's second-best petticoat?'

'Just remind me,' whispered Laurie. 'Why did we come in the first place?'

'Do you think he's her toyboy?' asked Sharon of Timothy, speculatively.

Timothy stared. 'Looks a bit like it to me,' he acknowledged. He was blest if he could see what a well-built young male could see in such a scrag-end of mutton. She was fifty if she was a day. Old enough to be his mother.

'Where I work,' mused Sharon, 'all the old blokes have girlfriends of eighteen. They pick out the juiciest students, they do, it's true. They don't realise we're watching. But we are. Have another sherry. Go on. You might as well. Mrs Pendlebury . . . Mrs Pendlebury . . . this here is Timothy Whitty, he's been dying to meet you.'

'Oh – is it really – is it really you, Timothy? Oh . . . how lovely . . . lovely to see you.'

She hadn't the slightest idea that this poor old chap, in his evident state of advanced physical decay, could possibly be the friend with whom she had enjoyed the magical correspondence.

'I *should* have realised,' she went on. 'But of course we've never seen a photograph of one another, have we, and so . . .'

'Marianne.' He managed, chokingly, to get out her name. But he found, to his intense chagrin, that tears were sparking behind his eyes and his face was working. In the moment of clasping the hand that had held the pen and had (so he felt) kept him alive through the winter of his loss, he forgot his disappointment at the plainness of her appearance, the shambles of her performance. The phantom Marianne whom he had constructed from the shape of her 'f's and 's's on the page, the loops and flourishes of her handwriting, fled away before the immediacy of the small, smooth hand which squeezed his, and did not immediately let go.

'Goodness,' she said, seeing his tears and drawing closer. 'You've come all this way. And I can see you're not well. It must have been a hell of a journey.'

'It was . . .' he croaked. 'Yes.' She had a small mole on her right cheek, he saw. Her eyes were a greenish-blue, wide-looking behind the round glasses. She wore no make-up. Her skin was not good. 'Worth it though . . . to see you . . . Marianne.' And immediately he spoke her name the tears sparked again. He had better stop saying it if he wanted to avoid making a fool of himself. 'I enjoyed your talk,' he said. 'Sorry I coughed at the beginning. Hope it didn't put you off your stride.'

Another of Marianne's illusions had crumbled into a powder of dust: Timothy. She had not realised how much she had invested in her image of this man whose letters had consoled her with their concern and evident pride in her attention. *Over the Peak*, she had thought of him. Her special person who lived in poetry and solitude, at altitude. His being up there, sending the beautiful messages gliding through the door week by week, had helped her through the rowing, the nappies, the babies' squalling, the sleepless nights. Through him, she had kept in contact with an estimable image of herself. She'd looked out of the window into the rainswept, redbrick mundanity of the street and thought: someone out there cares for me. But he'd been, in her imagination, a giant of a man, rugged, powerful, just a little beyond his prime of life; interestingly frail, not a positive relic.

This aversion caused her to squeeze the old man's hand more tightly; to lean over and kiss him lightly on the cheek. For she saw that he was moved; and was disgusted at the baseness of her own thoughts.

Had she wanted to lean on him then, that she'd conceived of him in such large dimensions? Had she somehow thought of him sexually? Not really. It had been the mystery that attracted.

'Well, my dear,' he said in his no-voice,' I meet you in my latter days. But we don't judge by appearances, do we? I've something for you in my bag if you'll hang on a minute . . . made it myself.'

He rummaged in an old blue shoulder-bag and brought out the box containing the bolero. Delight lit her face.

'Should I open it now or wait till later?' She held the long box between her hands with an exaggerated carefulness, to signal to the giver that his gift was cherished.

'Oh, later.' He'd wrapped it in tissue paper and drawn a candle on a piece of card to symbolise all that he'd thought they meant to one another. He didn't want all these strangers eyeing it. 'It's only a little thing . . . I just hope it fits.'

What with this old man who ought to be in a nursing-home by the sound of him cosying up to the lecturer, and that young man who was all over the professor who had claimed to be a docker, Eileen felt the dismay that darkened whenever she saw people in pairs.

Her mother came into her mind.

She should be tidily in bed by this time. The agency nurse should have given her cocoa, brushed her hair, sat her on the commode, tucked her up. The thought of Mum at once worried, irritated and consoled Eileen: a dappled feeling.

Her mother tweaked a cord at Eileen's ribcage, reminding her that she was needed. Perhaps Mum would call for her in the night, and she wouldn't be there. Muriel thought her hairnet was a tiara and the cats visiting royalty. One day she wouldn't be there. The hairnet would be brushed away like a spider's cobweb and the courtiers would mew for their invisible queen. She wouldn't be there. It was a complex feeling.

That young man's hand fascinated her. It prowled and roved. As Laurie Morgan debated earnestly with another woman, the hand crept under her green-silk blouse, which had ridden up at the back . . . very slowly . . . it crawled caressively into hiding. Laurie reached round in mid-conversation, and swatted it away. After a pause, the hand found itself on Laurie's left buttock, which it secretly massaged, round and round, as if in light conversation. Eileen repositioned herself so as to read Laurie's face. It was suffused with a smile. The secret hand now roved to the other buttock and continued its ministrations there. The buttock pressed back into the palm. Eileen saw it squeeze hard, and Laurie jumped, with a giggle, choking on her sherry.

'Duncan,' she turned and hissed. 'Will you lay off?'

'I haven't laid on yet,' he bent and whispered. '*Yet.*'

His teeth were exceedingly white. His hand was lean and hairless, with long, insinuating fingers.

'Behave yourself, child,' said Laurie, and, looking one another directly in the eyes for a long moment, both smothered a laugh.

'I'm so sorry,' said Laurie, turning back to the earnest pair of spectacles with which she was conversing. 'You were saying . . . You are a devotee of . . . Branwell. *Really?* Do tell me more.'

The young man fiddled with the stem of his sherry glass

and gazed over people's heads, insolent and bored and beautiful. The index finger of his left hand played in a Morse
code upon Laurie's thigh, dotting and dashing. Laurie's lower
portion was encased in black leather. She had a black leather
bottom. The doodling finger of the young man seemed all
the more obscene for that.

Was that fetishism?

Many men were supposed to be fetishists.

Some were known to dress up in brassières and suspender
belts. They sometimes throttled themselves by hanging by
bra-straps from doorknobs, their erect members sticking out
of frilly panties. This was true. Eileen had read it in the *Daily
Telegraph*, otherwise she would not have believed it. From
what she could tell, councillors, MPs, merchant bankers –
they all did it, or a considerable cross-section. It was confus-
ing; very. You wanted to be loved with a fiery burning
passion, and all that was on offer seemed to be males with
their heads in carburettors or hairy chests wearing 36B cups;
or young men with round metal glasses who reduced themselves to a forefinger circling on a leather behind. It was
hurtful, undignified and disappointing.

'Passion,' she said authoritatively (to hide the wound) to
the astounded young woman beside her. 'It's different from
sex, you know. The Brontës knew that.'

'You what?' said Sharon.

'It's engulfing – wild – extreme. You can't control it. Like
a fire devouring the moorlands. Indeed, you *shouldn't* control
it . . . when it's the real thing. You know what I mean?'

'No,' said Sharon.

'That's the pity – the pity of it. Youth today – they know
nothing but *sex*.'

The word 'sex' seemed to climax in the room, bringing
the swell of conversation to a sudden full stop. Eileen wore

her blush like a badge of office. Militant, and yet abashed, she was impelled onward across a plateau of arousal. She clutched the handle of her shabby handbag with both hands, as if hanging on to the reins of a runaway horse.

'*Sex* . . .' she exclaimed. '*Sex* . . . is nothing but . . . *sex*. What is wanted in the modern world, as Emily knew (and don't ask me how I know Emily knew, I just know she knew, that's all) is Passion. True Passion.'

Oh, my God, she's off, thought Marianne. She stuck her parcel under one arm. The whole room seemed to rock with unshed laughter, like a great storm brewing, as Marianne contemplated the demolition of her conference by the anarchy of mirth Mrs Passion always wrought. Her eyes appealed to Timothy in vain. He coughed discreetly, amused and vivified by the performance of the tombstone lady.

Eileen, in full spate, challenged the gathering to contradict her. Wasn't it important, she demanded, to give oneself for ever, fully, finally and freely? Heathcliff ought to be regarded as a role model. According to Eileen, he was a pattern of monogamy and fidelity; not legally married to Cathy, certainly, but subject to Higher Law.

Hilarity rumbled round the room like the beginnings of a storm. It broke out briefly amongst the semicolons men and ran across to the feminism corner. Eileen felt its scorching proximity; and waxed more heated still. She was accustomed to being sent up, laughed down. Outsiders always were, if they told their own truth. Laurie's young man pierced her deep in the eyes with his mocking gaze. She fiercely held the gaze, locked into it. *You are Sex*, she accused him, *but I am Passion.*

The handbag spasmed up and down in Eileen's two hands. It knocked down a half-full glass of sherry.

'Excuse me,' a voice interrupted, foreign, diffident. 'But if you didn't minded would you please repeat it?'

'What?'

'What you have back now just said. I am Japanese student. So interested in all these Brontës but I cannot write so fast.'

Eileen's molten heart glowed. The Japanese girl was taking notes from her words of wisdom. A surge of unprecedented sweetness rose in Eileen.

'Goodness me – you don't want to take notes of my witterings.'

'Oh but I do, madam. If you would please just say again, about Charlotte's passion – in Brussels, did you say she had it?'

Eileen explained about Brussels, supplying dates and names, and giving it to be understood that she had lately been researching into the subject. Nonchalantly, she swabbed up the pool of sherry with a mansize paper tissue. The young woman was wide-eyed, gentle; her short, straight hair was held back in a clip shaped like a butterfly.

'The butterfly is an emblem of the soul,' Eileen told the young woman for good measure. The young woman wrote that down too, using her companion's back as a rest for her notepad.

'I am grateful,' she thanked Eileen, dipping her head with the sweetest of smiles. 'It is really too much.'

'Christ,' said Sharon drunkenly to Timothy. 'What a load of crap. Words, it's just words, these people are all words – words meaning sod all.'

'Ah,' said Laurie Morgan. 'Did you hear that, Duncan. *Someone* agrees with me at last.'

Sharon stared uncomprehendingly into the gaunt, rouged face.

'You what?'

The toyboy was looming over the woman's shoulder and taking plentiful eyefuls of Sharon's breasts. He was juggling them like mighty jellies in either hand. She held in her breath in order to contract her stomach and press up the bosom. Sex was sex.

'Well,' went on Laurie. 'Words are just words – that's what you were saying. There's a gap between the word (the signifier) and the thing represented (the signified) – that's what you were saying.' Her hand crept round behind her to Duncan's crotch, to which it gave a soft, secret grasp.

'Oh,' said Sharon. 'Is *that* what I were saying?'

'Or words to that effect,' said Laurie. She stifled a yawn.

'So how do *you* know what I were saying, if words don't mean nothing?'

'I beg pardon?'

'If everything what I say don't mean nothing, then how the bleeding hell do you know what I meant when I fucking said it, excuse my French?'

'You are a bright girl,' said Laurie with some admiration. 'But now, if you'll forgive me, I think I'll just slip off. Time for bed. See you tomorrow. We can talk further then. Come along, Duncan, bedtime. Good night, Marianne.'

Under starlight in the touristless streets, Marianne allowed herself to wonder how the babies were. She hoped they were asleep and that Charlie did not have one of her bad dreams in the night, because if she did she'd not go back to sleep, but kneel and moan, rocking the bars of her cot, half-asleep. She could go on for hours, till she dropped to the mattress in mid-moan, when your nerves were at breaking-point. There was a slightly shameful pang of relief at not being there keeping vigil. Thomas and the babies seemed very far away – in another world. She had kissed them goodbye. She could care about herself for a change; enjoy just being herself. Surely that was not too much to ask? Letting herself into her room at the Three Sisters guest house, she stepped straight out of her clothes and into a hot bath, lying there steeping herself in the privacy of steamy silence, water lapping round her temples and hair-line. No babes. No Thomas. No hassle. No home. She almost dozed.

Later she recalled Timothy's present. It had been packed in tissue paper with infinite care. She opened it with answering care. It was a bolero or waistcoat, with no buttons, heavy in her hands. He had made it for her himself, the card said, using a local fleece. Marianne studied herself in the mirror, her wet hair turbaned in a pink towel, naked except for the bolero.

'My dear Timothy,' she scrawled in her eloquent, confident italics, sitting rosily nude at the dressing-table. 'I cannot thank you sufficiently for this unique and so beautiful present – I am wearing it at this moment . . .'

Chapter 6

Will the day be bright or cloudy?
Sweetly has its dawn begun;
But the heaven may shake with thunder
Ere the setting of the sun.

'Charlie, please,' wooed Thomas.

The youngest fruit of his loins, out of her mind with anguish, hurled herself backwards in his arms and bellowed.

'Be a good girl for Daddy,' he begged desperately, wrestling the top part of her body into some relation to her bottom half. She squirmed against him, kicking at his testicles.

'What's the matter? Tell Dada what the matter is, Charlie? Does your ear hurt?'

'Ear hurt,' agreed Charlie.

'Which ear?'

'This here ear.' Charlie poked at Thomas' own left ear.

'No, I mean your ears. Or have you had a bad dream? Tell Dada.'

'Bad dream,' confessed Charlie lugubriously. She had abandoned herself in his arms, entering a phase of cryptic melancholia. She flopped her doleful hot head against his shoulder and lay against his pyjamas like a stone. 'Bad, bad dream.'

'Well, the dream's over now, Charlie. All over. Back to bobo.'

'No bobo,' murmured Charlie into his collar, and placed her muscular arms round his neck, squeezing passionately.

'*Yes* bobo,' snarled Thomas, before calming himself to continue rationally and authoritatively. 'Charlie you will go bobo now. It's two o'clock in the morning. Come on, loosen your arms, Charlie, come on. Down to bobo. Daddy's tired.'

'Bad dream in the earhole,' Charlie confided, explaining why neither of them would be permitted to sleep for several hours and nestling up close in amiable expectation. She began now to babble, asking to go into his bed, mentioning her rattle, her clucking hen, the mice in the lamp, the wonders of the loofah, the lady on the lawn and various items which she understood to be of mutual interest.

'*Charlie*,' said Thomas, prising one arm from around his neck. 'It's two o'clock in the morning.'

'*Morning*!' beamed Charlie. 'It's morning!' And began to sing. The notes bubbled up in a stream of gospelling joy.

'Shut up! – just – shut – up!' he bawled.

Charlie burst into tears.

'You are a bloody manic depressive,' he informed her, hurling her into her cot. 'Now just pipe down and go to blasted sleep.'

Charlie huddled completely silent, wide-eyed. Her silence resounded; it accused him of criminality.

'That's right. Bobo,' he said with returning temperance. 'Cuddle teddy, that's right. That's the way.'

He padded back to bed; snapped off the light; inhaled some deep breaths.

The moaning began.

Andrew burst in. 'Dad, Charlie's woken me up. Tell her to shut up or I'm going to bash her.'

'Go back to bed, Andy. She'll stop it soon.'

Andrew rushed into Charlie's room and emptied a box of bricks over his sister's head. Charlie roared. The neighbour banged on the wall. At length Charlie tumbled aslant asleep as if shot.

Emlyn awoke at four thirty and peed in his wellington boot.

When Thomas found the boot of pee in the morning, he resisted the impulse to tip it over Emlyn's head and mildly remarked, 'You are a juvenile delinquent', before emptying it into the loo and washing out the boot. He was knackered. A curdled image of his wife had been churning in his mind throughout the night. Swanning round Haworth, he saw her, followed by a procession of fools. Off up the moors in hiking boots and backpack, pointing out significant places, showing off her colossal ignorance of the points of the compass. Sweet-faced at a lectern spouting words like 'free spirit', while the fools clapped.

He hoisted the nappy bucket on to the sink and let the bleached, shitty mass flop out. Turning on the cold tap, he began to knead, with distaste. He had never liked this kind of thing; was sensitive to odours and winced if he became aware that his shirt cuffs were even faintly soiled.

Charlie clung round his legs while he worked, swaying and crooning. He felt the weight and tug of her love.

'Shall we go and see Mummy?' he enquired, wringing the nappies and slinging them one by one into a second bucket. 'Go see Mummy in Haworth – have a nice day out?'

'Charlie see Mummy!' his daughter bleated enthusiastically, and scampered to the door.

Emlyn was not happy about the plan: he sulked as he was strapped into the car, pointing out at the top of his voice that he was supposed to be going to Banger's party, with Big Macs at McDonald's.

'Mummy'll give you ice creams,' promised Thomas, putting his foot down as he rode the outer lane of the motorway. 'And fudge – and cake – and Walnut Whips.'

He held his hand down on the hooter to budge a lorry; the lorry wouldn't move over, so he passed on the inside lane.

'And *Maltesers* – and *Mars Bars* – and *Coca-Cola*.' He added each item with a fierce lash of malice, like a whip-crack.

The children were silent in a row on the back seat, sucking their thumbs.

'And Mummy will take you for a nice walk on the moors with her nice friends and Daddy will have a nice, nice rest.'

Charlie raised the possibility that she might be about to be sick. Emlyn leaned his thin, scarred knees judiciously sideways towards his brother.

'You'd better bloody well not be,' said Thomas, shooting off the motorway; so she wasn't. Their communal shrieks as they shot round the roundabout were more hectic but less elated than on the Nemesis roller-coaster at Alton Towers.

Chapter 7

Methought the very air I breathed
Was full of sparks divine,
And all my heather-couch was wreathed
By that celestial shine.

Morning's milky light pooled upon the moors as the party set out for Top Withens. Not everybody had upped with the lark for this expedition, the semicolons men begging off on the grounds that they had seen the place before and, after a full English breakfast, would toddle over for a pint in the Black Bull, to savour the atmosphere. There they would crack jokes and exchange cricketing anecdotes.

Marianne struck out, therefore, at the head of a party of enthusiasts, yeasty and fizzing, unballasted by commoner sense. She strode forward in jeans and sweater, her backpack weighted with Mars Bars. She felt dubious about Timothy's insistence on coming. He scarcely looked fit to wait at a bus stop, but here he was, in the strangest of outfits, a spindling Sherlock Holmes, in a corduroy cap with earflaps, trousers resembling plus-fours by being tucked into his socks, and a tweedy jacket. Weighty climbing boots were a serious impediment to locomotion; he had wanted to look like the real thing. For he had once been the real thing. Really, he knew, he'd have been better in plimsolls . . . or not coming.

Long ago, he puffed to Marianne, as they began the ascent of the rough path, he and his wife had been big walkers – Helvellyn, the Cairngorms, Snowdonia . . . the list seemed set to go on for ever. He paused in his itinerary to cough.

Neil Thorniley and the Cumberland Shepherd overtook and strode ahead, debating vigorously. The Shepherd poled along on a carved and polished stick, appropriate to his imagined calling.

'See you up there,' they called back.

The Passmore twins and Ellen Rooney Herzog also caught up and forged ahead. The two gentle Japanese girls passed, under the tutelage, Marianne saw, of Mrs Passion, who seemed to be delivering an animated lecture, gesturing to distant hills and naming them.

'Hare Hill over there – see – to your left – on the horizon – the *brow* of the horizon – well, that is a most famous place in the annals of the area – that's right, take a snap, you can show it to your friends when you get home – tell them HARE HILL,' she boomed, as if the poor girl were afflicted not merely with foreignness but with deafness too. 'That was where Emily Jane and her boyfriend, a poor ploughman from Ponden who died at the untimely age of eighteen, are believed to have had their secret trysts.'

'Secret trips?'

'Trysts, dear. Clandestine assignations. Rendezvous. He was the model for Heathcliff, it is believed – or it will be believed, when the theory is better known.'

'Really? A model?'

'No, not a model in the sense of male fashion model, dear – no, I mean the *model*. Pattern. Original. The true fact.'

'Ah.' The young woman took photos of the incomprehensible hillscape with Eileen posed picturesquely in her tartan slacks, gesturing with one flung hand to the Beyond.

'Thank you, Professor,' she said. 'These are all thoroughly interesting.'

Eileen could not help it if people took her for a professor. Natural authority could not be camouflaged. She had become so accustomed to her honorary status this morning that it seemed authentic, even though she was having to invent much of the local colour. After all, what was a professorship but a piece of paper? So Emily would have said.

Nevertheless, she had shushed the girls as they passed Marianne, and only when she was sure they were out of earshot did she expatiate again, with manifold flamboyant gestures.

Kerry Richards passed with a pleasant greeting; Ron Hebblewhite, saying nowt; Sharon, struggling and panting in a baggy track suit, but not particularly conscious of the struggle, so headily happy was she.

She was enjoying it so much: the keen air, the expanses of grey-green hummocky grasslands, with reedbeds and the darkness of the heather and bilberry bushes. Sharon was unused to the countryside. At home on the estate there was just a square of green for 'recreation', where lads played football, and a scummy pond on which floated tyres and condoms. The skies seemed small and partitioned there. Here they arched for ever and immensely. Her heart hammered with the effort, yet she seemed to float. Her silky hair beat about in the gathering wind.

She thought she saw a hawk but it might have been a gull.

There was a sense of homecoming for Sharon in this shining gale, these free spaces.

She passed Marianne and the old fellow at a lurching

gallop. Marianne thought Sharon looked lonely and a pathetic odd-one-out, and reproached herself for the impulse of inviting her.

Laurie Morgan and Duncan Lascelles branched off down the wrong path and disappeared into a dip.

By befriending Timothy, Marianne had ceased to function as the group's leader. Indeed, they lost all contact with the others while he tottered on, eyes bulging, possessed by the one compulsion, to keep upright and to stagger onwards.

'I do feel,' said Marianne with gentleness, her hand cupped beneath his elbow, 'that we might perhaps . . . pause for rest . . . I don't know about you but I'm fairly tired.'

'Oh Jojo,' Timothy exclaimed. The world heaved sideways. He discovered himself foundering on a fibrous clump of heather, with his legs buckled under him.

'Timothy . . . I'm not Jojo,' Marianne ventured, with an air of apology. She sat hugging her knees beside him. 'Are you okay? We needn't go on. We can just sit here and admire the view together.'

When Timothy had inhaled his Ventolin, the horizons steadied.

'It must be so confounding,' he croaked, 'to live in an earthquake zone.'

'Er . . . yes, it must, I suppose.'

'The eternal rocks beneath,' he said. 'Rocking.'

A cliff of white stone was scooped from the side of a rounded hill. They agreed that the quarry added to the beauty of the vista, with its fall of pale underlying stone exposing what lay beneath the counterpane of turf. He told her to go.

'I don't want to leave you here.'

'Why ever not?'

'I'm worried you might not be well.'

'If I died here, what better place? But I'm not about to. I'll be waiting for you all to come back down. Truly. You carry on.'

She reached over and with a little shy swoop kissed him on the cheek before she left. He felt the kiss lingering there and fading slowly for a while after she had disappeared. Nobody had kissed him since Jojo. Nobody. In the arm's-length dissociation of the widowed he had missed human touch to the point where, had he let himself brood upon it, he'd have despaired. Now there was a new beginning, a fresh pulse of life.

Having scaled the hillside, she scrambled all the way down again.

'Are you sure you're all right?' she wanted to know. 'I looked down from up there and you looked so . . .'

'I'm all right,' he wheezed. 'Off with you. You've a conference to run.'

'Are you sure? I –'

'Marianne – dear. I'm not as pathetic as I look, you know. I'm sitting here thinking.'

On the far side of the hills, Jojo tenderly applauded.

Eileen marched her contingent off the main route along a winding sheep-path. She explained to her party, which had now grown to six persons including their director, that if they went along here – round there – and up again and round again – they should arrive at Withens ahead of anyone else and enjoy the advantages of vistas more panoramic and romantic than those available to the dull masses who kept to the broad, well-trodden path. The sheep-path, which ran bouldery and uneven, was also unpredictably circuitous, which Eileen explained would add to this experience.

They should all imagine, she advised, that they were lost in a maze or labyrinth.

Her knees twinged, and sharp gusts sporadically slammed into her mouth, striking her dumb.

When people began to drop back, muttering, she waited for them to catch up and administered rousing short lectures on the prodigious walking capacities of Anne and Emily Jane Brontë, in miles per hour, with distances covered.

'They thought nothing of walking to Keighley and York,' she told them. 'There and back in forty-eight hours flat.'

When a sceptic remarked that they must have been at it day and night, Eileen replied that people's legs were stronger in those days.

'Tough and hardy and sturdy,' she affirmed. 'Girls bred in Sparta. They don't grow them like that these days.'

She passed a pitying eye over the limp anatomy of the mutineer, who was lighting up a cigarette. The smoke wafted straight into Eileen's face. She batted it away, offended.

'Perhaps they were joggers,' said one of the twins, helpfully.

'Or else they rode on broomsticks, I don't think,' sneered the smoker. 'The Three Weird Sisters. Excuse me if I get back on to the path.'

Good riddance, thought Eileen, as the woman sloped off, dangling the fag between her fingers. One did not expect more of females with spiked-up hair dyed yellow and metal chains suspended from their earlobes. Her lips formed but did not pronounce the word 'vulgar'.

They trekked on. Eileen praised the bracing quality of the air and pointed out that there was probably nothing quite like it in Japan. The Japanese girls politely but unenthusiastically agreed with this, but they had taken to murmuring to one another in Japanese and seemed to have retreated into their shell. Reverence had subsided into docility. Eileen began to stumble; she realised with a sudden access of lucidity that she was tired out and hadn't a clue where they were heading.

The path now ran steeply up over a hillock and curved round, to command a new and really quite momentous view over the hills, bathed in mother-of-pearl light. The sky was filmed in thin cloud through which a radiance sheened the entire field of vision. Eileen's eyes travelled out across remote distances into a purplish haze. She stood silent on the scarp and looked her fill. Not knowing where you were scarcely seemed to matter, having rounded this corner into aqueous extensions of light over space . . . space which was light. It was a brimful moment which she was to remember all her life . . .

. . . not the least because, when she looked down into the dell beneath her, her eyes fell on two naked bodies copulating.

Two naked bodies.

Copulating.

In a sheltered basin of velvety grass beneath the great luminous skies and amongst the sheep droppings, two naked bodies were copulating.

At first she could make no response.

A silence possessed her.

Then the silence exploded in her chest like a firework and rushed up her throat, whooshed in her ears, disintegrated in sprays of sparks. Still she neither moved nor spoke.

It was an unusual sight, not only from the point of view of location but also given the degree of athleticism displayed by both partners. The man was standing upright, the woman lifted way up in his hands, which supported the thighs of the woman, who rode him, her legs clasped behind his haunches.

Like a monkey, thought Eileen.

Thus the two bodies were stacked on his two legs, amongst a scattering of shed underwear, and the male thrust, and the female rode; and he laughed while she grunted, and he ground while she quivered, her legs wound tight around his body.

Eileen stared, swayed.

Beasts. They were like beasts. She panted. She was hotly shivering in nameless places.

Did the man then see her watching?

She burned with the shame of it.

Did he toss back his head and laugh out loud, and did he really call out to her, 'Want a go?'

No – it must have been, 'Want to go?'

Depravity.

The woman – who was the docker – looked out of eyes that were drugged, unseeing; and indeed she couldn't have seen much for her spectacles were lying on her shed garments. But somehow her hold slackened and the mating pair came uncoupled. She lost grip, slithered down, crouched and grabbed at her clothes. The ramrod man, however, moved a step closer to the aghast Eileen.

And indeed he did invite her down to join him; and he did say, 'Come on and have a turn.' And he did scoff.

She had never seen one before, in her life.

She had seen dogs at it in the next-door garden or in the park. She had soused rutting cats with buckets of water where they yowled and scrimmaged under the rose trellis in the early hours, and Muriel called from her room, 'The baby's crying – go and see what's the matter with the baby, dear', and Eileen said, 'No, Mum, there's no baby – just cats', and Muriel, with a pained expression, sat up in her hairnet, shaking her head at her daughter's delusion of child-lessness.

Eileen had seen graffiti of cock-and-balls in the public lavatory of Oswestry station, and again when she attended the eisteddfod at Llangollen. She had also seen an aerial photograph of the Cerne Abbas giant with his club. But this was her first sighting of the member in the flesh. It swelled purple. It wagged when he stepped forward. It was as gro-tesque and fascinating as the young man who paraded it was insolently handsome.

Her straggling party of pilgrims was almost upon her. She heard their grumbling approach in her wake, and gathered her wits just in time to totter back and shoo them off back the way they had come.

'Back! Back!' she exhorted, chasing them before her like sheep, and (louder), 'Go back – back the way you have come, all of you', to cover the monkey-woman's shaken call of 'Bugger off – peeping Tom!'

The party expressed perplexity at their lieutenant's sudden volte-face, as she drove them before her to rejoin the main contingent. A certain relief was also discernible. Eileen's credentials as a guide in the wilderness had come into severe doubt. One of their number thought she had glimpsed fig-ures in the dell.

'What was it down there? What did you see?'

Eileen considered, scudding along the ridge, what exactly she had seen.

'Oh,' she said, manifesting unconcern. 'Nothing much. There were some animals, that's all. I just realised from getting my bearings that we were on the wrong path. So I about-turned, without more ado.'

Back on the right path, she trailed behind, seeing what she had seen, over and over again; seeing the man's eyes watching her seeing it. She felt curiously lopsided, and walked in a listing shamble, as if in the aftermath of a terrific swipe to the head. So that was it, she thought, that was it.

Fifty years old if she's a day, she thought. *And him young enough to be her son. Literally.*

She herself was only in her mid-sixties.

Impaled, she thought. Again the man's erection skewered her inner eye with blind brutality.

That's all we are, she thought. It was the saddest, most desolating thought; and coexisted with a thrilled voyeurism of her own that made it necessary to go over and over it again. She wished she could have seen the whole thing from the beginning. And yet she fled from these depravities towards the furthest horizon; and the furthest horizon would not be far enough away. She felt she had lived her life in illusion. She had never really known what it was all about. Now she longed to draw her customary illusions around her like a cloak, comfortingly intact. Buffets of wind raised goose-bumps all over her exposed skin, and she hugged herself in her own arms.

Eileen's mind drifted to women in general, her mother in particular. It came to her for the first time in her life that her mother was not a virgin. Eileen was a virgin but Muriel was not.

How odd that seemed. Her mother must – well, obviously – have done . . . *that*.

Another shocking thought: *with Eileen's father.*

Well.

She stopped dead in her tracks and swept the lonely hills with incredulous eyes. Her mother was not the innocent she seemed. She knew much that Eileen had never known. She had experience of sex. From this experience, Eileen herself had been produced. Had she enjoyed it? Did she just accept it matter-of-factly as something you had to do? How did women feel about it in general? She meant nice Ludlow women who wore hats lanced with pearl hatpins and attended St Laurence Parish Church for Eucharist, Matins and Evensong.

If she had married her Frank, she would half a century ago have known too. But surely, she thought (watching the clouds part like silver-margined curtains to reveal a triangle of blue), it would have been an initiation shy and gentle and tender – with Frank – not a crude shock of strutting flesh?

But how did you know? How did you know what men were like under the surface, in their private bedrooms? How did you know what you were like yourself? – hanging on with monkey grip with monkey grimace while he plunged and bucked?

You didn't.

She was very quiet when she reached Withens. Withdrawing to a position on the margin of the chatting group, under cover of extracting her coffee flask, she took a covert look in her mirror to size up the state of affairs as regards her hair-do. A wrecked bird's-nest met her eyes, on top of a pouchy face with hectic cheeks and a look of helpless alarm such as she sometimes caught on her mother's face when her mind half rose from the unfathomable depths of her dementia, to find herself cast adrift from her fantasy into the alien territory of the real.

'Top Withens is supposed to be the original of Wuthering Heights,' confided an elderly, headscarfed woman to Sharon.

'Yeah?'

'Yes. And the clue is – what clinches it – is that it begins with "W". And it sort of rhymes. "Wuthering" . . . "Withens". Obvious really, isn't it?'

Sharon refrained from replying. Plenty of things which appeared to the Brontëans obvious seemed to her a bit far-fetched. She looked down at the slate-grey semi-ruin of the farmhouse and the moorlands and grasslands rippling down beyond it, and it did not seem to her to make much difference whether it was or not. This was simply, in itself, a grand place. Her heart swelled.

'Well, of course,' put in a man's voice, 'there's a certain doubt about that. Bit of a myth, you know.' He tapped his nose. 'Put a question mark over that,' he advised, and he drew one in the air. A giant question mark hung over the landscape. 'I locate the Heights a *long* way from here.' He pointed towards a distant horizon. 'Over there,' he stated, 'to be precise.'

'Where?' There were no houses on that hillside, only a dotting of sheep, like toys among the fern.

'Halifax,' said the man triumphantly. He nodded with irritating complacency. 'You can't see it from here, of course.'

'Well, I were told,' objected the woman, 'that this here were Wuthering Heights.'

'You were told wrong then,' said the know-all.

'Then why have we come all the way up here?'

Sharon had noticed how they pecked snappishly at one another, these Brontëans. Though they all had one faith, their many creeds impelled them to perpetual quarrel over which were the real holy relics and which were just bits of common rock and dull soil, devoid of gleam.

'Does it really matter?' she muttered. 'After all –'

The quarrellers drew together, scandalised. Despite their disagreements concerning detail, both knew it mattered absolutely.

'I have personally studied the Parsonage laundry list,' said the man earnestly. 'What's left of it. Under a magnifying glass – for you must understand the list was burnt in some kind of fire, perhaps in about the year 1860, so that now only dots a fraction of a millimetre remain on the left-hand side of a notebook measuring two centimetres by twenty-three point four centimetres. I am attempting, with painstaking – properly scientific – accuracy, to piece together the items of this list. Piece them, you see, together.' His hands met at a variety of angles to demonstrate the dimensions of his quest. 'A certain amount of hypothesising is inevitable. But let no one doubt,' he challenged them, with a nervous twitch, 'that this is an important work.'

His hands trembled with emotion as he brought forth this revelation.

How could you get worked up about a list of dirty knickers? Sharon studied him with candid amazement.

'Important,' he maintained, defending himself against that barrage of mockers, both real and fantasised, who sniggered behind his back at so dedicated a life. 'The tiniest, humblest thing,' he said intensely, 'is significant to our great quest. The more we know, the more we understand. I have personally measured the steps of the Clergy Daughters' School at Cowan Bridge with a tape measure, and calculated (with the aid of a seven-year-old child, kindly loaned by one of my acquaintances, also an *aficionado*) the eye-line of the young Charlotte when she first entered that fateful establishment.'

'That were Lowood in *Jane Eyre*,' put in the busybody, to illumine Sharon's welcome ignorance. Sharon was understood to be a hole for filling with nuts of information. There weren't many such empty receptacles about. They all came jam-packed with opinion, mostly off-beam but sometimes disappointingly infallible. 'Charlotte were right unhappy there. The Reverend Wilson, he ran it – Brocklehurst in *Jane Eyre* . . .'

'William Carus Wilson,' interposed the old man. 'We must in all things be exact. Brontë scholarship has been notoriously prone to gush and gossip – old wives' tales. Fortunately I am now retired and have time and leisure at my disposal to devote to the excavation and reconstruction work on properly scientific principles.' Future generations, he gave it to be understood, would have reason to bless him for his orderly and masculine intervention. 'You see,' he added, 'I was for thirty-five years a teacher of mathematics at Kenge Clough Grammar School. Yes, indeed.'

Sharon felt that explained a lot.

Marianne arrived, panting.

'Oh,' she said. 'Ah. Everyone's here, I see. Well. Such a good day for it. Nice and blowy. Just get my breath back. Sorry I was held up . . . I had to leave Timothy back down there – not really strong enough to – but he says he'll be all right. Now . . . now then,' she said. 'This is Top Withens.'

On the way down, the party ran into another party on the way up.

'Odd bods,' murmured the descending party to one another. They stood aside as if in deference to a communal eccentricity far more categorical than their own. Besides, the ascending party was accompanied by a group of photographers and a film crew who would lope alongside or dart out ahead of the objects of their attention; and who waved the downcomers aside as if they had formally requisitioned the hillside.

The ascending party announced itself in a tempest of barking. It consisted predominantly of dogs straining at their leashes and snuffling at the grass in the vain hunt for urine samples from fellow dogs. All were massive beasts built on the heroic scale, shaggy and lugubrious, Irish wolfhounds and bulldogs, all yearning forwards over the odoriferous universe.

The human participants seemed curiously secondary to the pack, being dragged forwards on chains by the powerful shoulders which muscled upwards to the tune of 'Whoa, boy!' and 'Just hold it there!' from the cameramen, whose professional commitment seemed to outstrip their grasp on the canine ability to subdue instinct to art.

Heading the team came a statuesque woman of considerable height and stride, who billowed up the hill in a pea-green coat, with a flying scarf to match and tossing dark hair that fanned out on the air. This handsome apparition looked serenely right for the part. She swept forwards, smiling with her eyes, head high, gloved fist firm on the leash of the dog to which she was attached.

'What's going on? What are you?' shouted a member of Marianne's conference.

'We're the Keeper and Grasper Lookalike Competition and mass dog walk,' called back the tall woman, in a gravely amiable voice that seemed to rule out any absurdity inherent in the proceedings. She halted, throwing the pack into a state of tumult in which every dog was at its neighbour's throat.

Marianne recognised Annabelle Willis of the Hardy University of Dorset, which had graduated from polytechnic status by buying in some very big names.

'Annabelle!' she effused, and, skirting the wolfhound, exchanged pecks on the cheek with her renowned acquaintance.

'It's okay, relax, he's gentle as a lamb,' Annabelle reassured her. 'Sit, Lennox.' Lennox sat. 'Just a bit of fun,' she explained, from the high ground of her stately carriage. 'Not my idea and not my dog, but (sit, Lennox, I said, sit) publicity for the Brontës – keeps them in the news. I say' (she button-holed one of the photographers) 'what about this rock?'

Annabelle, Lennox and a mastiff named Fred posed on the rock. Annabelle gazed out romantically over the hills. Fred lay with his dolorous, grizzled head dumped on his paws in a state of terminal boredom. Some disgruntlement could be detected amongst the members of the mass walk, dog owners who had devoted weeks to grooming their pets to look glossily fierce for the occasion, and who had travelled (so hissed a disaffected woman with a Wiltshire burr) hundreds of miles to take part, literally hundreds of miles. And after all this trouble their dogs were to be wilfully excluded from the picture.

'Group portrait at Top Withens!' promised their leader sensitively. 'Thank God Lennox didn't win, I'd have been for it,' she confided to Marianne, with a rueful grimace. 'Sorry – must fly – see you anon.'

Lennox flew Dr Annabelle Willis off up the track towards the summit. She belled out behind him in full sail.

'Emily's dogs were called Grasper and Keeper,' the indefatig-able busybody explained to Sharon. 'She loved them dogs better nor any human being. Thought them more faithful, you see, and a deal more intelligent.'

Fuck a duck, thought Sharon. She was thinking of chicken and chips, with mushy peas and gravy, eager now to get back down to civilisation.

The pack of hounds had passed Timothy like something out of a dream. Indeed, he had dozed on his bed of heather, head pillowed on his folded raincoat, aware as he dropped off of the breaths of warm wind that came and went, came and went, and lifted the frail tang of heather into his own breathings. His half-closed eyes had focused on the stems of heather that thicketed his view and swelled through proximity and near-sleep to gnarled forest trees.

A hum of insects travelled near and receded. An aeroplane passed overhead; a lapwing mourned, skimming the heath. Then, all being quiet, his mind dipped down.

It would have been a wonderful way to die. Not in a ward stuck full of tubes but out here, warm and relaxed, on this lap . . . but no, either his own barking cough or the barking of the dogs woke him, and he hacked and wheezed his way back up to consciousness, spitting out a gob of phlegm into the heather. He struggled to suck in enough air to keep him from fainting.

The pack had passed by the time he had composed his shattered body. But no – for, looking up in the direction from which the party had come, he was in time to see a final figure, detached from the main group but proceeding at a cracking pace, come up round the bend with her dog.

It was a young woman, got up in fancy dress. She charged forward, her face all thunder, as if she had just come away from a dispute in which her mind was still engrossed or perhaps was quarrelling inwardly with itself. She was thin, narrow-faced, long-nosed, short-haired, wearing this singular fancy dress of silver-grey material covered in a design of (he squinted) crescent moons and lightning-flashes. In this busy gear she stomped on, yanking the dog's lead, which was wound twice round her painfully thin hand; and the great bronze bulldog didn't seem inclined to put up any resistance.

He recognised her of course, almost at once.

He had never previously seen her by daylight. Perhaps then he was indeed dying. It would be beautiful to die in this way.

The bad-tempered girl, still discussing furiously within herself, came flouncing on without giving any sign that she noticed him. To her he was immaterial. But he would touch: yes, this time he would reach out and touch. This time: yes, he would dare to satisfy his desire.

Her skirts swished, soiled at the hem from the mud she tramped. He reached out.

Emily looked down.

Timothy looked up. Pins and needles tingled in the fingertips that had darted out to handle the forbiddenness of her garments.

Her eyes said that she hadn't minded. She comprehended that need. She did not precisely compassionate it but disinterestedly withheld judgement. Somewhere beyond her along the same curving plane stood Jojo. Jojo with both breasts intact, but diminished, refracted and at a peculiar angle to reality.

The texture of her dress resembled cobweb or the furred body of an insect. His arm shimmered with the electricity of the contact.

She neither looked through him nor avoided his eyes but took the pressure of his gaze. Her reply seemed to confirm that, though rather a poor specimen, he belonged to the same earth that had been her own native land. The dog accorded no such respect. It walked straight through Timothy as if he weren't there, and came out the other side.

She was on her way, sweeping round the green curve. She did not delay. She made haste to leave him. Yet she had afforded a fraction of a particle of her presence (a particle which was a wave; a wave which was a force-field; a millisecond of the eternity she had entered).

And yet he had not died. That was the sad and unaccountable thing. Here he was, stranded on the wrong side.

He rubbed at his numbed arm to induce some feeling, trying to remember every detail of what he had seen: the back of her shabby and ill-fitting dress, for instance, which was seated and baggy; the frown lines on her forehead; the painful thinness of her wrist and hand – and the shadowy hollow behind her collarbone; the affecting blue beauty of her eyes.

And she had a bosom. That must not be forgotten. Thin she may be but flat she was not.

When Marianne came round the knoll and saw him sitting there, unlit pipe in mouth, looking out over the hills, her heart squeezed. She had thought him so tottery he might have died there and then, where she left him; and she would always have grieved at her willingness to abandon him. He looked so small from where she stood, a faded and temporary grey figure within the wide scene.

He said he was fine, though she could see he had been crying.

Neil Thorniley and Ron Hebblewhite made a chair for him by clasping their hands, and bore him downhill. It was not an effort. Timothy was no weight at all.

The Cumberland Shepherd said he would sing, if nobody objected. The urge had come upon him.

Nobody objected, though a few eyebrows were raised and grins went round.

'I have set Emily's "No Coward Soul",' he explained, 'to a tune of my own composition. Dedicated, in all humility, to her Glorious Genius. The melody came to me in the bath one night,' he added. 'Quite out of the blue and spontaneously, and I leapt out like Archimedes when he had discovered his principle, wet as I was, to note it down before I forgot it. The tune is in the key of F major. All are welcome to join in as and when.'

He commenced.

Really, after you had got over the embarrassment of people bursting into song out of their little pink mouths in the middle of nowhere, Sharon thought, the old chap had quite a voice on him. A dark sonorous bass, suited to his magnificent stature, girth and beard. The tune was not difficult to get hold of, though you had to hold protractedly certain notes which went with particularly significant words. By and by the walkers all joined in, then they began again.

They warbled that no coward soul was theirs.

They bragged that they were no tremblers in the world's storm-troubled sphere.

They revealed that they saw Heaven's glories shine.

They affirmed that Faith shone equal, arming them from Fear.

Those who did not know the words sang 'La la la' but, looking up into the blue-grey haze and around over the grey-green earth, they felt that they were in the spirit of the thing.

Sharon sang blushfully, defiantly, 'La la la'.

Laurie Morgan and Duncan Lascelles, fully clothed, skin tingling lax from fresh sex and fresh air, caught up in time to join in. They sang with scorn how the thousand creeds that move men's hearts are vain, unutterably vain, worthless as withered weeds . . . But they looked round with a certain apprehension for the poor old dear who had stumbled upon their quick fuck up there on the hillside.

Eileen caught wafts of singing tossed back on the wind as she winced along far in the wake of the party. She had turned her heel in these silly shoes which looked sensible but she'd known quite well weren't; and the ankle had inflamed. Every step was agony. What with the shock of this, and the other more intimate shock like a wounding, she had entered a state of concussed numbness. Her sole

130

thought was to get back into that guest-house room and lay up on the pink candlewick bedspread with a cup of tea and a couple of paracetamol. Otherwise all was confusion and she did not even begin to grasp what people were doing singing hymns out here on the moors. Or perhaps they were strayed football hooligans. If so, she hoped they were not coming in her direction.

She held tight to her handbag in one hand and selected a large jagged stone to wield in her other, for the purposes of self-defence. Eileen did not lack for courage. She would go down fighting.

The tabloid headline PLUCKY PENSIONER BEATS LAGER BEASTS flickered through her mind, in company with a photo of herself looking noble, modest and forty.

Long-lost Frank, finding his eyes drawn irresistibly to the picture, sitting (unmarried) at his breakfast table (or widowed) would recall in a flash (eating marmalade) the bright freckled face of the girl from De Greys Café.

These fancies cheered her, despite the fact that she would not like Frank to be the sort of person who read tabloid newspapers, so that she was able to make better progress.

The tabloid newspaper would probably have been left by the woman who came in to clean for Frank. He would have picked it up and flicked through it casually.

A drift of music again reached her on the wind. 'With wide-embracing love . . .' sang men's and women's voices together. She seemed to be catching up with the choir. 'There is no room for death,' she gathered. Taking heart, she put on speed and met up with group and the minibuses on the Stanbury road.

'We were wondering where you'd got to,' said Marianne, though they hadn't been.

With her last remaining ounce of energy, Eileen heaved

herself into that minibus which did not contain the forni-
cators. She flinched away from the very thought of what she
had witnessed, which she packed back into the obscurest
recess of her mind, where it throbbed, dark and hot.

Chapter 8

Was I not vexed, in these gloomy ways
To walk unlit so long?
Around me, wretches uttering praise,
Or howling o'er their hopeless days,
And each with Frenzy's tongue –

Dreamily Marianne passed across the car park, quieter within herself than she could remember having been for months. Dreamily she threaded the milling visitors, smelt the coal smoke on the air. And as if in a dream she saw her own children being propelled across the car-park by their ireful father. Saw Charlie in the buggy, Andrew in a baseball cap being tugged along by Thomas, and Emlyn head-down, trailing in their wake. Witnessed Thomas savagely bump the buggy down the steps towards the village; and saw them disappear.

But they were not a dream. This weekend was her dream and these, her real children, had broken into it.

What did he want? Why was he doing it? Was there an emergency? If so, he'd have phoned the guest house. No, there was a malignity about the set of his shoulders and the way he'd charged the buggy at the steps and only pulled up at the last moment. She saw now quite clearly, he'd had enough. He'd come to wreck the conference by dumping the children on her or by creating some unholy scene in the middle of the afternoon seminar. He was quite capable of it. His temper was tightly elasticated . . . he held it and held it . . . you held your breath and held it . . . then he'd let go, having carefully aimed at your softest points.

Right. That was it. She was leaving him. And taking the children with her.

No. There was something wrong with the logic of that. The car-park reeled. An ice-cream van drew up, playing 'The Happy Wanderer'. A wave of children rushed forward and foamed about it. Car doors slammed. Grandparents, unpacking themselves from back seats, called for wafers and cornets. Marianne considered her own position, with a sense of faintness. Taking your children away from their father because he insisted she be an adequate parent was ridiculous. And she didn't want to look after them; not now anyway. And yet they were beautiful, and part of her, and they loved her and needed her, and she loved and needed them. Instead of which she marched up and down hills with a cornucopia of Mars Bars which she forgot to distribute on a windy summit to motley strangers.

Marianne crouched on the low wall between the car-park and the West Lane cottages. Here she could internally agonise concealed between a Volvo and a Range Rover. She squinted through at a world of accusation. Family values were exhibited in every quarter. A jolly father placed a Frisbee on a boy's head. An aged, blind man was half carried from a car up towards the Parsonage. Twins in a pram sailed across her line of vision, each having a balloon attached to his wrist by a string; their mother bounced along behind the pram, beaming at her cherubs and their bobbing balloons, showing her family off, relishing its life.

Thus the virtuous world passed by and Marianne was not a part of it.

Sharon thought she must have shed a pound or so even in the three hours it had taken to climb to Withens and back. Her thigh and calf muscles had gone to jelly with the unaccustomed exercise; it must be getting her fitter and toned up. She had read that if your muscles grew, your fat deposits shrank.

Her stomach gnawed, however, and she nipped into the first café that looked affordable. She would just have sandwiches, to keep her strength up, nothing fattening. The waitress was dressed up in the black uniform of a Victorian maidservant, with white frilled apron and a mobcap. The walls were hung with heavy brass mirrors, samplers, portraits of blindfold pink babies carrying bows and arrows, feather dusters, a warming-pan and the whole head of a deer with saddest eyes. Next to Sharon stood a blue and white chamberpot, from which a wax-leaved plant coated in dust sprouted. Sharon liked the cluttered place and examined everything. Old things always interested her.

The waitress marched off flat-footedly, her soles slapping on the rush-mat floor. She was wearing yellow plastic flip-flops, Sharon noted, which spoilt the kinky old-fashioned look of her get-up.

'One sandwich – ham. Tea for one – India,' she bawled to her colleague behind the counter.

The tea came soon; the sandwich took an age. Sharon felt sick with hunger. She followed the waitress around with her eyes and tracked her movements when invisible by listening out for the flip-flops.

A bowl of home-made tasty and nourishing Yorkshire

soup with crusty roll arrived at the next table. Someone else got a scone with a miniature pot of real strawberry jam.

At last the ham sandwich advanced through the gloom towards her famished eyes.

It was about the smallest sandwich she had ever known. Cut into four tiny quarters, its ready-sliced edges curled to reveal a single slice of supermarket ham. Beside the paltry sandwich lay a scatter of wilted salad.

'You must be joking,' she objected.

'You asked for a ham sandwich.'

'Yes, but . . .'

'That's a ham sandwich.'

Cheated and aghast (for it would cost her £2.50), Sharon fed herself the morsels on the plate. Her whole world seemed to cave, its walls crumbling inwards. She should have demanded a proper sandwich. She should have stood up for her rights. Instead she had got done for £2.50 and been left with a craving stomach.

She would never come to Pamela's Pantry again – not after this. Never. As she chewed the scraps of cress and raw cabbage, a sense of total betrayal swept over Sharon. She had tumbled down from the high ground of the morning into the everyday region of betrayal where they screwed you for all you were worth and laughed at you behind your back as a plump lump. She had asked for a ham sandwich and been served a stone.

'UP YOURS,' she wrote on the back of the bill, and dashed through the door without paying; straight into the Wildfell Café, where she ordered sausage, bacon, egg, beans, mushrooms and chips.

She was blissfully shovelling in the yolky chips when the figure of Marianne Pendlebury flashed past the window, downhill.

Sharon sopped up the residue of tomato sauce and egg yolk with bread, feeling much restored. She contemplated pudding.

Marianne Pendlebury raced back past the window in the opposite direction.

Sharon, eating a mound of apple tart with custard, craned her neck to gauge what was going on. A man with a baby-buggy was standing in the middle of the road bellowing Marianne's name. An anxious-looking boy, having snared Marianne's hand, was gently leading her back down to the shouting man and the wailing children. Her face was red and blotchy; her posture at once hangdog and defiant, like a child caught out in some forbidden game.

Thomas ceased bellowing and enquired of Marianne what she meant by running away from her own children.

Marianne demanded to know what Thomas meant by interrupting her at a conference during which he had agreed to take charge of the children, as being their legitimate parent with equal responsibilities for child-care.

Thomas replied in a measured, civilised voice that he was damned if he was going to be used as a nanny so that she could go off making a fool of herself.

Marianne pointed out her rights and his duties.

Thomas riposted with the twin arguments for gender-specialisation from biological design and immemorial custom.

Marianne asked when did he think they were living, in the nineteenth century?

Thomas said she evidently thought more of a bunch of dead Victorian spinsters than her own children. She must be some kind of necrophiliac.

Marianne expressed surprise that he would wish to leave his offspring in the care of a professed necrophiliac.

Thomas confessed to strong reservations about her sanity.

'Get me out! Go up of Mummy!' shrieked Charlie, launching herself from side to side in the straps that detained her in the buggy.

'Shush, lovey, do,' said Marianne. 'Daddy and Mummy are talking.' She crouched down and held one chubby hand in hers.

'Out! Out!' roared Charlie, deducing victory from this concession. Andrew laid his head against Marianne's crouched back, and wound both arms round her body. Pinioned thus, she was at a tactical as well as an emotional disadvantage. Thomas stepped free from entanglement and looked down with dignified disdain. Emlyn disappeared, embarrassed at the scene his parents were making in full public view. He went and fiddled with a tray of keyrings outside a shop.

'Right then, I'm off,' said Thomas. 'See you all Sunday night. Toodle-oo.'

'Please, Thomas – don't, *don't* do this.'

She couldn't believe he would actually do it.

But he was doing it.

Charlie under one arm, she dashed after him, begging him to see reason.

Thomas said he had had it up to *here*. Up to *here*, he said, slicing at his throat with the side of his hand. He gave her a look of desperate bale such as she had never previously witnessed on his face, sick of her, sick of it all, as if he'd seen through her at last. He took the steps into the car-park in two light leaps; slightly hesitated at the top of the flight as if off-balance, and was gone.

'What a shit,' Marianne kept repeating. 'What a shit.' She was at a loss what to do, and had been grateful for Sharon's sudden appearance, holding the hand of her elder son, whose impersonation of an abandoned waif was undermined by a furtive chuckle, for he had filled a pocket with filched articles.

'I found your lad,' said Sharon.

'What a . . . shit,' said Marianne. She could do nothing but shake her head and marvel, in the middle of the chaotic thoroughfare where ice-cream eaters with cut-off jeans shoaled round her family group, at the excremental character revealed in her husband. 'Hello, Emlyn. Where have you been?' she greeted her son vaguely.

He refrained from answering, dismayed by all this coming and going, shouting and about-turning. All three children studied their mother in silence to see what she would do next.

'What a . . . what a . . . *turd*,' she resumed, as if still lost in wonder at the revelation.

Sharon coughed into her hand. She suggested ice cream all round. Marianne followed her into the tea-shop like a lamb and wedged the squirming children one by one between the fixed chairs and the table. Sharon produced five ninety-nines.

'So what are you going to do?' she asked curiously. They all licked.

'Christ knows.'

'Will your guest house take them?'

'They might. But how am I supposed to find a babysitter?' She asked this vindictively, as if addressing the truant turd.

Then, like one awakening, her eyes lit calculatingly on Sharon.

After all, Sharon was lower class. Sharon didn't really fit. She wasn't literary or even, probably, all that literate. And Sharon was grateful to Marianne – or ought to be – for noticing her and being nice to her, so in a way Sharon might feel she owed her a favour, or a kindness.

'I suppose . . .,' she began cautiously, giving Sharon one of her sweetest looks. 'I hardly dare ask but, as I'm in a fix, I suppose you couldn't . . .'

Sharon saw it coming. She recognised the look in the eyes, as soon as they began to stroke her. Mrs Pendlebury wanted to use her; saw her as a convenience. Her hackles rose. She'd paid £76 for this weekend and all she'd had so far were two glasses of sherry, a boring evening and a walk up a hill.

Marianne, in the middle of 'suppose you couldn't', recognised the smoke pouring from Sharon's ears; recognised also, with a painful wince, the justice of Sharon's resentment against being used as a dumping ground.

'I suppose you couldn't . . .' she repeated, and Sharon's face blackened further; '. . . ring the Three Sisters and ask them if they can take the children for the night. Say I'll have Charlie in a cot in my room – the other two could share. *Do* you mind, Sharon? I'm so sorry to impose.'

'In with Mummy . . . for the *night*,' exclaimed Charlie, speaking round her thumb, proud and blissful as if accepting a prize. She looked forward to a night of companionship, bouncing cot-springs, catnaps and affable chats.

'Well,' muttered Sharon. '*I* could take them off of you if you wanted . . .'

'Certainly not,' said Marianne. 'This is your weekend. I wouldn't presume.'

'No, really. I wouldn't mind,' she lied. She felt she ought to make the offer. On the other hand, she felt Mrs Pendlebury oughtn't to run off and leave her toddlers – them being so little. No wonder the husband put his foot down. Yet she hadn't liked the way the husband was. The way he jabbed his glasses up his nose and blinked when he thought he'd scored a point. Also she objected to his naff shirt with navy and white stripes.

Marianne hesitated. It would be so much easier to accept, off-load the problem.

'Thanks so much, Sharon. But no. If you wouldn't mind just making the call . . . and buy some disposable nappies . . . the shop by the kiosk. The children will just have to attend the conference. I'll bribe them. You never know, they might learn something.' She smiled a watery, tense smile.

What a shit I am, thought Marianne.

Timothy, lying on his back with his feet on a pillow to ease the swelling, thought as he drifted off to sleep of how tender Marianne had been, how dear. She had taken time off from her schedule to be with him and make him feel special. Now that he had become accustomed to her unremarkable appearance, her very ordinariness touched him to the quick. It made a bond between them, a kinship.

The Emily meeting, belonging as it did in eternity, he put aside in his mind, to meditate when he arrived back in Hayfield. It was in point of fact less miraculous than the plain fact of this achieved closeness with Marianne – the first time since Jojo disappeared that he could turn over, as now he did, and rest on the solid ground of an affection which he knew to be reciprocated.

He slept right through Gillie Deneuve's electrifying discourse on Brontë autosexuality and, though if he'd clapped his dentures in his mouth and run, he'd have made it to Mulryne's twenty-minute divertimento on 'Who was the Stranger at Anne Brontë's Funeral?', he turned over instead and dreamed on.

Eileen dozed fitfully. She had swaddled her inflamed foot in cold compresses and raised it on a pillow covered by a folded towel. Her deeper inflammations could not so readily be poulticed, though a cup of tea and then a second did console her, as tea always did. She added two heaped teaspoons of sugar as treatment for shock.

Whenever she surfaced, it was to the sense that something had changed which would never be the same again. That the world was not the place she had taken it to be, or rather that a passage had been forced to her sanctum, blinkers had been ripped off her eyes.

The rough thrust of young loins fascinated her inner eye. The blind Cyclops eye of the staring penis tip.

The monkey-woman grappling, her posteriors parted, as if she'd split.

Shivering, jittery, Eileen perched on the edge of her bed in her petticoat. Should she pack up and leave the conference; go home to Ludlow and mother, and let these impressions fade in the round of duties and pursuits – as they surely would?

She bowed her head. Frank must have been dead and buried years ago; or married to some nice little woman – which was equivalent to dead and buried, as far as she was concerned. 'Rest In Peace,' she thought and laid his ghost in her mind with tenderness, like a childhood puppet in a box.

The painting she had picked up in Brussels was not authentic and she had forged the signature. She had no revelation to offer. Nor was she in any way related to Ellen Nussey; she'd made that up.

Passion was a credulous word for sex.

Sex was that grunting coupling she'd viewed up there on the moors, necessary to procreation and evidently highly enjoyable, but not the answer to the boundless desires and hopes she'd cherished in secret for so long.

Eileen roused herself. She tested her foot against the ground and gradually tried her weight on it. The injury was minor, just a slight sprain. One could live with that. But how to live with this dismaying world that was exposed when you stripped it of illusion, she could less easily say.

Really she should have had a proper education and a fulfilling career, like Marianne Pendlebury, she thought, combing the wild frizz of her hair out of its madness. All she'd been was a secretary and then a carer for her mother. For a person of intelligence, this did not fill your life. She'd been expected to marry; marry and breed. But this could not always be arranged. And in those days parents had not judged it a good investment to educate daughters. Hence, compared with someone like Marianne Pendlebury – *Dr* Marianne Pendlebury – Eileen had lost out.

Her hair was now under control, but had lost bounce. Eileen did not know how to induce bounce. She left these arts to her hairdresser.

She could have made just as much of her life as Marianne; more. The edge of grief abated under the access of resentment. She prinked her hair up with her fingertips. Really this younger generation of women had it all.

Marianne stood on the dais with her youngest clinging round her neck with both arms, peeping occasionally round at the coughing, shuffling audience and then hiding her face in her mother's neck. As time went by, the peeps became coy glances, graduating to winks and brazen flirtations. A natural yen towards theatrical display blossomed impromptu. Thus encumbered and strangulated, Marianne carried out her duties as chairperson with a composure born of despair. Her career, she saw, was over.

'I have pleasure in introducing . . .' she resolutely stated.

Emlyn and Andrew sat in the front row on either side of Sharon Mitchell. Emlyn's fair head lolled back against his chair and flopped loosely from side to side. His mouth was open; his eyes were fixed on the ceiling, a topic of exhaustible interest, as he was already beginning to feel. Andrew stuck his tongue out at his sister every time her head spun round to woo the audience, which corporately wondered where these detestable kids had come from and who had let them in.

Marianne sat down; Gillie Deneuve arose.

Most people except those in their immediate vicinity at once forgot the children. Gillie sprang at her audience like a panther; she chased and harried them; she picked them up by the scruff of the neck and shook them from side to side. Blessed with a naturally penetrating voice, she also had a nervously intense intellect which, as it stimulated itself, poured forth words torrentially; words which tended to the aggressive and vulpine, the further her brain heated.

She spoke of the erotic, the neurotic, the phallic mother, Oedipus, castration, the female orgasm, cunnilingus, incest and the way the Heights could be viewed as a gigantic nipple. She made scoffing reference to Kavanagh's cock-and-balls theory and pulverised the critics who had equated the windows of Wuthering Heights with a vagina, through which phallic presences were forcing in (and out, which was another form of in, viewed in the light of dialectical theory).

'Huh?' she kept enquiring combatively. 'Huh huh?'

Terrific use was made of notepads and pens in the body of the hall, for this colossus of Brontë scholarship was known to be the latest and very newest and most radical thing in the field. She was saying things no one had ever thought or said before; things no normal person could possibly have thought up for herself. Because of this, and because of her personal ardour and the explicitly sexy nature of the ideas, her discourse aroused its listeners. But so dynamic was the thrust of delivery that not everyone could follow the furious pace with which her thoughts were belted out.

Viv Passmore wrote, 'Out is in. But in is out (not) ★★★.'

She experienced a burst of illumination as she took this down. She saw, perhaps for the first time, the looping of truth which explained everything which the previous twenty-three years had left obscure. Later she was to stare in perplexity, then ennui, at these hieroglyphics. The dialectical loops of which she had been convinced would come to seem mere loopiness, away from the charisma of the speaker.

Val Passmore wrote, 'In/out. Out/in. Windows/Phallus – old-fashioned theory.'

Then they both wrote down in unison: 'CLITORICITY NOT HISTORICITY.'

Here was something they could put their finger on. The clitoris as the focal point from which all critical theory and practice must ray out.

Viv Passmore could imagine a T-shirt bearing the logo 'CLITORICITY NOT HISTORICITY'. How this exciting new concept related to *Agnes Grey* (Gillie Deneuve insisted that it did) Viv did not – as yet – grasp. While she did not feel convinced that Agnes would have known what a clitoris was, she did suspect that, if she had been informed, Agnes would certainly not have approved. Nor would Anne Brontë have exulted to hear this word CLITORIS aired in public, let alone shouted as a sort of war-whoop. But this, apparently, was not the point. This was archaic dodo-speak.

Some in the audience thrilled through less with the electricity of intellectual discovery than with scintillations of wrath. They glared affronted at the black-clad, elegant figure. Hand on hip she stood, undressing their saint, directing a strip-tease. Irene Nelligan's heart pounded at the thought of leaping to her feet and mounting an attack on the speaker as a pornographer, innocent of the fact that Gillie liked nothing better than a challenge. Shy Irene sat tight, diverting her thoughts to plaice and chips, with petits pois and a slice of lemon.

Laurie Morgan and Duncan Lascelles, possibly the only persons in the room who truly understood what Gillie was saying, listened with respect and interest. Laurie sat forward, elbow on knee, tapping her underlip in concentration. Here was the real thing; the genuine article – a postmodern mind through which the texts of Irigay, Derrida, Althusser, existed in a state of traversal, disseminating themselves in stereo-graphic plurality. The fact that Gillie was *wrong*, stupendously *wrong*, did not undermine her pleasure at witnessing a brill-iant mind at work; on the contrary, it augmented such pleasure, since at every stage one's own yet more brilliant mind could take its arguments to pieces. Laurie sat there dismembering Gillie, uncoupling her head from her body, unscrewing her hands from her wrists and generally disjoint-ing her logic with a serial killer's anatomising insight. If you understood how Gillie's brand of feminism was put together, you knew how to take it apart. Laurie looked forward to a set-to after the show in which she and Gillie would wrestle.

Once Laurie and Gillie had indeed wrestled naked, in the light of an Anglepoise in a visitors' suite at Harvard. That had ended interestingly. She sat and thought for a while of Gillie's pubic hair. Gillie's was an unusual *mons Veneris*. Her rival recalled its delicate sparseness of hair. ('Do you shave? Surely not,' she'd enquired. 'No, I'm just not that hairy a person,' Gillie had replied. 'Whereas you . . .') While Gillie's brilliant mind whirled words like CLITORIS at her enthralled audience, Laurie sat forward with her chin pillowed in both palms, oblivious of Duncan.

Susy Sugimura had a dreadful earache from being out in all that wind and wondered when the noise was going to stop. She had stuffed a piece of cotton wool in her ear, an expedient which had taken the edge off the oratorical drilling effects.

Neil Thorniley practised his liberal humanism by endeavouring to see the enemy's point of view. He strove to make sense of the sexual fireworks being ignited as technical terms and going off like rockets past his ears, but evidently he was not striving hard enough, for all he could keep his mind on was the possible size, shape and texture of Gillie's breasts . . . which one could not readily estimate in those loose-fitting garments. This remained, along with Deneuve's meaning, a mystery. He yawned and rubbed his balding cranium with both hands. He was too old, too lazy and too amiable for this kind of thing – thank Heaven.

Christ arrived at the Reverend Ron Hebblewhite's feet in the form of a child.

He looked down, looked up again, stared down and blessed his soul. The boy's round face, with wide blue eyes and a snub nose, returned his stare. An urge welled in Ron to shove the child away. He resisted the urge.

Andrew, growing rapidly bored, had slipped down from his seat and crawled out of Sharon's reach. Having scurried to the end of the row, he sat for a musing moment bouncing quietly and then crept along the second row of the audience, which was largely empty. He was therefore able to crawl through the tunnel provided by the row of metal chairs trawling for coins, buttons and other objects of interest along the way. The two ladies on the end of the row pretended not to notice Andrew, even when he poked his face up and bo-peeped them several times.

He headed into the third row, beginning to feel depressed, and raised his head lugubriously upon arrival at the Reverend Hebblewhite's knees. Like a tortoise he poked his head out and insisted upon being noticed. He then reached out and pulled at the papers balancing on the clergyman's knee.

Ron perspired. 'Shush,' he whispered kindly and placed one finger over his lips. Andrew mimed the gesture. 'Shush,' he said back, a playful glimmer entering his eyes. The minister nodded agreement. Andrew mirrored the nod. They nodded together.

The word ORGASM broke like a summer storm above the conference. It had had to come. It had been a long time pending. Now it came, in a deluge of synonyms. Gillie's lecture crescendoed in the word CLIMAX, at which some trembled and others tittered.

At the word ORGASM, the chairperson, in whose arms Charlie lay fast asleep, sucking a handkerchief, discerned her younger son mauling an elderly vicar in the third row. She looked imploringly at Sharon. Sharon half-rose and, craning to see where Andrew had got to, made signs to him which he could not see. She shrugged helplessly up at Marianne. Marianne, rocking her daughter, patting her damp behind, raised her eyes to the ceiling.

Gillie was almost done now. Her verbal energy had slackened, a torpor was setting in. But she was the kind of speaker who finds it difficult to finish. She dribbled on, speaking of the post-coital enervation of the second half of *Wuthering Heights*. At last the fountain dried, she sank into her chair: a little death, deliciously applauded.

Andrew Pendlebury sat on the stranger's knees, smelling

his fusty jacket and inspecting at close quarters the bristly, bulbous face.

'Clap then,' encouraged Ron Hebblewhite. 'Clap the lady.' Although God knew, the lady deserved spanking rather than clapping. Andrew clapped slow-motion but steadily, and continued when all the others had ceased to express their rapture.

Suffer the little children . . . thought Ron. A tender feeling arose in his breast in a rainbow bubble as he went on with his inward quotation . . . *and forbid them not . . .* and he handed the little fellow his fob-watch, which Andrew wonderingly clasped . . . *for of such is the kingdom of Heaven.* Andrew laid the aged timepiece against his ear and listened gravely to its measured wisdom. Patting the child's dungareed back, the retired clergyman sat beaming and feeling the bubbles of tenderness rise and pop in his chest. He confided the words 'Tick-tock' to his young acquaintance.

Marianne expressed the audience's gratitude to Gillie Deneuve for her powerful and exciting talk. Her arm muscles burned from holding the dead weight of the sleeping Charlie; she lugged her daughter up her shoulder and invited Alex Mulryne to reveal the identity of The Stranger at Anne Brontë's Funeral.

'We are all agog,' she said, collapsing into her seat as Charlie, awakening, began to squirm and whimper and look around, appalled at the sea of alien faces. 'Shush, Charlie, shush love, please, for Mummy,' she begged, and popped a Smartie into the mouth that was squaring up for a good bellow.

Happily, Mulryne's paper on the Stranger was short and sweet, consisting of a list of candidates for the unknown mourner, each one being scornfully ruled out as having an alibi or being already deceased. With each elimination,

Marianne popped in a new Smartie. Charlie opened her beak and demanded more.

When the box was finished, she occupied herself by attempting to introduce her little finger into Marianne's nostril.

'Just bloody well stop that,' Marianne hissed, arching back from the probing finger.

Having heard Mulryne's lecture several times before, she knew that, by the time he reached Herbert Shaw, the Scarborough apothecary, he was nearly through his list (for he proceeded methodically, in alphabetical order); the afternoon's torture was almost at an end. She grasped her writhing offspring in an unfriendly hug.

'Finally . . .' announced Mulryne, turning a page.

Andrew Pendlebury slithered down from the Reverend Hebblewhite's lap and legged it with Ron's grandfather's fob to the back of the hall, where he began to climb a grand piano covered by an oilcloth. Emlyn Pendlebury, head down so as to avoid the communal glare, trotted back to join his brother. A crashing fragment of tunelessness boomed into the piano's body and died there in a prolonged echo of modernist *Angst*.

'Oh my Christ,' said Marianne Pendlebury. 'Sorry,' she declared. 'Sorry. *So* sorry, everybody,' she apologised to the conference, giving up all semblance of control and thus permitting Charlie Pendlebury to wriggle out of captivity, patter down the steps and scurry to join her siblings in their music-making at the back of the room. As she skipped, she emitted exhibitionistic squeaks and chirrups as being likely to entertain the gathering.

Ron Hebblewhite tussled with the child of God over possession of his fob.

He commanded its instant return, for this was a priceless

heirloom, handed from father to son from generation to generation. It was vital that it should not be scratched or suffer concussion. From his prodigious height (the tallest vicar at Synod in 1964 by a clear three inches) Ron found it curiously difficult to engage with such a slippery flyweight opponent, past master of the dodge and feint.

'Give – it – back – boy,' he ordered, breathless.

Sharon disappeared under the piano to grapple with Andrew at close quarters. Andrew, overwhelmed, let out a siren wail, and was dragged out by the feet.

The fob was restored.

Charlie, having toppled backwards off the piano stool, experienced a minor apocalypse of her own, as her mother (who disapproved of corporal punishment) administered two vicious slaps to the back of her legs.

She roared.

Emlyn jumped down from the lid of the piano and disappeared out of the side door into a pungent room full of mops, buckets and Ajax, where he sat subdued with his hands plunged in his keyring-filled pockets, peering from the ajar door at the scuffle without.

Sharon dragged the remainder of Mrs Pendlebury's bawling brood out into the street. They quietened at once, looking round with puzzled eyes at the fresh light and prospect. As the hall abutted on to the Methodist chapel, it seemed natural to climb the low wall and roll around on the graves, waving their legs in the dappled air and chanting a mildly indecent rhyme. Sharon settled herself with her back against a headstone and closed her weary eyes.

Marianne Pendlebury, scarlet, remounted the dais and issued a further statement of abject apology to audience and speaker. While the audience rather inclined to mirth and sympathy than to a feeling that it had received less than its money's-worth, Mulryne gave no sign of recognition that anything untoward had occurred. Returning his half-moon spectacles to his nose, he took up where he had left off and disqualified the final candidate for the Unknown Guest, Arthur Henry Tressant, the well-known Moravian philatelist from York, with whom Anne Brontë might or might not have had a correspondence concerning the existence of hell.

This done, Alex Mulryne removed his spectacles once more and pronounced his conclusion.

His conclusion was that the identity of the Unknown Mourner at Anne Brontë's funeral remained Unknown.

This deduction was doubly satisfactory in exhibiting a classic simplicity and preserving the mystery vital to the legend. Mulryne nodded and blinked in response to the applause and was graciously thanked for his revelations by Marianne, who reminded the conference that after supper they were to enjoy a private viewing of the Parsonage. She then charged from the hall into the graveyard, where Charlie was still tumbling on the mossy surface of the stone belonging to Hannah Pigshead, relict of Joseph, died 1848. Andrew, however, having stung himself on a nettle, was lamenting loudly.

'Where the fucking hell's Emlyn?' asked Marianne.

'I thought he were with you.'

Emlyn ambled out of the door in the charge of Duncan Lascelles.

'Found your son, Marianne,' he remarked. 'In a *broom cupboard*.' He managed to make it sound a bizarre novelty never met with in the cultivated south of England.

Marianne took a swig from a can of lager and lathered the bodies of her two sons in the bath at the Three Sisters. Foam slid down their slick skin. They were languorous and peaceful, dreamily murmuring comments on the size and shape of the taps, the red dot on the shower attachment, the plastic curtain with buttercup patterns. To them all objects were fresh and interesting, for they refused the dull distinction between meaningful and meaningless which hampered the perceptions of their elders. Marianne too had calmed, under the influence of the beer and in the knowledge that nothing much worse could happen to ruin things than had happened already. She lounged against the bath, sleeves rolled high, up to the elbows in the hot water, her glasses steamed up. Neil Thorniley would be superintending the Parsonage tour.

She lifted them out one at a time, their warm wet bodies swathed in yellow towels; and as each was delivered, she kissed his forehead as she always did after the bath, in exactly the same way, and cuddled his glowing body close. And each child's eyes spelt the same secret smile as she hoisted him out and said to each his special poem. To Emlyn she recited, 'O thou my lovely boy'; to Andrew, 'Little lamb, who made thee?' Then she dried them vigorously and they ran into the bedroom wearing her T-shirts to have a cup of hot chocolate in front of a television which was wonderfully special because it was not familiar, even though the programme was the same.

Then she and Charlie got into the bath and soaped one another's bodies, singing of their intention to row, row, row their boats gently down the stream.

Charlie was in a gentle, mellow mood. She lay between Marianne's legs and wafted warm water over her mother without splashing. Marianne half dozed. Charlie turned and knelt. She began to scoop water into her palms and to ladle it with all possible tenderness and method over Marianne's shoulders, her breasts and tummy, her arms and thighs and knees.

'You feel nice now, Mummy,' she advised. 'Udderwise Charlie do it again.'

'Go on then, Charlie. It was lovely. So relaxing.'

Charlie repeated the dousing, naming (where known) the anatomical parts to which she was ministering.

'This is the life,' said Marianne, floating her arms out in the water.

'Do it again?' offered Charlie. 'Not bored,' she reassured her mother.

'Do you want me to do it for you?'

'Only *me* do *you*,' insisted the child with professional authority; but dropped her mask of severity at the words 'Hot chocolate' and began to scramble out of the bath. Marianne snared her in the towel and tied her wet corkscrew curls in a turban before she sped out in the direction of the promised drink.

'Not spill it you naughty, naughty boy,' Marianne heard her admonishing her elder brother. 'Mummy be sad again.'

'It's not you that make me sad,' said Marianne. 'It's me – or the world or something – but never you. Anyway, I'm not in a bad mood now, am I?'

Watching television with the children, in her dressing-gown, her own hair piled up in a turban, drinking hot chocolate, Marianne realised that for once she did not feel ('sad' was not the word but the only way Charlie could interpret what emanated from her mother) driven, hunted. One half of her conflicted life had been shorn away – the public, working self, with its compulsion to perform, assert control. It had just fallen sheer away and left her private self alone with her children. The burden of their need seemed

154

at this moment less crippling; the abundance of their love stabilising.

She could just be with them. She had no need to rely on Tom. She had no need of reputation. She did not need the Institute. When all these props to identity were withdrawn, there was still someone there. It was almost miraculous, the sense of freedom . . . but she cautioned herself, as she rubbed her hair dry, not to exult rashly. Take it a step at a time. Later, she knew, she would register disorientation, failure, tedium. At present there was plain relief.

The phone rang.

'Er . . . er . . . Marianne?' enquired Thomas' wobbling voice.

'Yes.'

'Oh God . . . *Marianne* . . . I'm just . . . bloody hell . . . I'm so . . . are you there?' He had been drinking.

'Yes.'

'Are you all right?'

'Yes.'

'Oh.' He was silent, as if stunned at the list of neutral affirmatives. Finally he asked, 'What can I say?'

'That would be up to you.'

'Christ, Marianne. It was a bloody thing to do. Bloody. Can you ever forgive me?'

'Actually we're watching television and it's rather a good programme. You won't mind if we cut the conversation short here.'

Replacing the receiver, she fleetingly considered the question of whether she could forgive him. It seemed irrelevant. He seemed so far removed. Let him remain so.

But no.

'Marianne.' Urgently.

'Yes.'

'Shall I come up now and take the kids home? There's still time. Just say the word.'

'No.'

'But where are they now? Who's with them? How are you managing the . . . conference and so on? I mean, I'm worried about you. I feel dreadfully bad about this, I really do . . . Marianne?'

'Don't come. The children are with me and we're all fine. Don't ring again please.'

'Marianne . . . let's be reasonable about this – work it out together rationally, like we always do. I'll get in the car now; be with you in an hour and a half. It's the obvious answer.'

'Look here. Just sod off, will you?' She crashed the phone down, trembling with new-sprung rage. It was the advice about being reasonable that had got to her.

'Rude words,' observed Andrew, scandalised but simultaneously gratified at the licence her explosion conferred to exchange select obscenities with his siblings. He wasted no time in telling Emlyn that he was a little bummy bugger.

'Oy,' said Marianne. 'Cut it out.'

'Marianne,' said the phone.

'If you insist on disturbing the children when they are settling for the night, you drunken oaf, I shall have no option but to take the phone off the hook. Good night.'

'Well, if you're sure . . .' replied the phone doubtfully, and did not intrude again.

Chapter 9

He comes with western winds, with evening's wandering
  airs,
With that clear dusk of heaven that brings the thickest stars;
Winds take a pensive tone, and stars a tender fire,
And visions rise and change which kill me with desire . . .

Timothy was cruelly disappointed to realise that Marianne
would not be leading the Parsonage tour. He could make
little sense of the garbled explanation of her absence gleaned
from the conversation of the others: something to do with
having her children suddenly turn up.

'*She's* got her hands full.'

'Poor old Marianne. My heart went out to her.'

'. . . but when the little lad went mountaineering on the
piano I really honest to God thought I'd burst . . .'

It seemed that while he'd been snoring, Marianne had
undergone some public humiliation which he'd have hated
to see her endure but at least his sympathetic presence might
have encouraged her. He almost turned tail and went to her
lodgings, but wouldn't he just be one more burden, having
to be helped wheezing and doddering up the stairs, then
fussed over and entertained?

Taking the ankh which hung round his neck in the palm

of his left hand, Timothy inwardly murmured a spell to ward off harm from his friend. He would think of a candle-flame every hour on the hour; and that flame should stand for Marianne's welfare. Such inward and spiritual pledgings of solidarity, for what they were worth, were all he could think of to offer.

The queue was admitted for its privileged viewing, the ropes which barred out the public from the Brontë family's private spaces having been removed. They might all wander freely from room to room, and in the sweet thrill of this once-in-a-lifetime access, Timothy let the anxiety about Marianne sift to the back of his mind. Neil Thorniley, who had sunk a pint or two, and was looking forward to sinking a couple more, handled the visit in a vague and informal way. He didn't insist on doing a guided tour but, reminding the visitors that they'd been requested not to touch items on display, ended, 'Well, just sort of . . . feel free to, er, roam round and do your own thing.' Neil was an easygoing sceptical fellow, not without a glint of cynicism concerning the whole Brontë charade. Questioners who approached him were referred to noted bores amongst their number, sentencing them to a thousand lashes of the tongue: 'I think you'll find Smedley can fill you in on that.'

Timothy stood in the Reverend Patrick Brontë's study, beside the cottage piano on which Emily had played Haydn, Mozart and Beethoven to her blind father. He too was a lover of music and yearned to push up the lid and place his fingers where Emily's had been. Music was always for Timothy an experience of haunting, listening in to the mind-patterns of people who had long ceased to exist as more than dust but who had left scores of their inmost being to be reproduced from generation to generation. The ghost of Emily would be in the music. She'd been to Brussels and had been offered the finest piano teacher in Belgium; played transcriptions of the Prometheus Overture and the Seventh Symphony on that very instrument. Furtively, he ran his fingers over the cover. It seemed too trivial an instrument either for Beethoven or Emily: a mighty woman at a doll's piano. And if those keys could be made to speak now, the notes would probably come out quite unstrung and out of tune.

And here was Mr Brontë's place set out for him to eat his posthumous meal in solitude at a table which bore his magnifying glass and a book of psalms in case his peckish ghost should chance to return with a yen to sing a glad song unto the Lord, blast his enemies or hang his harp upon the trees of Babylon.

All seemed to Timothy faded and off the point. These were just leftover objects in a reliquary, nothing more. He twinged with disappointment: just when you held your breath with quivering expectation at the thought of entering the inner sanctum, brimming with presence, you found yourself flung further away than ever.

People exclaimed, admired, queried, qualified. His ears were invaded by the tramp of footsteps over squeaking floorboards and the clack of high heels up the cold stone staircase; floral skirts swirling in and out of doors.

'She died there – Emily. On that sofa. She turned her eyes from the pleasant sun, as Charlotte so nobly put it.'

All eyes stared at the sofa. There seemed hardly room for a tall woman of five foot seven inches to die on that perch, which had been transformed to a Sacred Sofa which, how-ever tempted, none of their number would violate by depositing upon it her own backside.

Electrical replicas of oil lamps had been lit in each room, conferring a glow of authenticity which softened the edges of tables and books, threw a commotion of long brown shadows from the visitors on to the wallpaper and reflected in the black mirrors of the sash windows a second oil lamp which lit faces in the frames of transitory portraits.

Most people now had filtered upstairs, leaving Timothy alone in the kitchen; alone, that is, save for Eileen James, the forthright lady who'd handbagged the hennaed professor claiming roots in dockland. A formidable lady. She glared at him now, over her beaky nose, and the lamplight caught her hawk-eye. Each read the other's wish for him or her to back off and relinquish the delicious privacy to commune with whatever wisps of ghost might still be extant, like spiders' webs in crannies. Each resisted, silently asserting prior right to be present, though Timothy emitted a small, apologetic cough to signify that he understood his rival's need to be alone and regretted that his own was equally imperative.

Eileen did not cough. She turned her back on the stranger, hoping he would withdraw. The old man's harsh and laboured breathing seemed to fill the quiet room with intimations of mortality. Crossing to the great black kitchen range, she surveyed the copper pans and utensils.

'I believe we met on a tombstone,' Timothy tentatively addressed the brown wool costume and the flat back of a beehive hairstyle whose front elevation was all façade, after its trouncing by the elements that morning.

Eileen turned reluctantly to the poor old wreck.

'I believe we did. It was extremely hard upon the coccyx. One does not like to be disrespectful to the dead but there are times when one simply must take the weight off one's feet.'

'Of course,' croaked Timothy. 'In any case, the dead aren't really there, are they? Just a pile of bones. There's nobody there. The dead are' (where were the dead?) 'elsewhere.'

'Still,' observed Eileen, 'one must draw a limit. For instance, crisps — bags of chips — cans of Coca-Cola — should *not* be consumed on gravestones. I draw the line there.' But in general she did not disapprove of the sentiment, what she could hear of it.

'Anyone's welcome to eat chips on *my* gravestone.' Timothy gave *carte blanche* to future diners. 'Or a five-course meal, come to that. After all, I shan't be there to see it. Better for folk to enjoy their life than mope and moulder. The dead,' he announced, with something of jubilation, 'are there to be danced on.'

Who said that? It was pure Jojo. Jojo speaking through him. Her opinion, to the life.

'Well,' said Eileen. 'Well.' She liked the spirit of the man: a bit of a revolutionary old bird under that dull, dun plumage. Still, she did not believe for a moment that Charlotte Brontë would have been best pleased with the kind of riff-raff that trailed around the graveyard, consuming hot dogs and burgers. Miss Brontë had had a blunt opinion of the lower orders.

'Charlotte would have sent them about their business,' she observed.

'I believe she would.'

'To think,' went on Eileen, setting down her handbag on the kitchen table, 'that Emily kneaded her dough and read her German books at this very table. Here, where we are standing, Emily was. Well, she was, wasn't she? And she could not know that we'd be standing here, in her very place, 150 years later, talking about her. It's a singular thought, isn't it? Isn't it though?'

She stroked with her fingertips the irregular surface of the table, smoothed through much scrubbing. Many women's arms had scoured that surface, among them Emily Brontë's.

'It's a thought,' agreed Timothy, endeavouring to think it.

But there was a block. He couldn't reinstate the perished woman, not a strand of her hair, not a shadowy fold of sleeve. There were just the two of them in the room, with all their present aches and preoccupations.

'I wonder if she liked a cup of tea,' meditated Eileen. 'I don't believe it says anywhere, in the records – at least from what I've read. But I expect she did. Most English people do, don't they? My mother – she's ninety-two – is drinking tea all day long. As soon as she's had one, she's looking round for another. "Mother," I say, "you've just had a cup of tea", but, no, she won't have that. So I just make a new pot. The whole day's one long brew-up. Of course, her mind's gone – it left her sixteen years ago now and it hasn't come back. She lives in a world of her own. But she's happy there.'

'Does she know who you are?'

'Oh yes, normally she does. Though she occasionally tells me I'm in the wrong house, I'm someone else's daughter, she forgets whose. I take no notice of course. She forgets what she's said as soon as she's said it.'

'It cannot be an easy life for you,' said Timothy. Having nursed Jojo, he understood and was quick to compassionate those carrying such burdens. 'Not easy at all. I looked after my wife – Joanna – in her last months. Strained my heart lifting her about. . . . But I mustn't complain,' he reminded himself, for he could feel himself launching off into the long saga of his ills that made people's eyes glaze and had them shifting from foot to foot. 'She was a brave, proud woman,' he stated resolutely. 'And a great lover of the Brontë sisters.'

Eileen could think of no reply. But she reached out her left hand (she who compulsively preserved twelve inches of body space at all times) and patted the old man where his rough sleeve met his thin, mottled hand. Skin met skin.

They exchanged names, and potted life histories, and

Timothy was huskily explaining to Eileen how he was a fan of John Tavener, and wondering if she had ever heard his music, so tuneful and spiritual, and Eileen was making a note to listen to it, she had often thought of investing in a Walkman, when Neil Thorniley put his face round the door and asked if they'd mind just turning the lights off when they'd done.

'Let yourselves out,' he said. 'You'll find us at the Black Bull. Welcome to join us. Going off duty now.' He fled away with relief, having delegated.

Yourselves. Let *yourselves* out. Now they were *we*, a couple.

It was strange to switch off and unplug the downstairs lights of the Parsonage, plunging the rooms one by one into darkness. Eileen pulled the plug on the dining room and Mr Brontë's study; Timothy turned off the lights in the kitchen and Mr Nicholls' study. They climbed slowly up the stone staircase, side by side, past the grandfather clock, as *we*. They ascended, Eileen thought, like an elderly couple going up to bed for the night.

Sharon saw a lad in the Black Bull she really fancied. Just as she was sitting on the margins of her group, so he was on the edge of his, a gathering of local lads and girls. The lads told jokes and stories against absent friends or the weaker members of the group, and the permed girls squealed with helpless but robotic laughter, as though someone had just turned them on.

The lad Sharon thought she fancied was a tall, slender youth, no older than seventeen. He sat listening at the edge of the bench, smiling at the stories as he flipped and spun a beer mat on the rim of the table. He did not seem to have a girl attached to him, as the more dominant specimens did. He looked, Sharon thought, like someone's younger brother.

'. . . and so she pulled them down, and I got out me tackle, and Christ what a pair. WHAT a pair . . . I said, WHAT a pair . . .'

Roaring; stamps; hyena laughter.

'So then Atherton came in for his innings,' said one of the semicolons men. 'Well, you know Mike Atherton . . . and he had scored a century in the previous series. Met him once,' he digressed. 'Pleasant chap . . . Gatting . . . de Freitas . . .'

The semicolons men droned on like a radio set. Their world was a portable cricket pitch, a green cloth which they carried from Lord's to Old Trafford, from Haworth to Houston, and could unfold in any milieu, laying out at will their little white wicketkeepers, batsmen, fielders and umpires. In the persons of their 'men', they bowled heroic bouncers, they caught impossible catches in the slips, rolling head over heels, howled Howzat! and brandished the Ashes in the Black Bull at Haworth; and invisible crowds roared them on. They had another pint.

The feminists and postmodernists kept well out of the way of the ball. They looked upon the cricketers as the intellectual kin of Winnie-the-Pooh and Eeyore; or as the harmless relics of a desiccated imperialism.

'By God, we thrashed the Pakistanis that year.'

'I'd ban all competitive team sport,' observed Gillie Deneuve. 'Male team games are a stylised form of militarism.'

'There's a theory,' said Ellen Rooney Herzog, 'that it siphons off their destructive energy. Keeps them from gang-raping us.' The fierce women regarded their hypothetical attackers with forensic curiosity. The unsuspecting suspects sprawled, mild hands on cardiganed paunches, and 'Out for a duck!' exclaimed one. 'Just like that. Bails flying everywhere.

Nothing for it. Had to walk.' He shook his head. 'Another round?'

The innocent rapists agreed to have another round.

'You ladies having another?'

Laurie Morgan denied being a lady. Gillie Deneuve did too. Ellen Rooney Herzog remarked that she was a woman, plural women, spelt WIMMIN. Sharon stated that she would have another half of Webster's. So far she had not paid for a single drink.

'And a bag of peanuts, please,' she added. Nobody commented, but Sharon was aware of being considered a political liability. She had no objection to being called a lady if it meant free drinks and peanuts. She spied the silken interior of Gillie's purse: a wedge of tenners her privileged fingers riffled through. Sharon sniffed as Gillie slid past her to buy her fellow wimmin's gin and tonic.

The well-fit lad flipped a beer mat too many and it sailed down at Sharon's feet. She bent and handed it back. Eyes met eyes. His were brown, long-lashed; his long hair, parted centrally, flapped down over a fashionable undercut in a pair of glossy wings.

'Thanks,' he said and, blushing, hung his head and returned to his dreamy flicking.

'She were a right slag,' observed his neighbour. 'Marilyn. Marilyn she were called. But, way-ay, you should've seen her knockers.' He cupped his hands and weighed in them a ghostly pair of global breasts.

'What – bigger nor our Julie's?'

'Hey, watch your mouth, cheeky bugger.' The group's eyes communally assessed Julie's magnificent bosom. Its owner squirmed in embarrassed delight. Flat-chested girls loured. The thin boy flashed a sidelong look; blushed deeper, drawing in his chin; built a house of beer mats, which collapsed.

'Marilyn were nowt like Julie. She were a right ho. Any-body's for a frigging pound. Us lads ud line up for a go. Now she's wed to a right eppie.'

'So I got out me tackle . . .'

'He got out his tackle. Come on, let's see it mate.'

'I don't wholly go along with the neo-Freudian view,' said Gillie intensely. 'The problem of the phallus is just too intertwined with issues of class to be, of itself, paradigmatic . . .'

'. . . bowled a remarkable series of googlies in 1962 . . .'

'. . . put it up her arse . . .'

'. . . and then, as regards the workings of the *id* . . .'

'. . . poetry in his bat . . .'

'. . . could do it fifteen times a night . . .'

'. . . the problem for women has always been . . .'

Rival conversations clashed and crashed around Sharon as she chewed her salted peanuts. Balls and bails flew. Pricks played Punch and Judy. Long words fought for airspace. She felt weary of it all and gave a great, uninhibited yawn. When she closed her mouth, the lad was looking her straight in the face.

'Have a peanut,' she invited him.

He accepted a peanut.

'Have a few. Hold out your hand. Go on.'

He didn't speak. He was a blushful, bashful boy. But he held out his delicate palm to receive the last scraps of peanut and a shower of salt. He licked the salt from his palm.

'Another drink?' he murmured, his blush deepening. Sharon, aware that it would be hard for him to stand up and fetch her a drink in front of his well-lubricated Saturday-night mates, said, 'No, let me. What'll you have?'

'Hey up, Mark, you're well in there.' She heard it from the bar: the chorus tuning up.

'Bit of a lard-arse though, Markie. Still you can't have too much of a good thing, so they say . . .' She heard it all from where she stood (and the barmaid refused to notice her), presenting to them her rear end, upon which they felt free to philosophise. Part of her prickled and cringed, pondered bolting for the door and going home; the other part endured, strengthened by wrath, made stoical by long discipline to wanton injuries.

She refused to allow them to damage her.

Turning, Sharon gave the morons a baleful stare. That transiently quenched them. They shifted their eyes, whistled, snorted behind their hands.

'Thanks,' said Mark. She had expected him to be more daunted by the peer-pressure; but, though fiery red, he allowed the two flaps of hair to curtain him from the attack. 'Sorry about them,' he said. 'They're all right really, my mates. Had a drink too many.'

'Oh, that's all right. I'm Sharon.'

'Nice name, Sharon. I know two Sharons. I'm Mark. You from round here then?'

'Oh no,' said Sharon. 'I'm at a . . . conference. Just thought it might be a bit of fun,' she apologised. God only knew what he would make of the company she was keeping. Gillie Deneuve, at the prodigious top of her voice, was challenging the semicolons men with the theory that the cricket bat was a stylised phallus by which the batsman proved his potency against the rival males of the tribe, and Stan Smedley was yelling (for Gillie was in unstoppable flow) his question, 'So what does that make the ball then?'

Gillie paused; but she was not to be stumped.

'The ball,' she replied, as if to a child or simpleton, '*of course* represents the challenge made by the male community to the individual to prove his sexual prowess . . .'

The semicolons men guffawed as one team.

Sharon coughed; shifted in her seat. She didn't want to be identified with these people.

'Nutters,' she explained quietly. 'Sad cases. I got brought along on false pretences. I were interested in the Brontës, you see, and Mrs Pendlebury (she runs the conference) said I might like to come – but she never told me one half were sex maniacs and the other half off their trolleys.'

'Oh. Right.'

'So what do you do?'

'I'm on YT. I'm training in Freight Forwarding.'

'What's that?'

'I don't rightly know yet. I've only started last Wednesday. Something to do with sending goods from A to B. All I done so far is make coffee and answer the phone. I have to say, "Good morning, this is Mark at Hibden and Laing Freight Services, how may I help you?" in a pansy voice. Then the guy at the other end asks something like, "Can you quote me a price on ten tons going from A to B?" Of course, I never know the answer, so I have to pass them on to Derek or Andy. That's what I do. Dead boring like, but I'm hoping it will improve. What do you do?'

'Waitress. I have to carry cups of tea from A to B. I've got some good mates there. We have some great laughs.'

They were getting on well. Her spirits rose. Mark's hair was glossy-dark, his face narrow and soft-featured. It seemed to be in permanent retreat into the mantle of hair, which he alternately shook down to veil him from view and peeped round to spy what was out there. He was gentle; and treated her like a person.

'How you doing, Markie Mark?' A hand on his shoulder.

'Fine,' said Mark. He was almost off the edge of the bench, so heavily did his shaven comrade bear down upon him.

'What's her name?'

'Sharon.'

'Hi Sharon,' said Baldie. 'Chatting you up, is he? Want to watch him. Hunky Spunky they call him down Mytholmes Road. Right, girls? Right? Hunky Spunky. You watch out, love. This guy is a stud, I'm telling you. Known for it.'

'Shut up, Daniel,' said Mark in a weakly voice.

'So . . . it's Sharon, is it? Lovely curvaceous Sharon. Didn't I see you on Page Three last week?'

'Shut up,' said Mark, less feebly.

'Wouldn't fit on,' said another wit. 'Spread over into Page Two.' He snorted into his beer.

'Stop it. Leave her alone,' said Mark, choking.

'Piss off, you wankers,' retaliated Sharon. 'You're dormant, you. You're spack. Scran. Just fuck off or I'll fist you one where it hurts.'

The landlord, pulling a pint, paused and looked over vigilantly to where a fat girl was threatening to beat up disreputable members of his clientele. She looked as if she could do it too. Built like an ox. Was on her feet. He hoped she'd take them outside first.

Laurie Morgan heard Sharon Mitchell take on a gang of yobs; saw her rise and confront one. She was impressed. She elbowed Gillie in the ribs to give over. Gillie, raving climactically, couldn't.

'Nice way of speaking,' observed Baldie, coolly lighting up his cigarette and blowing smoke in Sharon's face. She was towering over him but trembling violently. 'Ladylike. Good manners. What do you see in a beefy slag like that, Markie?'

'Do you have some kind of psychological problem I could help you with?' enquired Laurie Morgan of Baldie.

'You what?' He gaped at the old bird with hennaed hair.

'Do you suffer from some affliction of the brain?' Laurie

went on solicitously. 'Which surgical intervention might cure? Just say the word. We'll see what can be arranged.'

Sharon sank down into her seat, quivering. Taking her hand, Mark squeezed. Baldie, muttering about farts and tarts, made a tactical withdrawal into the heart of his group where, however, public opinion did not receive him with unanimous acclaim.

'You didn't ought to of been so tight on her,' said a girl. 'She didn't do you no harm, Daniel.'

'Yeah. She can't help having a backside like a double-decker bus,' said Daniel's mate. Laughter was muted. When Sharon and Mark left, they did so under cover of Laurie Morgan's high-powered forensic enquiries into the ethical foundations of Baldie's patriarchal creed; Baldie's demand to know what the effing hell she was on about; Gillie's redirection of her tirade against the hairstyle of Baldie, which she defined as an example of that tumescent modern fantasyland in which the males of our species strove to impersonate their own pricks.

'So that,' she said, 'you get this *phenomenon* of big pricks marching round waving little pricks.

'And the abolition,' Laurie said, 'of the cerebellum.'

'Sure. Their brains (which were never highly developed and the education system has not helped) are absolutely shrivelling – shrinking. Civilisation gone into reverse.'

'These people,' said Ellen Rooney Herzog, 'are in process of recidivism. Upright earthworms.'

'But worse than earthworms, Ellen,' objected Gillie hotly, 'since not only are earthworms – the genus *Lumbricus* – in point of fact hermaphroditic but they serve some purpose in the recycling of decaying matter – but what possible purpose,' she queried, 'is served by a prick like that?'

They both gazed earnestly at Baldie as if to deduce the

answer to this scientific problem. Baldie scratched the tattoo of a mermaid on his arm, then hid his head by nuzzling his girlfriend's left ear with his tongue, and pretended not to know that he was the subject of scrutiny and debate.

'Well,' said Laurie, 'it is possible to argue . . .'

Neil Thorniley and the semicolons men had decamped to Haworth Old Hall Hotel, where they had only to contend against the resonating thud of the juke box.

'Ten years ago – or fifteen,' sighed Neil, 'women like Laurie Morgan had not been invented.'

'Forty years ago,' observed Stan, 'there were hardly any women about. Just one or two earnest bibliographers. And then of course if they married another member of staff that was it – career over – they got the boot.'

'A hundred years ago,' said Neil, 'they couldn't even be students. Of course,' he added, 'that was a damned unfair state of affairs.'

'I sometimes feel,' said Stan, tamping down the tobacco in his pipe with his forefinger, 'that the pendulum has swung a smidgeon too far the other way.'

Neil, who had downed several pints more than was customary, was hazy about whether he had locked up the Parsonage properly. He supposed he had.

'One last round,' he proposed.

'Golly,' said Eileen. 'Crikey. I do believe we're locked in.' She was incapable of masking her schoolgirlish elation.

'Let me have a go.' Timothy ham-fistedly fiddled at the lock, puffing and blowing. He'd left his heart pills and water pills at the hotel. It would be no joke for him to be stranded all night without them. The lock wouldn't budge at all. 'They'll come back for us,' he quavered.

Forty-five minutes passed.

'Someone will remember. Or see the lights,' he repeated.

Eileen wished he would stop trying to spoil the sole exciting thing that had happened to her (she suddenly realised this) all her life. She wished he'd stop dithering there by the door and bobbing between the shuttered windows, trying to locate a passer-by to hail. Sooner or later one would turn up and see the panicky old man knocking; and they'd be let out, the Parsonage locked up, and that would be that.

'Timothy,' she said. 'Hadn't you thought? This might have been *meant.*'

'How do you mean? *Meant?*'

'Well, look,' she said. 'It's quite a strange thing, isn't it, for two people like you and me – people who've lived with the Brontës all our lives practically – to find ourselves locked into their house, don't you think? I mean, it's hardly a run-of-the-mill event, is it? Personally, the only thing I regret is the absence of tea-making facilities. At my guest house there's a grand little alcove in the room with everything you could think of – nice modern mini-kettle, teapot and matching willow-pattern cups, five sachets of Nescafé and five PG Tips teabags . . . Of course, the Long Life milk isn't ideal, but one puts up with it. I suppose we're going to have to do without these home comforts tonight. So are you coming back upstairs, Timothy, and we'll sort out sleeping arrangements?'

Dazedly, Timothy followed his self-elected landlady up from the souvenir shop, through the room displaying books and manuscripts, through Branwell's 'studio' and into the hall which gave on to the bedrooms. Busily, Eileen squeaked into each room in turn.

There was only the one bed.

It was a reproduction of the Reverend Patrick Brontë's half-tester bed, dark wood, brocaded, severe. It looked approximately as comfortable as those on which Timothy had kipped down when doing National Service. On the bedspread were draped a man's white nightgown and a nightcap.

'Well then,' observed Eileen in a matter-of-fact voice, 'we'll just have to share . . .'

'Take turns, you mean.' He nearly tumbled down on Mr Brontë's bed there and then, he felt so weak. Ankles pulsating, he gazed longingly at the mattress. As a gentleman, he ought to concede priority to the lady. As a wreck, however, he felt he must prefer a claim.

'There's perfectly adequate room for two persons,' she pointed out. 'After all, we're both adults – and no spring chickens at that. We need our rest.'

Having first removed their outdoor shoes, Timothy and Eileen lay side by side to try out the bed for size, their heads raised on a steep bolster.

'Well, what do you think?' he asked.

'Horsehair. Lumpy.' Eileen giggled. She turned her head to survey the unfamiliar male face beside her on the bolster. It was mainly beard and eyebrow. 'I think you ought to try on the nightgown,' she suggested. 'For authenticity. Go on. Then I'll know how it felt to go to bed with Charlotte Brontë's dad.'

Jojo laughed. Somewhere out there in the beyond, Jojo went off in a characteristic peal of laughter.

She'd been an exhibitionist. Buying a bed in a department store, Jojo would test the springs of half a dozen, in an orgy of barefoot bouncing.

Timothy caught the spirit of the thing.

'How do I look?'

He had not removed his trousers. Modesty forbade. His spindling ankles and wrists poked out of the voluminous garment; his nightcapped head met its addled likeness in the reflecting glass of a picture.

'Like Wee Willie Winkie.'

His figure cast a ballooning shadow out behind on to the wall. He was wearing the nightclothes of the dead. Daring their ghosts. Filling out the space they'd vacated between collar and cuff. It ought to feel creepy. Instead it just felt fairly silly. He struggled out of the robe, coughing with inhaled dust, and folded it neatly at the end of the bed. Why keep dead people's clothes anyway – bits of their hair, Aunt Branwell's mouldered metal clogs, Charlotte's minuscule slippers, lace collars? He'd taken Jojo's clothes straight to Oxfam.

Now he paced the rooms, looking for two vessels to use as chamberpots, and met Charlotte Brontë headless in a glass case.

She gave him quite a turn. By daylight amongst crowds of living voices chirruping 'Wasn't she small?' . . . 'Hardly bigger nor a child', the model caused no dismay. But to Timothy trespassing in the forbidden zone, by night, the headless Charlotte in a glass case came as a shock.

Day by day eyes roamed her. They roved her bodice, girdled her tiny waist, glanced off her full skirts, looked straight through the space where her head should have been – that so very shy head that swivelled away from guests at the tea-table, so as to perform by gradual stages a forty-five degree turn from the feared eyes of her fellows. A neat head of perhaps rather rough hair, in the close-fitting style of the Victorian miss. The head that housed the storming mind. Now the reclusive Charlotte stood condemned to display herself to all and sundry, beheaded and handless. Charlotte's silent scream ricocheted around the interior walls of the transparent box.

Timothy would pee in Mr Brontë's spittoon. For Eileen

he secured a chamberpot, the genuine article, which he presented to her with some embarrassment.

'Excellent,' she acclaimed it. 'You wonderful man.' She didn't seem a bit troubled by the intimate details of her partnership with this stranger. She felt like a bride on her honeymoon, serenely thrilled at her new estate. 'I shall keep my chamberpot in Aunt Branwell's room,' she announced. 'You may like to place yours in Charlotte's. I shall know not to disturb you there.'

So he would piddle beside the headless body of Charlotte. He'd be up and down all night of course. He mentioned this to Eileen, sketching out a rough picture of the state of his bladder.

'Well, if you must, you must. Of course.' She took it philosophically. Seemed listening out for something, her head cocked to one side, hands on her lap, feet in their snagged stockings crossed tidily on the bed. Her feet were broad and high-instepped, he noted. Her legs were rather sturdy than elegant. Her hips were broad. Her bosom . . . he checked himself from thinking of bosoms.

He wondered what ghosts would be stirred by the breathings of these unbidden guests; what dreams would effloresce in the depths of the mind, when one had taken up residence in the abode of those dead wild dreamers. He sat down on the bed and hemmed, wondering whether it would be acceptable to remove socks and trousers; his braces would cut cruelly into his shoulders if he left them on. Postponing these radical acts, he compromised by removing his tie, which he rolled up and placed in his shoe.

'I cannot offer you a cup of tea, I'm afraid,' he wheezed. 'But I always carry about with me a small hip flask, ready for any emergency.'

'Oh my goodness, now that *is* strong,' she exclaimed, as

the brandy burned its way down her throat. 'Elderflower wine is my usual tipple.'

Warmth diffused through Eileen's joints. It flowed sparkling down her legs, inducing a melting torpor in her thigh and calf muscles. All the knots of her being slipped slack. Her tongue loosened and she was flown with loquacity. She snuggled down beside the man's friendly body. She seemed to have known him for years and years. He seemed always to have been there. Eileen murmured nonsenses to him, their heads upon the one bolster, nonsenses that were also profundities. Deep sayings rose as froth. She laughed; she cried; the old man sat up to cough rackingly; he drew a cover over the two of them, put his thin arm round her shoulders and hoarsely said they should sleep now, it was time for them to rest. Her leaden limbs sank into inertia and she snored her way to oblivion.

Timothy dipped down into sleep and came sharp awake with a shock. He thought the ceiling had fallen on him. There was a walrus-weight of woman against him, lolling almost on top of him. His flimsy ribcage took the burden of a petticoated stranger. He eased from the bed. She gave a surprising snort and tumbled over in the other direction.

Of course he went to Emily's room.

On bare feet over the smooth boards he padded to her doorway. The narrow room was shadowed and still; and it was Emily's room.

He closed the door behind him and opened the shutters to admit the moonlight and the starlight. On the floor stood a shadowy wooden crib and a child's miniature chair: this had been the Brontë children's nursery before it became Emily's room – but then and for ever it had become Emily's room.

Here she sat with her lap-desk and wrote her secret words.

176

Her pen nib would have snagged and scratched as it bit along the paper; her breathing would have come slow and deep. These trees would not have soughed as now, for she lived before their time. In the night silence she divined the winds and their directions; listened in to their breathings, and was stirred or lulled by them in moody alternations. She looked beyond to the night skies and the stars' outsiderly gaze returned her own.

> Thought followed thought – star followed star
> Through boundless regions on . . .

He had never felt more peaceful, never as gathered, as here at the window of Emily's room.

> . . . while one sweet influence, near and far,
> Thrilled through and proved us one . . .

Eileen, awakening, knew immediately where he was. She lay waiting for him to come back to bed. It must be no joke having a bladder like that. When he didn't return, she began to wonder if he'd had some accident – tripped and fallen, perhaps, or even suffered a small stroke. The long years of looking after her mother rang the alarm bell in her mind. She clambered from bed, mouth sour and dry, mind still blurred from alcohol, and knocked gently at Charlotte's door, where he had stationed his spittoon.

'Timothy – are you all right, dear? Not in difficulties?'

But Timothy came out of Emily's door.

He took her hand.

'Did you wonder where I was?'

'Yes.'

'I was in Emily's room – listening. Will you come with me?'

Hand in hand, they stood at the window of Emily's room, listening together.

'Best whisper,' said Sharon. 'The landlady's an old dog.'

Sharon and Mark crept up the respectable staircase under the eye of a dusty chandelier on a chain. They silently skirted the many-tongued aspidistra on the turn of the stairs, and escaped into the mazy corridors of the guest house, covered with busy red floral wallpaper.

Sharon snapped the lock on the door.

'Here we are. My pad.'

Persons unknown had tidied her scattered garments into a seemly pile and lined up the bottles and sachets on the dressing-table as if for parade inspection. Sharon's magazines had been placed face-downwards on her bedside cabinet, as if such reading matter had been judged and condemned as vulgar.

The room was small and poky. You kept falling over your own shoes in the attempt to fill the kettle, which could hardly be manoeuvred into the tiny wash-basin so that the tap could wedge into its spout. She caught sight of herself in the mirror as she struggled to couple tap with spout. The unkind light revealed a scared, puffy face and a bulky body. She backed away.

'Here, let's have a go.' Mark managed it first time. Then he tore open the coffee sachets and picked open the lids of the milk sachets; asked her if she took sugar. He seemed happier doing something. They sat side by side on the pinkly sagging bed, sipping decorously, daintily.

A gurgling roar went up beyond the opposite wall. The cistern rumbled and clanked. Footsteps departed.

After this musical interlude, there was silence. Sharon tried to think what to say.

'The ornaments are stuck down with superglue in case anyone walks off with them,' she informed him.

'Who'd want to?'

The cistern gurgled again.

Then a rush of water began on the wall behind them. A thumping and squeaking ensued, followed by a tremendous sloshing. After some time, a plug was pulled; torrential waters drained away.

'Blimey, there's a bathroom on one side and a bog on the other,' said Mark. 'Not going to get much sleep tonight, are you?'

I hope not, thought Sharon.

They put down their cups simultaneously on the window sill. She felt faint and hopeful and fearful in case, in his shyness, he should just get up and go; and alert lest, up his sleeve, he should be mocking her. *Please, please don't be.* She cast him a swift, complex glance.

He caught the glance.

'I'm sorry about all that in the pub,' he said. 'It were right shady on you, Sharon. He thinks he's major smart but he can be a joey – he's not always like that, just when he wants to make out he's big like,' Mark pleaded.

'Uh huh.' She looked down; would rather he'd not referred to it at all. The angry humiliation, the casually brutal face, flooded back.

'*I* think you're gorgeous, Sharon,' he went on breathlessly. 'Gorgeous to look at and intelligent like. I hope you don't mind I'm not into books and that lot.'

'You're not laughing at me, are you?'

'*Me* – laughing at *you*? You must be joking.'

His lips were tender and hesitant. They seemed to speak

the truth, in their soft tellings of kisses that were entirely new to Sharon. Hours they lay there, kissing only. Giggling when the cistern went. The walls were so thin you could hear the men pee: long gushes of what had been pints of beer; an occasional relieved sigh of 'Aah!'

Once Mark got up to go. He peed discreetly: she didn't hear a thing until the cistern went into its routine uproar. Sharon shifted up on one elbow and examined the time: two thirty. She didn't want the night to end. Ever. Her lips were tender and swollen with kissing. She brushed them lightly with her fingertips.

Generally they poked their tongues into you and thrust them in and out; roughed up your boobs; shoved their finger or dick in or got you to suck them off. So she'd found. After this they jerked up their flies, lit up a fag and strolled off to play the fruit machines.

Mark kissed lower. He seemed to want to drown in her breasts. He ran their large softness like liquid over his face; stroked and tongued the nipples, murmuring, then quiet, then half-crying; she was all silk, rippling round him.

'Have you got a . . . you know?'

'No,' he said. 'Have you?'

'Yes.' She had almost denied it, thinking he'd think her . . . but he didn't. She rummaged for the rubber. He fixed it on, not very expertly.

'Not hurting you, am I? I don't want to . . . hurt you . . . Sharon . . . love.'

'Not hurting . . . oh, not hurting.'

He came, with a rasping cry as if of pain. The metal cry echoed like a bell. Sharon had an image of a landlady in a housecoat, irate at the door, demanding to know . . . They both listened. Nothing. Then the cistern roared, clanked, glugged. They dissolved.

Dawn came up. The room grew grey-blue over all its surfaces.

'There . . .' said Sharon in an emergency voice. 'There . . . again, there. Do, please, yes, don't stop, please, Christ, God, yes, Mark, yes . . . oh.'

Chapter 10

– So said I, and still say the same
- Still to my death will say –
Three gods within this little frame
Are warring night and day

Early morning communion was celebrated at Haworth Parish
Church where the Reverend Patrick Brontë had held forth
with apocalyptic vehemence on the occasion of the Ponden
Bog Burst. The parishioners communally agreed that they
had left undone those things which they ought to have done
and done those things which they ought not to have
done, and that there was no health in them, while Mr
Brontë's wife, son and four noncommittal daughters slept
under the stone floor.

At the Catholic Church in Ebor Lane the host was raised
and blessed. At West Lane Methodist Church, chrysan-
themums shone like suns. Next door West Lane Baptist
Church and Hall Green Baptist Church on Sun Street strove
for the allegiance of the flock and the ears of God by
outsinging one another. West Lane poured out its soul in
passionate strains of 'O Love that wilt not let me go,' while
Hall Green rocked to the music of three guitars and a tam-
bourine belting out 'The Lord of the Dance'.

Church bells woke Neil Thorniley, instilling unease. A suspicion that he had done something he oughtn't or not done something he ought nagged at the corner of his mind, as he lathered up, razored his chin and snipped his moustache. But what the hell was it?

A mackintoshed man in a cloth cap sandwiched between placards was patrolling the cobbled road beneath the mullioned window. Neil gathered that The End Of The World Was Nigh. The prophet of the millennium cast a long early-morning shadow in the hazy sunlight.

Neil placed a fragment of the *Yorkshire Post* over the bloody nick etched in his chin. He watched the prophet out of sight. Two girls carrying Bibles in their left hands walked in his wake, wearing their Sunday best and evil smirks. He saw the little sinners toss the Bibles to one another and back again. Gold-edged pages riffled in the sunshine. The shadows of the flung Bibles winged like birds to and fro between them. The purity of their white anklesocks passed out of sight.

He remembered something. More precisely, he remembered he'd forgotten something.

Christ. It dawned.

He'd locked the buggers in.

As he ran, his paunch walloped along in front of him: not fit, too fat, hot, awash, and falling apart.

There they were, waiting with their coats over their arms as if his coming had been foreseen. Their serenity was entirely baffling.

'How *can* I apologise?'

'Don't mention it,' the beaky lady reassured him. 'It was an oversight that could have happened to anyone.'

Neil muttered about refunds.

The woman came in quickly with, 'That would be most acceptable.'

The old chap mumbled about pills. Neil, perspiring, steered him down Main Street, the woman commanding his arm on the other side in a marital manner. Together they acted as brakes on Timothy's accelerating totter down the steep incline.

'You may leave us here,' said the woman, with something of a stately manner. 'We shall take some refreshment, I shall attend Matins, Timothy shall rest, and we shall no doubt see you again at the workshops.'

The semicolons men ordered cereal, grapefruit juice and full English breakfast. They would each have sausage, bacon, two fried eggs, tomato and mushroom, followed by toast (white and brown). Tea for all.

'Couldn't look at it at home,' said Stan Smedley. 'Where's Neil got to?'

By the time Neil slumped down into his place, Stan had already skewered one of his fried eggs in the eye; it wept yoke over the bacon.

'That looks good,' said Neil. Habitual optimism, along with the smell of fried rashers, was triumphing. 'My wife won't oblige at home. It's all oat bran and wholemeal bread. This reminds me of Blackpool when I was a lad.' He dispensed a few well-garnished amusing recollections of Blackpool in the forties, unfurling his napkin on his lap.

'Full English, sir?'

'Oh, yes please. I'll have my eggs scrambled though. And any chance of Worcestershire sauce?'

The landlady toured the tables individually, asking each patron if he or she had what he or she desired. She wore her apron to indicate her culinary role but offered literary observations as a kind of intellectual side dish. Her face was worn, wholesome and mild; her outfit starched as a nurse's.

'Good morning, sir. I trust all is to your liking? I am a long-term admirer of Daphne du Maurier's biography of Branwell. So well written', was the tidbit she presented to Alex Mulryne. Then she turned to Neil Thorniley: 'Enough milk, sir? Good. I consider *Shirley* to be Charlotte Brontë's most underrated novel. I don't know your view? Ah, here comes your bacon and egg.'

Neil dug in.

'By the way,' he remarked. 'I accidentally locked two of our number into the Parsonage all night. Excellent bacon. Good Yorkshire cookery, you can't beat it. But they seem to have survived with no obvious ill-effects,' he elaborated. It was already on its way to becoming one of his anecdotes. In ten years' time he'd hardly know how much was real and how much legend.

The semicolons men watched the large girl at the next table furtively butter ten slices of toast and conceal them with several potlets of marmalade in a paper bag. She sat awkwardly with her arms crossed above the paper bag in her lap while the landlady conducted a brusque interrogation concerning her satisfaction with the service. *She* was not favoured with any literary supplement to her diet.

Sharon had considered and rejected the feasibility of transporting cooked elements of the full English breakfast up to Mark in some kind of box. Or introducing Mark as a surprise breakfast guest. But whereas the first expedient seemed too messy, the second was beyond her powers of imaginative explanation or dramatic execution. And besides, it occurred to her that the landlady might recognise him, being local.

When she arrived back at her room with the paper bag, the landlady's hangdog daughter was advancing from the other direction with a turned-on vacuum cleaner. Sharon stood her ground and glowered.

'I'm not out yet,' she objected, above the roar of the motor.

'Vacate by ten.'

'It's not ten yet.'

'I never said it were ten. But t'room's got to be empty *by* ten so we can *thoroughly clean it*.' She made this statement offensively, as if Sharon's ilk were under suspicion of being a contaminant, with filthy habits.

Sharon flounced in, whipped the 'Do Not Disturb' notice off the inside of the door and hung it on the outside.

'Ten o'clock prompt,' said the voice outside.

'I heard you the first time.'

'Good.'

A pale, slim youth lay fast asleep on her bed, completely naked, his face cushioned on the crook of one arm, his beautiful hair flung back. The soft penis tilted sideways over his groin. She gasped at his beauty.

The landlady's daughter must have had an eyeful.

'Toast,' she whispered to the sleeping Mark. 'Sorry to wake you but we have to be out by ten.'

'Out by ten, Miss Mitchell,' said yet another female voice in the corridor.

'I *heard*.'

'Just a reminder.'

The vacuum cleaner was switched on again and seemed to make vituperative dashes at Sharon's door while they ate their toast, urging its message of universal hygiene.

In the room diagonally opposite to Sharon's, Eileen let herself in, having nearly tripped over the flex of a roaring vacuum cleaner in the hands of a rude girl who was shouting, 'On your way by ten o'clock, mate.' Such uncouthness would under normal circumstances have rendered Eileen incensed enough to demand to see the management, had her head been less fogged with sleeplessness in combination with a hangover one part brandy to one part sheer joy. As it was, Eileen had contented herself with demanding, 'Are you addressing me, young woman?'

'No – her in there. And Loverboy.'

Observing that her neighbour had hung out her 'Do Not Disturb' sign, Eileen swooped in and swooped out again to do the same. It might keep the vacuum cleaner from bursting in and careering round her personal territory, as it seemed threatening to do. Sabbath calm was sadly lacking. She had left Timothy tucked up in bed with a hot-water bottle, having administered his pills and supervised his undressing with the same efficient care she routinely bestowed upon her mother, though Timothy was a light stick-person compared with the doughy bulk of Muriel. Eileen had been shocked at his wasted legs, as she threaded them into his Marks and Spencer pyjama trousers. For the first time she saw him as a sick man.

'We'll have to plump you up a bit,' she had observed.

'Oh, I've never been the chubby sort. "The spare young man", they used to call me.' The pyjama trousers did not fit to his waist. He had to bunch the top together in one hand to hold them up. He hoisted his legs into bed with a sigh of relief.

'Well, spare young man, that may be so. But you need feeding up.'

'Eileen – I'd never be much use to you, you know. In fairness and honesty, I should say that.' The rasp of his gravel voice told the same truth. Anyone could hear.

'But this,' she had pleaded, crouching down by the pillow, '*is* special? Has been special?'

'Will go on being special,' he affirmed. 'For as long as . . .' He had already been drifting off to sleep.

She was parching for another cup of tea.

Passion had come to Eileen in a manner she had little dreamt: a seeing along the same eye-line with another human person, looking out of the window together into the all-but-lightless world. Passion had very little to say for itself and nothing whatever to do with sexual gymnastics. Having occurred in the realm of the unsaid, it would rest always in the world of the untold. They had held hands at Emily's window: that was all.

And it had meant absolutely everything.

This was why she felt such an urgent need for a cup of tea: to help her cope with the effects of extreme emotion. Cups of tea could always be relied upon to soothe and steady.

Aghast, Eileen confronted the dingy white plastic shelf which was home to the tea-making equipment. Only the kettle remained; the rest had been removed – snatched. She panted with dismay.

Accosted the vacuum-cleaning girl, who was thumping down the corridor with a mound of blue bedclothes.

'Someone's taken my cups and teabags.'

'For washing. Standard procedure.' She thumped on.

'But I want them.'

'Out by ten a.m.'

'It is *not* ten a.m.'

'Nearly.'

'It's an absolute disgrace . . .' Eileen began shrilly. 'A person cannot rest in her own room (paid for, mark you, in advance, and overpriced at that, I might add) but she is chivvied – and hoovered at – and harangued by the chambermaid (you ought to be ashamed of yourself, who taught you your manners?) – and chased out – and lastly denied access to the tea-making facilities to which the brochure expressly states she shall have a right.' Once launched, Eileen was not easily deflected, and though she demanded to know what the young woman meant by it and what she had to say for herself, and though the girl attempted to bawl an answer, Eileen simply swept on, livid as lava.

A jangling miscellany of crockery was slammed down on Eileen's dressing-table. The girl flounced out, ostentatiously glowering at her watch.

Sipping her tea, Eileen wholly failed to recapture the exalted mood which she had brought from the Parsonage. Instead she felt the world slipping sideways; electric discharges in her head. It would no doubt be better when she moved into the room she had booked at Timothy's hotel, next door to his; they had agreed to stay on in Haworth an extra two nights.

She must ring mother to let her know. She hadn't rung last night of course, on account of being imprisoned. The Ludlow Home Care Agency was a tried and tested organisation which would have sent the two helpers in to give Muriel her wash and put her to bed, so she hadn't any worries on that score. And of course, Muriel hadn't much idea of time; but she might unconsciously have noticed that Eileen's voice wasn't there when it should have been. Eileen's habits were regular to a fault.

She rang the number: waited. No answer.

Rang again.

And again.

Tried through the operator. Waited. Nothing.

Rang Ludlow Home Care. Number engaged.

Rang again. Number still engaged.

And again. Cooing voice in recorded message advised callers to try again in an hour's time.

In a sweat, Eileen rang the next-door neighbour; got his Ansafone. Rang her mother again. Nothing.

Spasms of panic.

Rang Timothy's hotel to leave a message for him that she'd gone home, giving her phone number, saying she'd return if all was well.

Rang Marianne Pendlebury's hotel.

Rang for a taxi.

In the event, Neil Thorniley ran her to Hebden Bridge; the least he could do, he said, considering his awful bloomer of last night. He didn't like the look of the old girl at all and hoped it wasn't the result of his damn stupid foul-up.

He saw her on to the train.

She looked ill and bleak, clasping her navy handbag to her chest like a spongy shield against the future. Hands in pockets, jingling his small change, Neil watched the train out. The station was full of walkers wearing fluorescent backpacks, woollen hats and clumping boots. When they moved out of the view, the train had disappeared and that was that. Their weekend faces had a cheerful, robust look. They marched out of the station car-park towards the Heptonstall Road. Neil passed them as he began his return drive; was furiously hooted and tailed by some maniac driving a Vauxhall Cavalier. Neil, who in his quiet way took a pleasure in passive resistance to these speed freaks, at once braked and moved out. He pottered along in his shirtsleeves, window open, arm lax on the window, enjoying the woody view over Hardcastle Crags. The road above the precipitous cliffs ran twisty and narrow, allowing no room for overtaking; Neil's ostentatious amble simply reinforced the point satirically.

The maniac overtook as soon as they had climbed out of the valley on to the straight road over the moor. A scatter of early Sunday trippers in lay-bys looked up transitorily from their deck-chairs as the hell-bent motorist roared past.

'Please, Marianne,' begged the maniac. 'Let me make up for yesterday. I've not slept a wink. It was a bloody beastly thing to do.'

The children leapt on their father from three different angles. Marianne reproached herself: there was no excuse for having mated with a man who said things like *bloody beastly thing to do* like a public schoolboy.

'I don't need or want you to take them.' She looked him straight in the eye.

'Please, Marianne, please.'

'If you and they really want to.'

Interrogation commenced. It appeared that half of Charlie wanted to go home with Daddy to see the peacocks at Pets' Corner; the other half was adamant about staying here for ever with Mummy, whose legs she fervently embraced. Andrew said he wanted his kangaroo, which was at home. Emlyn sulked and shrugged his shoulders and said he didn't care. So disaffected did he feel with the parental choice on offer that he seemed to be looking round for some third party to claim as a fosterparent.

'So that's decided,' Thomas concluded. 'Home with Daddy. Who wants a piggyback?'

Charlie and Andrew scrambled for the piggyback. Andrew won but Charlie thumbed him in the eye; so they both cried.

'You bring the push-chair, Emlyn, there's a good boy. Emlyn, for goodness' *sake*. Stop crying, Andrew, you're putting it on, you're perfectly all right. I'll put you down if you carry on like that and Charlie can have first piggyback.'

Andrew stopped crying. Charlie grizzled on. Emlyn tipped

back the push-chair, rocketed up the cobbled street, narrowly missing the Reverend Ron Hebblewhite on his way out of the newsagent's, having purchased his *Sunday Telegraph* on his way to church, where he would assess the performance of the incumbent on a scale of one to ten. Spotting his little friend, the Child of God, riding high on his father's shoulders, he forgave him his trespasses the more readily for perceiving that he was being carted off to another place. He tapped Andrew on the head with his *Telegraph* but the child's blue eyes looked amazed and stared through him without recognition.

'What that old man bopped me for?'

'When I get back,' Marianne cautioned Thomas, enunciating clearly, 'we're going to talk about the whole future. Okay?'

'Okay.'

'I mean, seriously.'

'Yes — sure.'

You see, I've decided not to fight to stay on at the Institute. I'm giving notice when I get back.'

'Oh — Marianne.' A melting look suffused his face. It was what he'd always wanted: Marianne to stay at home with the kids; order and serenity; meals on the table. But you couldn't in this day and age ask such a sacrifice of a woman; she had to offer it herself. It had to come from her. It *had* come from her. 'I'll make it up to you,' he said. 'You could carry on evening teaching if you liked — or even take up some new study of your own.'

'Such as — flower-arranging perhaps, or t'ai chi? What do you suggest? Some nice yoga perhaps, to calm me down?'

'Of course not.'

'I don't think you understand. I'm not staying at the Institute. But I'm not staying with you either. So, if you want to take the children home now, and they want to go, take them by all means – but please note, everything is going to change.'

He said no more. He knew her well: a dreamer, with her head in the clouds. All crackpot schemes and airy gestures. How often had he said to her, 'Feet on the ground, Marianne. We have to live in the real world'? Not much of what she said translated into actual deeds. And this time he must admit to having grossly provoked her.

'Wave to Mummy, children,' he said as they rounded the corner out of sight. But Mummy was not there to be waved to.

'Gone,' said Andrew. 'Gone and gone and gone.' With each 'Gone', he drummed on his father's head with both fists.

'How was your night?' asked Kerry on the coach.

'Choppy,' said Marianne. 'I was sharing a bed with my daughter. She doesn't sleep in the night, on principle, and if there's company she has a party – a rave. She spends hours just bouncing. Bouncing and chatting to imaginary friends – that's if she doesn't think you're awake; if she knows you're awake, she chats to you and the imaginary friends.'

'A bit of a budding Brontë, by the sounds of it.'

'Christ – I hope not.' They both laughed.

'The bed-springs were going next door to me.'

'What – Gillie Deneuve?'

Kerry nodded, creased-faced with suppressed laughter.

'But – who with?'

'Laurie Morgan. I'm sure it was Laurie,' Kerry whispered, face up close. 'Honestly. Yes, honestly. I didn't twig at first. Then I realised it was a woman not a man. Then I heard the name. They weren't being particularly quiet about it.'

193

'But what about – Duncan?'

'Vomiting all night in the en-suite bathroom. Some scampi he'd eaten, according to Laurie.'

'So Laurie wasn't ministering to his fevered brow or holding the bucket?'

'Reactionary Florence Nightingalism apparently.'

At Hare Runs Hill they all piled out of the coach for their first Scenic View. Marianne suggested people might care to walk a little way, meeting up again in half an hour.

The strong wind flowing over the heath at once revived and relaxed her. Her anxiety about the mishap to Timothy and Mrs Passion bowled away on the wind as she walked; the sudden jolting arrival at the end of the road with Thomas, and with the Institute; the problem of what to do with her life and where to live it, and what to live on – the wind relieved her of responsibility for the present by tossing these burdens off her shoulders into the general commotion of fir boughs, beaten reedbeds, scudding cloud.

Marianne took a stony path over a grassy mound towards the moor. She walked alongside the dry-stone wall of a farm, past a rectangular field in which sheep were penned, bleating raucously. She climbed past the farm with its barking sheepdogs; past a fir plantation and a deserted house with its windows boarded; through a farm gate and on to the plateau of the moor. A figure was staggering after her, wind inflating the hood, body and arms of a green anorak; and others in twos and threes straggled up, bending forwards against the slamming wind, searching out a Scenic View.

Being ahead guaranteed a measure of solitude. Turning into the wind, she strode on over puddles in the track which rippled in blasting gusts. Banks of heather and bilberry fled away on either side to reedbeds. Above, stone-grey masses of low cloud sped eastwards towards a morosely dark horizon.

194

Wading into the heath, she plumped down on a hummock of grass. When she lay back in the heather with her hood up, there was a sense of passing away out of sight, into isolation and stillness. Down in this grave of growth, gnarled stems wove a shelter against the booming wind. Her face was scalded, as if from the sea. Marianne lay and viewed the clouds streaming before the wind. She thought of nothing. Nothing mattered.

Nothing.

'Mind if I join you?' Laurie Morgan in a billowing hood, wearing no make-up, nose and cheeks reddened from the wind, loomed.

'Of course not,' Marianne felt bound to say, and, struggling up, got a great clout of wind smack in the eye.

'I envy you,' she heard Laurie say. But Laurie wouldn't have said such a thing. She stared at the face, which seemed embarrassingly nude without its make-up. It was wrinkled; and these were not laughter lines, but furrows of anxiety or concentration.

'Pardon?'

'I said, I – envy – you,' Laurie shouted against the wind.

'Why?'

'Oh – everything.' The gaunt face looked away, towards the horizon; one hand fiddling with a rusty sprig of last year's heather. 'You should have seen yourself up there on the platform yesterday – your little girl in your arms. That was something . . . I could never experience, you see . . . I don't mean having children, I couldn't manage children . . . but you with the little girl asleep in your arms, speaking in such a natural way . . . something so moving about that. Much against my better judgement, I found myself envying it.'

'You needn't. It was an illusion. I was just making a fool of myself – I hope for the last time.'

'Pardon?'

'I can't cope with both. Work and children. No good. I'm giving in my notice. Reached a crisis.'

'No, Marianne – don't.' Laurie placed a hand on Marianne's sleeve, as if to detain her. The wind lulled. 'Now really, don't. Seek some support. You and I don't think alike. But people like you live in a world that's real to more people. You inspire affection. You have the common touch. Whereas people like me,' she added, 'tell it not in Gath – haven't.'

Marianne looked down, struggling with tears.

Laurie looked up.

'Glory,' she exclaimed. 'What kind of a bird is that?'

'What?'

'There. Look.' She pointed.

A winged creature was sailing the air currents, soaring, plunging, executing surprising arabesques and manoeuvring into dramatic volte-faces. All over the heath, people stood stock-still, their exclamatory faces tilted upwards to view the flight of a pennant-flying craft.

'Hang-gliders,' said Susy.

'CHARLOTTE,' read Ellen, pausing in her efforts to scrape sheepdroppings from her sole. Charlotte vaulted and sidetracked, tore up, swooped down.

'EMILY, that one says EMILY,' shrieked Viv, with delighted astonishment.

'And ANNE, here comes ANNE,' said her twin.

Anne held her course onwards and upwards until it seemed she would disappear into a cloud. Emily was an artful dodger, veering leftwards, catching a gust, speeding forwards in virtuoso display.

'BRANWELL,' read the Cumberland Shepherd from where

he perched on a tussock, peeling a banana. But Branwell was in evident trouble. He plummeted, caught a cross-current and wavered with every appearance of terminal decline.

But there were more where those came from. Coasting across the plain from the hills came craft after craft: Maria I, Maria II, Eliza, Patrick, Aunt Bran. One after another they rose from the dead and floated across the ashen skies.

A dozen cameras were raised and triggered. Flashes went off. But since the targets would not stay still to be photographed, the lenses framed a patch of sky, a seagull, a dangling pair of legs. The eye of Tom Lassiter's camcorder roved the heavens.

Branwell was in a bad way. He seemed to possess only the most rudimentary notion of the principles governing flight. He struggled crazily in mid-air, rocking and plunging. A hysterical gust tossed him high but he was incapable of capitalising on this advantage. He faltered and began to die in the air. The Scenic Viewers ran towards the probable site of impact.

Branwell touched down almost gracefully, on tiptoe. Ran a few steps. Capsized in a heap.

'Are you all right?'

Hands lifted the contraption aside; supported the gloved, helmeted and goggled aviator, who giggled uncontrollably. He was helped to a grassy mound, and there gently lowered. The Scenic Viewers crowded around, with helpful suggestions. Tom Lassiter's camcorder zoomed in for the kill. Overhead, Branwell's next-of-kin streamed away south-westwards one by one, only the Reverend Patrick cruising in broad arcs overhead as he mourned the downfall of his Icarus son.

The fallen hero stripped off helmet and goggles. A freckled face emerged, pale-skinned and green-eyed. A mass of curly hair flopped down on her shoulders. For Branwell was a short, squat girl.

She got up and waved to the parent in the skies.

'I'm all right,' she bawled. 'Go on! Carry on!'

Kicking his feet, Patrick sailed into the airstreams where only hawks and eagles fly.

'Who are you?'

'We're the Brontë Hang-gliders, Balloonists, Microlight Aircraft and Parachutists Association,' said Branwell. 'We're out most weekends. Haven't you seen us? Who are you?'

'We're a conference.'

'This is my first-ever flight,' said Branwell. 'Brilliant. The most brilliant thing I've ever done. You should see the world from up there. You really should try it. A sense of eternity,' she said earnestly, 'is what you get. But I got so tangled in eternity I forgot which way I was supposed to push the damn bar. You have to do it back to front, you see.'

She demonstrated the principles of her equipment. The lightness and simplicity of the technology were much admired. Branwell was happy to tell the camcorder what her organisation was all about.

'Well, originally we started as a radical breakaway group from the petit-bourgeois reactionary boring Brontë Society. We think they're too – well – pedestrian. Earthbound. They have no wings. They're like a ladies' tea party – too polite by half. Always tittle-tattling about trivia. The Brontës weren't like that. They were – more – well – you know – *birds*.'

'You are just breaking me up,' said Gillie Deneuve. 'You guys are about the most incredible thing I've seen here and, boy, have I seen and heard some incredible things.'

'Good. We are meant to be incredible. I mean, weren't *they* incredible?'

'When you are saying the Brontës are *birds*,' asked Susy, 'what do you mean? They could fly? Fly really? Or in the *mind*? I think you mean in the *mind* they fly. Not with the arms.' She flapped hers a bit to emphasise her distinction, full sleeves belling and rippling in the wind.

'Certainly,' said the Cumberland Shepherd, 'they were ornithologically inclined. They knew Bewick's *History of British Birds* intimately; and consider all the birdlife in *Jane Eyre* and *Wuthering Heights* – thrushes . . . hawks . . . sparrows . . . martins . . . skylarks . . . what else? . . . I've got a complete list somewhere.' Tapping his pockets, he began investigations of their contents. No one was listening, for the newly alighted Branwell was the celebrity of the hour.

'By birds, I mean creatures with wings. I mean, these women *flew*. We want people to look *up* when they see us coming. We do these stunts to take their eyes off their everyday pursuits. Sometimes we hang-glide, other times we do parachute drops on to Haworth Moor. We're collecting for a Brontë Balloon. Do you happen to have any transport?'

Collecting up Branwell's gear, the party made its way to the coach. The excitable Branwell, whose legs seemed to be buckling under her, was assisted along by enthusiasts.

'Bird-brain,' observed Gillie.

'Well, I don't know.' Laurie's spirits had risen and along with them her appetite for debate. 'You could say that this airborne Branwell-girl reproduces the threshold or interface between male and female, immanence and transcendence, signifier and signified . . .'

They were off. First they practised jumping on the spot. Then they beat their pinions and plumed themselves. Now they took off and flew. Way above her comprehension and beyond her lexical reach, Marianne watched Gillie and Laurie soar and spar.

Faraway-eyed Sharon stumbled along beside her. '*What* were that lad on about?'

'Not a lad. A girl pretending to be a lad. About how the Brontës were birds.'

'Pigs might fly,' observed Sharon.

'Emily had a hawk,' said Marianne. 'It was injured and she rescued it, and tamed it in the process. She called it Hero. She wrote this incredible poem to it:

> Give we the hills our equal prayer;
> Earth's breezy hills and heaven's blue sea;
> We ask for nothing further here
> But our own hearts and liberty.
>
> Ah! could my heart unlock its chain,
> How gladly would I watch it soar,
> And ne'er regret and ne'er complain
> To see its shining eyes once more.
>
> But let me think that if today
> It pines in cold captivity,
> Tomorrow both shall soar away,
> Eternally, entirely free.'

'That's really lovely,' agreed Sharon. Her heart was flying miles high above her body, but not like a bird, like a kite attached to her ribcage, where it tugged at its moorings in spasms of painful pleasure, as she remembered . . . and remembered . . . and remembered. And she longed to tell Mrs Pendlebury that she'd met a lad, his name was Mark (the most beautiful name ever) and he'd spent the night with her, and he'd gone back home to his mam's because she'd expected him last night and she'd be mithering about where he'd got to, but that she'd be seeing Mark (the most gorgeous lad ever known) that afternoon; and she was going on a diet, *definite* this time.

'It might be prudent to skirt round this reedbed,' said Marianne. 'Just in case. It'll be boggy.'

The reeds were high and rust-red, interspersed with the white heads of cotton grass, nicknamed 'bog-baby-warning' for obvious reasons. Cotton wool on stalks; how Charlie would appreciate that.

Looking up into the racing sky, she recalled the hang-glider's assertion, 'These women *flew.*' Yes, she thought, throwing them up into her mental sky in a tempestuous rustle of petticoat. They wished for wings. Passionately. But once they were up there, they'd have been pining for earth; and once their feet touched firm ground they'd have been itching to get airborne again.

Laurie had been the same: 'I envy you,' she'd said; and she envied Laurie. She was desperately endeared to her babies; but when she was with them, she was hammering against the doors of her captivity, to be out at work. That would never be resolved. She was two people in the one body: two people who didn't get on. Though the pair of them longed to live at peace with one another, they tore at one another's roots to break free. She was not *in* a bad marriage. She *was* a bad marriage.

They reached the farm on the downhill path.

'So how have you liked the weekend, Sharon?' she enquired doubtfully.

'Best weekend of my life,' replied Sharon devoutly. 'I just wish it could never end.' She itched to say the word 'Mark'.

Marianne briefly stared. You never knew about people.

'You could always do an Open University degree, or a

part-time degree at the Institute,' she suggested. 'Plenty of people do who've missed out for some reason or other.'

Missed out? Sharon wished she could express how deeply she'd been filled in, taken up, included and embraced. Every door that had ever been closed stood wide open.

She would come here often. It was her kind of place.

'Thanks for the invite, Mrs Pendlebury,' she said. 'If it hadn't of been for you . . .'

Marianne could not hide her pleasure. She'd got something right at least. Perhaps she'd started Sharon off on a new career of reading – and just one person, just one who'd been touched, made it more than a fiasco.

'This afternoon of course,' she said, 'we've got the two eminent Brontë biographers to talk to us. I think you'll get a lot of insights from them, Sharon. There's Linda Gerard-Smith from Oxford and Dale Stevens from Macclesfield.'

They had reached the main road, in time to see the hang-gliding equipment installed in the coach and a motorscooter draw up. The rider stood astraddle, revving for effect; then took off his helmet, and tucked it under his arm as he peered round shyly.

'Oh – it's *Mark*.'

Up on the pillion, arms round his leather waist, Sharon looked ready to faint with ecstasy.

'Can Mark come this afternoon, Mrs Pendlebury? He likes books and that.'

Mark and Sharon roared off towards Keighley, there to feed each other greasy fish and chips out of paper in the car-park. Mark told Sharon at some length about a video game he'd just bought in which a superwoman-type stingray kills hundreds of sharks and giant crabs with a poisoned dart. He felt this would appeal to her sense of equal opportunities.

'And then you get to Level 4,' he explained, 'and all these squids come pouring out of a hole in the rock . . .'

Sharon listened, but did not precisely hear, with a quiet sense of beatitude. Everything he said was of interest to her, because he was interested in her. His mouth was soft and full, and it had been on hers, and all it said was dear; his tongue that had been in her mouth told her wonderful things. She watched his mouth move.

'And then when you get to Level 5?'

'. . . all these little sea-horses come out and you have to save them from conger eels . . . ZAP POW.'

'And what happens at Level 6?'

'I don't rightly know. I've never got to Level 6. It were solid. So-lid.'

A glimmering came through to Sharon that Mark was not all that bright. But that did not matter. It did not make a difference if you really loved someone that they hadn't much up top. It was who they were that mattered; not what they knew about *Wuthering Heights*. She'd listened a lot in these past two days; listened and analysed. From feeling edgily inferior she'd shifted to a kind of condescending pity. What was the difference between Mark's conger eels and sea-horses and these Brontë birds landing on the heath and barmy women arguing at the tops of their voices about whether the Brontës wanked or not?

'Want to come home and see my games?' Mark asked.

She paused fractionally: felt she'd promised Marianne to go and be bored rigid.

'What about your mam?' she asked. 'Won't she mind?'

Mark shrugged. 'She'll be asleep. She works nights.'

'Okay,' said Sharon, beaming. She could and would deny him nothing.

Timothy and Marianne sat in a dimly lit corner of Haworth Old Hall Hotel restaurant, picking at prawn cocktails. In the intervals of conversation, Timothy could not prevent his mind from recurring to the disturbing theme of what the Parsonage custodians had made of the used but unwashed spittoon and chamberpot which he and his companion had been obliged to leave when Mr Thorniley released them from captivity that morning. He had intended to mention these mortifying tokens of their fleshly occupation, but it had slipped his mind in the excitement of emancipation.

He related his adventure to Marianne, avoiding the problems raised by the exigencies of human functions, and the fact that he and Miss James had shared Mr Brontë's bed. From his account one would have gathered that the two old people had stood to attention all night long by the back door.

'I was truly horrified,' she said, 'when I heard. How dreadful for you – for you both.'

'Quite an adventure actually,' Timothy wheezed. His gums were raw, and speech an effort, for he had not felt able to remove his dentures throughout the night, out of a combination of vanity and consideration for the other party. He felt disinclined to inflict his death's-head nightmask on a lady of immaculate dental endowments. 'I see you're wearing my bolero,' he added, to turn the subject, chewing tentatively on an experimental prawn. 'How does it fit?'

'It fits beautifully. I shall always think of you when I wear it.'

The easy tears sprang to his eyes. Marianne had the gift to say a caring thing so naturally: few of his acquaintance had that sensitivity to know and the concern to say the tender words. The initial impression of her plainness and embarrassing public ineptitude had faded in the mere two days of their proximity. Her stubby figure, tired face, poor skin and owlish spectacles no longer defined her reality for him.

'Your conference,' he said, 'has been a great success. I heartily congratulate you, Marianne.'

The main course had not yet arrived but the wine had been poured. 'To your career, Marianne.' He raised his glass.

Her face fell.

'Did I say the wrong thing, my dear?'

She poured out all her woes. He saw it all: Professor Price saying 'Dead wood', the student complaints, the three children keeping her at full stretch, her own inadequacy, the child-minder with earache. It was a mess. And she didn't seem to love her husband; and the non-feeling was apparently reciprocated. Timothy listened with dismay. She was so different from her handwriting.

'I'm leaving work. I'm leaving him.'

'But how will you live?'

'Not sure yet, Timothy.' She had recovered balance. 'I suppose the answer is, "With extreme difficulty".'

Perhaps it was running away; certainly she would regret it. There could be no resolution of conflicts – only a fresh set of contradictions.

'And shall we still . . . correspond?' he asked. 'You have no idea what those letters have meant to me, Marianne. None in the world.'

'Of course. Of course we shall. We have a bond.'

We have a bond: he must be sure to remember that she had spoken these words, here in Haworth Old Hall, and in his emotion he averted his head to where the first spatter of stormy raindrops was striking aslant the leaded pane. *We have a bond*. So precious did the words seem that he had to restrain an impulse to pull out a notebook and write them down for safekeeping.

'You see, I am faced with the problem of having lived on after my own death. It's as if . . . I don't mean to be self-pitying . . . but half of me has died, or so it feels. I'm no more than half a person.'

He squared up the cutlery around his place-setting, with finicking fingers, clearing his throat.

'Whereas I am double. There always seem to be two of me battling it out. I'm sick of myselves.'

'I've been told to fatten up. Eat more roast beef and rice pud. It isn't the least bit of good. Not just that my dentures won't let me and I've the appetite of a bird. But how would you fatten up a ghost? . . . oh, if Jojo could hear me now, she'd be so damn cross. She abhorred self-pity.'

'Tell me about Jojo, Timothy.'

He remembered that afterwards: *tell me about Jojo*; and how over the gulf that isolates teller from listener, his stumbling tongue struggled to pass across the perished reality of Joanna. Nobody nowadays ever spoke her name; he didn't either. Just occasionally he said 'my wife' as if she'd been an append-age that had fallen off along the way. 'My wife' was absolutely dead but her darling name lived in him; and he knew it lived because of the pang it cost to speak.

Of course it was useless. You couldn't describe a person, especially your life's companion, any more than it would be feasible to detach and objectify your own arm or leg. Through the uneven pane the outside world shrank and dilated, awash with rain. Candles were lit in the grey gloom of the restaurant and guttered in red tear-shaped glasses.

'Uh huh,' responded Marianne; and 'I see'; and 'I can imagine'. She listened indefatigably; it was the least she could do. Looked carefully at the photographs of Jojo, a stout, jolly-looking figure like thousands of other stout, jolly-looking women who pass you in the street or have already completed their journeys.

Part of her sat apart, twiddling its thumbs and wondering when on earth the main course would arrive.

'You must be bored.'

'Not a bit.'

Vegetable lasagna and salad arrived. Timothy picked at his. Marianne wolfed. The storm intensified. To divert him, she told her companion a spiced-up version of the Branwell-bird. Timothy remembered that he had clean forgotten (in the glow of the younger woman's presence) that eccentric lady, Eileen. Continuing to forget her, he too now ventured an anecdote.

Chapter 11

Blow, west wind, by the lonely mound,
And murmur, summer streams,
There is no need of other sound
To soothe my Lady's dreams.

Velvet cats cruised her legs, mewing their violent hunger. She could hardly get in and close the latch for the seething of the creatures about her legs. Stained-glass light fell upon their furry swarmings. She clapped her hands to shoo them back.

Their bowls were licked clean. The air carried a sour-sweet odour, different from the familiar staleness of an elderly house which had not been redecorated for a quarter of a century.

She called out, 'Mother! . . . Mother?' Her heart beat harshly as she sought her in one room after another.

Muriel couldn't, of course, climb the stairs. But Eileen went up anyway, just to be on the safe side. The cats pressed round her in a mewing mob.

Her mother sat open-mouthed in Eileen's own armchair in Eileen's own bedroom. Her hair had come partially adrift from its bun and fell disordered over one shoulder; her head was bent and her eyes half-closed. Her walking-stick, still clutched in her right hand, pointed at her daughter's dressing-table, whose drawers gaped, their contents spilling out.

'Mum, what have you been doing? What?' A surge of chaos welled in her breast and, although she was aware of the inappropriateness of calling an unconscious body to account, she went on, 'What the heck have you been up to now?'

Her private secret world lay in dishevelment, open to view. She knelt amongst the scatterings of tissue paper, tarnished watches, lockets with curls of dead hair, watercolours and other memorabilia she'd hoarded. The cats were everywhere: on the bed, in the drawers, everywhere. Eileen shouted at them; shoved at them.

The cats kept clear of Muriel.

Seeing this, the living woman sucked in her breath.

'Mother. You've gone, haven't you?'

Later there would be time to know that she was free. There would come the sensation of lightness as if she'd been for years bowed down and now could stand up straight; correct her spine; flex her muscles. Her appropriated life would revert to herself.

Later too would come the desolation; the perception that no one remained who needed her. There would be no mooring. No one to fuss over, set to rights, go from and come home to. No infuriating crackpot conversation. None of those sensitive pauses or restrained words of endearment by which she knew her mother understood; cared; forgave, through all the fog of confusion.

But in the immediate interim, there was a remote and unreal calm. She phoned the doctor and funeral director; then fed the cats, while Muriel sat cold in Eileen's bedroom. She also made herself a cup of tea, dimly aware that this was a course of action Muriel would have counselled.

When Muriel had disappeared, darkness had taken her

place. Switching on her bedroom light, Eileen drew the curtains against the squally night; automatically crouched to tidy the mess her mother had made of her personal possessions.

But rather than replace the contents in the drawer, she found herself matter-of-factly dropping them in the waste-paper basket. She rid herself of her box of sacred illusions as if they had been so much junk.

The next-door neighbours came in and condoled.

'Let's face it, Stanley,' Eileen said bracingly. 'Mother was in her ninety-third year. She was demented. She didn't live in the real world. One can hardly have wished for her life to be prolonged.'

'True enough. Still, she was a character. It won't be the same without her.'

Neighbours came and went; she put the bottles out for the milkman; the cats plunged in and out of the cat-flap; and still her Timothy had not phoned.

Chapter 12

Heavy hangs the raindrop
From the burdened spray;
Heavy broods the damp mist
On uplands far away

Rain sloshed down upon the slate roofs of Haworth, dousing the mid-afternoon tourists pelting uphill or downhill for the shelter of their cars. Their hair stuck to their scalps and their T-shirts clung to soaking torsos. The man with the guitar singing 'O what a beautiful morning' sitting on a low wall on Main Street balanced a newspaper on his head and continued to sing. He ogled the lolloping breasts displayed through drenched cotton. Only when the rain had soaked right through his newspaper did he call it a day, pick up his cap of coins and decamp.

The harpist who had been playing traditional Irish melodies on the church steps was helped by her fiancé to transport the gracious but unwieldy instrument into the shelter of the church porch.

The Heathcliff Café was wedged with moist and grumbling families; the Villette Coffee House, the Shirley Tea Shoppe and Jane's Eyrie were soon full of customers. Dismal faces mooned behind windows watching the rain sluice down the cobbled hill. Pamela's Pantry did a fast trade in extortion-ate scones, with a scrape of real butter and a blob of home-made raspberry jam.

Anthony Carew, proprietor of the Locus of Desire, a university classics lecturer who had taken premature redundancy in order to have a stab at 'something really different', breezed in and out of the restaurant bearing platters of *gâteaux* and *Kuchen*. The Locus was situated at the top of the hill, a superior position he liked to think, nursing his gnawing inferiority complex by despising his customers, whom he felt bound to educate, by informing them that they were sitting on genuine antiques and drinking from authentic Victorian tea-services. Actually they were replicas, but the cretins couldn't be expected to know that.

Few ever returned for a second slice, and his business was slowly folding. Bad weather could be relied on to blow in a handful of innocents. They paused at the door, nervous at the smell of cinnamon, the rush-mats and the aggressive host who charged forward to herd them into seats. There they sat peering uncomfortably around, huddled in to one another, whispering behind their hands. The menu had to be loudly translated for them. Some stealthily escaped when Anthony's back was turned. He murmured in ancient Greek against barbarians.

Bales of dark cloud rolled down on to the village, emptied their contents and were displaced by new banks, piling up as far as the eye could see.

Bartholomew's Baubles cursed the buggering weather. The owner ran in and out, fetching in trays of dingy Haworth tea-towels which had spent years alternately flying in the open air and mouldering on a clothes-horse in the cellar. Damp postcards were salvaged until only imperishables such as giant pink shells from the Pacific Ocean and spherical marbled stones of uncertain origin were left in the downpour.

Angrian Artists sold its only picture of the day, an oil painting by the gallery owner of 'The Parsonage Seen by Sunset'. The buyer was treated to a rendering of a poem in Yorkshire dialect by a Yorkshirewoman wearing clogs, a free offer which it was alleged he could no way afford to refuse.

Fathers ran with hot packets of chips inside their anoraks through the chill downpour to feed their hungry families. They beat on misted car windows to signal the arrival of the feast, and intimated that if you didn't shut up your squabbling in there, you'd get no chips, it was up to you.

The cars began, one by one, to pull out of the car-park, which would soon be empty of all but local vehicles.

The Brontë biographers were not discouraged by the weather, which exerted an effect at once tonic and inspirational. They clumped up to the dais in their gumboots, one pair green, one pair black, and seemed rather complacent than otherwise with the aptness of their wear (they had brought no change of shoes) to local conditions.

Linda Gerard-Smith and Dale Stevens, despite their espousal of different sisters, were close friends who wore their eccentricities partially concealed under an outer layer of apparent common sense. Though well respected in their field, they were subject, both singly and jointly, to extemporisation. The inspirations of one might trigger new inspirations in the mind of the other, discharging themselves in a circuit of mental energy whereby the obvious generated the unlooked for; the unlooked for shot into an empyrean of strangeness astonishing to behold. This did not always happen, but they had become something of a celebrity double-act, much in demand at literary festivals, and Marianne had been lucky to get them for the conference for the small fee she could offer.

Solid and well built, reassuring and normal, they looked down into the well of the hall, at where people were shaking umbrellas, wiping wet faces with handkerchiefs, assorting papers.

'Yoo-hoo, Tommy!' Gerard-Smith had spotted Tom Lassiter and the bibliographers. She and Stevens knew everyone on the circuit; knew how their minds worked and how they might behave.

'Trouble in the fourth row,' whispered Dale, leaning over to her colleague. 'Trouble times three.'

'Oh, don't worry. We'll be fine.' They smiled at one another supportively.

Laurie Morgan sat wedged between her two loves, with a sensation of migraine aura, her mind split between opposing loyalties, a constellation of stars spinning in her right eye. For Duncan and Gillie had explosively confronted one another in a hotel lounge at lunch-time. Laurie had not foreseen this, nor did she comprehend what all the fuss was about. She saw no reason why she should not have both of them.

She had explained this rational standpoint to the warring parties as they stood in a triangle before the log fire blazing in the dog-grate. The residents, sipping coffee in the depths of armchairs, had listened in with interest. Laurie had been truly staggered when Gillie and Duncan stopped savaging each other and turned on her. Duncan had called her a selfish bitch and a bull dyke. Gillie had called her feminism resoundingly into question for allowing PENETRATIVE SEX (she yelled it at the top of her voice) with the Enemy.

'I do not believe this,' Laurie had riposted with scorn. 'Patriarchal commodification of woman as consumerist artefact on the one hand and fucking baloney on the other. But in point of fact,' she had stated, 'you are two of a kind. You both want to own – and exploit.'

The exploited victim tossed her head and marched off in injured innocence, her exit marred by catching her foot in the rucked hearthrug and stumbling on the tail of a basking golden retriever, which burst out barking. Laurie gathered herself together and marched out.

Duncan and Gillie stomped along in her wake, Duncan pale and black under the eyes from his night of gastric affliction, Gillie flaming with self-righteousness.

'You are not as young as you were,' Duncan told Laurie coldly in the foyer.

'And you are far less bright than one had been led to believe,' she retorted even more coldly.

Duncan's prospects of tenure hung by a thread, as they stood there and the rain beat down outside.

'I didn't mean it,' he recanted quickly, and put a hand through his shock of hair. 'I wanted to get back at you. I truly didn't mean it. I just feel so – bloody hurt.'

Laurie took the trouble to explain why he absolutely shouldn't feel hurt; why her attachment to Gillie (which went back a long way) was not susceptible of comparison. But with Gillie breathing down her neck all the while, this was difficult to do convincingly; and besides, she could not rid her mind of the echo: *You are not as young as you were.*

Now she sat between her rival lovers, hostile to each, bored with each, in equal measure.

She would ditch Duncan when she got back. He was little more than a cock on legs. Let him fend for himself in the jungle of academic competition.

A cock on legs. But what a cock. And what legs.

She peeped sideways. His athletic tallness sprawled in a don't-care attitude beside her, one tapering hand lying on the inner part of his thigh, one tapering finger stroking the cloth. He was sucking a peppermint. She might have had a son his age. She shivered.

Her eyes strayed the other way. Gillie was not beautiful; not young. But she was dynamic. Her hair was the colour of rusted iron.

You are strong, she inwardly told Gillie. *You are brainy and gutsy and original. You have power. But he has fair hair and all his own teeth, milky white with youth. Yours are all expensively capped.*

So are mine.

Laurie sat, in distress of conflict, between her two affinities; and strove with her twin desires to place a hand on the crotch of each, claiming both for her own, and her need to whistle them off as incidentals.

A woman she had never seen before turned round from the row in front and stared out of unfriendly blue-grey eyes at Laurie. After a long moment she turned back again.

Marianne had introduced the double-act.

The two biographers expressed little short of ecstasy at having been offered the opportunity of being there. They loaded Marianne with praise. They felt they were among friends. They beamed down like seraphs.

'Today we want to tell you our new ideas about the whereabouts of Charlotte's letters and the lost Gondal saga,' confided Dale Stevens. 'It's a little bit of a detective story, in fact. I don't know if any of you admit to being hooked, as I am, on detective stories?' Nods all round; chuckles; but no cosy admissions from the postmodernists, whose eyes the blinking biographer sought to avoid.

'It was Linda actually who came up with this brilliant idea – reading *Villette* one day, she came upon the pages in which Lucy Snowe movingly describes the effect upon her of the letters from Dr John, which alleviate her terrible loneliness in the foreign city – and the whole world is a foreign city to the unwanted Lucy. If I may just read to you, to refresh your memories – '

Timothy swallowed hard. He knew the passage that was coming, almost by heart, so perfectly did it express his desperate need for Marianne's letters – these messages of surrogate joy that lightened his toiling heart and yet made it heavy with the burden of dependency and shadowed with possible loss.

Yes, I held in my hand not a slight note, but an envelope, which must, at least, contain a sheet: it felt, not flimsy, but firm, substantial, satisfying . . . I experienced a happy feeling, a glad emotion which went warm to my heart, and ran lively through all my veins. For once a hope was realised. I held in my hand a morsel of real solid joy: not a dream . . . It was a godsend . . .

'You will recall,' commented Dale, 'that Lucy puts it away for later, to have something to look forward to; that when she opens it in the attic, she hopes it will be long and kind, and it is long and kind. It brings food for her hunger and drink for her thirst, although, being Lucy, she never kids herself that it means as much to the writer as it does to the reader, famished as she is for affection. When the malnourished Lucy finally gives up her hope of love from the attractive but shallow sender, she cannot bear to destroy her collection of letters but buries them in a hermetically sealed bottle beneath a pear tree. "I was not only going to hide a treasure – I meant also to bury a grief." And so she bottles up and represses her hope and inters it in the earth where root meets soil.'

Timothy had heard it maintained that only women could understand the Brontës. No, it was not so. For he had been there, where Charlotte's Lucy stood, desperate for any crumbs that might fall from her beloved's five-course meal. He too had felt the message as 'a morsel of solid joy'. You could hold and keep a letter, as never a phone call, or a life. He looked up now at Marianne; and it seemed she returned his serious gaze. Yet he must equivocate to cover the extremity of his need. Such knowledge must burden and might alienate her. Timothy turned his eyes away to a woman he had not noticed at the conference before (but then, there were shoals of strangers here). She seemed to be reading personal correspondence, her short-sighted eyes close to the page, breathing hard and short.

'Now Linda will take over,' said Dale. 'After all, the idea was her baby.'

Linda described the baby. She spoke easily, eloquently, as if she had been born and brought up in an Oxford common room, and there astounded the learned doctors with her gifts of mind. At the base of her neck was pinned with many grips a loaf of grey-brown hair, which she intermittently tested with her fingers to assure herself of its survival.

'Our actions,' she said, 'have had as their provenance the incomplete and irregular transmission of the past inherited from tradition, document and hearsay. And so we have found ourselves operating in the gap between fact and illusion, where angels fear to tread. But not us,' she added, inspecting her handsome galoshes. 'There are times,' she went on, 'when the impetus of desire, or design, is so powerful, that you honestly feel you have no option but to dive head-foremost into the world of speculation, or imagination, even if you find yourself waist-deep in a bog or ditch and looking rather a fool. As we two enthusiasts have sometimes done. Or, as happened last night, I am happy to say briefly, in a police cell.'

The Passmore twins, with several others, had plunged into note-taking almost as soon as Dr Gerard-Smith had opened her mouth. As soon as she reached the word 'provenance', they realised this was the real thing: that language of the high-flying intelligentsia, slightly mystifying and therefore impressive. Both Val and Viv would in years to come advertise the provenance of this or that, in a manner so authoritative that their innocent friends would pick up on it and break out in a rash of provenances.

Viv Passmore wrote down 'desire or design' for its pithy resonance. When the lecturer approached the ditch or bog, however, she felt confused and her pen hesitated. And at the words 'police cell', she looked up with a frown, driven to the edge where the glamour of suave metaphor tumbles into the mud of vulgar usage. Did the woman really mean she'd spent her last night in prison? Here indeed was a question of provenance.

As Val and Viv raised their heads, they became aware of two young women they had not seen before. The two, who were standing shyly at the side door, arms twined around one another's waists, were about the twins' age. The taller winked at the shorter, who smothered a grin. Evidently the latecomers found seats, for when Viv and Val glanced up again, they were no longer there.

'Let me explain,' Linda continued, 'the connection between Lucy's letters in *Villette* and the night Dale and I spent in police custody which is, so far, obscure.'

Susy Sugimura wrote down 'Obscure' and, wondering what it meant, placed an asterisk beside it, to remind her to look it up in the dictionary. She noticed for the first time the thin-lipped, mirthless and disapproving-looking woman sitting beside her: on her lap lay a piece of embroidery bearing the text, 'For me to live is loss, To die is gain.' Susy felt cold. She concentrated her attention on the lecturer who would now illumine the obscurities.

'The question exercising my mind as I leafed through *Villette* was, what happened to Charlotte's precious letters from M. Heger, her beloved *maître*, when she married Mr Nicholls. Had she burnt them in a sacrificial pyre? When Mrs Gaskell visited M. Heger in Brussels after her death, he (who understood her as few could) told Mrs Gaskell that Charlotte would under no circumstances have destroyed the letters. The letters were sacred to her spirit. So what *did* she do with them?'

Oh do get on with it, Ron Hebblewhite inwardly implored. In his sermons it had been his practice to instruct the congregation in plain terms what to believe, giving three reasons why they should do so; and then shut up shop after no more than nine minutes. He could claim without vanity to have been the most popular preacher in the diocese. He also regretted having eaten the roast lamb for his lunch: the fattiness did his gall bladder (overdue for keyhole surgery) no good whatsoever. The old chap next to Ron, whom he had not previously detected as clerical, was sitting with his arms folded, evidently not attending to the fiddle-faddle on the stage. With his massive build, high starched collar and air of edgy, gloomy aloofness, he somehow reminded Ron of a Paisleyite Ulsterman; and he turned away, shivering.

'At about the time of Charlotte's marriage,' Linda went on, 'local oral tradition has it that she personally planted the two Corsican pine trees which we can see today in the garden of the Parsonage. Two young trees – and a bundle of old letters; a new life to be entered upon as a bride – an old life to be laid to rest for ever. What more natural, I thought, than that she should have buried the beloved letters at the base of the Corsican pines?'

'And what if Charlotte at the same time had buried Emily's and Anne's Gondal saga along with the letters?' broke in Dale Stevens.

Marianne smiled at all the ebullient 'what if 's'. When she looked down into the hall towards Timothy, she was surprised to notice he had a companion, a dark figure, ample and bosomy, sitting terribly close; almost on top of him, making one aware of how little space he took up. Timothy, nodding off, seemed unconscious of sitting in her shadow. A swirl of irrational anxiety passed through Marianne, who averted her attention.

'With these ideas in mind, what could we do?' Linda appealed to the audience.

'Dig 'em up!' shouted Tom Lassiter.

Neil Thorniley threw back his head and roared with laughter. The young woman beside him, whom he'd hardly noticed previously, also threw back her head and laughed, as if in mockery of his gesture.

'Thank you, Tommy,' said Linda, also laughing. 'Got it in one. The more we thought and talked about it, the more certain we were not only that the papers were buried under the tree but that we must get out with spades and forks and dig them up. Unfortunately – unfortunately . . .', she wavered, and addressed a tiny woman she had not previously noticed on the front row, 'Was it wrong . . .' she asked doubtfully, 'to disturb the quiet earth?' The woman was tiny, but her strong, characterful face was full of purpose and, at the same time, brittle, nervous and hypersensitive.

The woman nodded categorically.

'I can't go on. You take over.' She tottered back to her seat, from which her view of the front row was blocked.

'Well,' said Dale. 'It was a hoes and mattocks job. Heathcliff over the grave of Catherine. We waited till it was completely dark and your conference had left the Parsonage, and then got down to work. (By the way, you left the lights on in there, all night.) Damn hard work. But, you see, we felt, somehow, we *couldn't not*. It was a cool, breezy night, but luckily not rainy. We set up our lamps and began to dig. Well, of course, we got more or less nowhere for ages. The ground's turfed and compacted, and wherever you dig, your spade hits root. But we kept at it. And there was this wonderful feeling of trespass that kept me going. I thought, "Well, why *shouldn't* we dig up Emily's secret world, which I'm sure Charlotte was ashamed of and hid away." I thought, "If we're right, I'll rescue Gondal for posterity – edit it for publication – get glory – give it to the world – be on *Woman's Hour* – " I was going over all this in my mind when there was a sort of groan – I suppose we were in that highly wrought psychological state, we both threw down our spades and shrieked. Then a burly male figure appeared from the bushes and arrested us for trespass and causing wilful damage.'

Duncan Lascelles lounged with his legs crossed, arms folded, eyes closed, in an attitude of sickened boredom. He longed to be lying flat under a duvet, cuddling a hot-water bottle; longed to be cosseted and little-boyed. He glanced sideways to see if Laurie was taking any notice of him.

She was not.

Next to him, a ginger-haired person whose presence Duncan had not consciously registered yawned and fidgeted. He seemed a brat: either a puerile man or a prodigious boy who evidently wanted it to be known that he was not enjoying the show. He scratched his head, kicked his heels, then fell to picking his nose with assiduous concentration. Duncan closed his eyes. When he reopened them, the brat was sketching the lecturer hanging by the neck from the gibbet of a Corsican pine, gumboots dangling. 'She would not shush so Rogue has had to silence her,' Duncan read. The brat now began to decorate the margins with inky devils and skeletons dancing.

'*So,*' said Dale Stevens, 'we found ourselves in the nick. Quite an unlooked-for adventure. But I must say the police officers could not have been more friendly and hospitable. They served us tea and biscuits in our cell, and we had a delightful talk with a detective inspector about the cultural history of the area, which is one of his off-duty specialities, it seems. In the end, we got off with a caution. Meanwhile, the quandary of the buried letters remains. To dig or not to dig . . .'

A general stir arose in the audience.

'Leave them be!' said some. 'Let them rest in peace. If Charlotte buried her letters, she meant them to be private. What right have we . . .?'

'No no, I don't agree with that – every scrap of their lives is precious to humanity . . .'

'Dig 'em up!' shouted Tom Lassiter again, seeing as it had gone down so well the first time.

'They're not there, it's just fantasy.'

'But they may be.'

'They *may* be anywhere. You'll have to excavate the whole Parsonage – dig up the whole blinking moor . . .'

Cries of 'Nonsense!' and 'Of course it is!' and 'How can you say so?' competed. Each man's hand was against his neighbour. Marianne was foxed as to what to do to quell the riot.

Laurie was moved to leap to her feet and denounce the whole lot of them.

'The Brontës are dead!' she exploded.

Shock. Heresy. All eyes turned on this monstrous mocker.

'Yes, they are! Of course they are! Dead and buried. They've been dead for 150 years. When are you people going to realise that and start thinking about what matters and what's real *now*?'

'No! Never!'

'They don't exist,' she told them. She looked round with forensic eye. She had seen and seen through each one of them here; no one had escaped her eagle-eye. 'You are hallucinating if you think they do – a mild form of group psychosis. You are seeing things. Your capitalist imperialist society wants you to see things that aren't there so that you won't notice the things that are – poverty . . . injustice . . . homelessness . . . oppression. *Real things*. When are you nice kind liberal middle-class folk going to wake out of your dream and confront real issues? When? The Brontës are *dead* – ' (cries of 'No!') 'Yes they are! Dead!' ('No! Never! Sit down!') 'You don't seem to like the word dead, but that's what they are. And we're alive – some more so than others – *now* – and we could change the world and free the suffering masses if we didn't prefer the company of the dead to the predicament of the living. THE BRONTËS,' she shrieked 'ARE THE OPIUM OF THE MIDDLE CLASSES!'

'Aw yes, un whear do ya think ya'll be Pro-fessor, coom t'Revolution? – Aw'll tell yer if ya loik – shull Aw tell yer? – Scrubbin t'lavatory flooers, that's whet them Bolshevik boogers ull hev ya at, comrade, cum t'Revolution.'

'I should be proud – *proud* – to scrub floors in an equal state where all were fed and clothed,' said Laurie superbly.

'Ya say saw nah. Bud yah'll be smoiling on t'uther soide o' yer face then, ya'll see.'

The elderly man, to whom Laurie had outlined her general position on the first night, but who had abstained from any comment but a sequence of grunts, now nudged his neighbour in triumph and tapped the side of his nose.

'In any case – ' Laurie stood her ground, ignoring the dig about the lavatory-cleaning, which she had heard before in sundry variations – 'my point is plain and indisputable: the Brontës are dead. You won't find them breathing messages to you through the wind in the trees, Dale, or buried at the roots – because they are simply – and for ever – and undeniably – and absolutely – dead.'

Laurie sat down as if felled at the word 'dead'; and, being a small woman, became invisible to most of the audience.

Duncan and Gillie simultaneously reached out to squeeze her hand. But she seized advantage of these symmetrical gestures by grasping the hand of one and crushing it into the hand of the other.

'Be friends,' she commanded.

Duncan and Gillie forced themselves to smile across the gap between them. As they showed their teeth to one another, Laurie let out a long sigh of release.

When Laurie had burst forth, Marianne had ducked. She had no intention of getting involved. Linda, who had recovered, suffered from no such inhibitions, considering Laurie Morgan to be a fairly effective example of her kind, and less of an ass than most. Positioning herself at the lectern again, she put up her hand for quiet and opened her copy of *Wuthering Heights* at random, as if to seek the leading of inspiration. Of course it could not in practice constitute a random experiment, for her elderly, much-read, pencil-annotated paperback automatically cracked open at its heart. In her resonant, expressive contralto, she read aloud Cathy's famous speech:

'surely you, and every body have a notion that there is,

or should be, an existence of yours beyond you. What were the use of my creation if I were entirely contained here? My great miseries in this world have been Heathcliff's miseries, and I watched and felt each from the beginning; my great thought in living is himself. If all else perished and he remained, I should still continue to be; and, if all else remained, and he were annihilated, the Universe would turn to a mighty stranger. I should not seem a part of it. My love for Linton is like the foliage in the woods. Time will change it, I'm well aware, as winter changes the trees — my love for Heathcliff resembles the eternal rocks beneath — a source of little visible delight, but necessary. Nelly, I *am* Heathcliff — He's always, always in my mind — not as a pleasure, any more than I am always a pleasure to myself — but, as my own being . . .'

When her voice had ceased, there was mesmerised silence throughout the hall. Some eyes were closed; others rested dreamily upon her face, with a hypnotised quiescence.

They sighed, stretched, awoke.

'What are you crying for? Why are you crying, love?' both Duncan and Gillie asked Laurie.

'I'm not crying — I never cry — my eyes are watering.'

'And so,' said Marianne, 'our conference is at an end.'

Although she'd dreaded it, and made a fool of herself, and longed for it to be over, she was now overwhelmed with a sensation of permanent loss.

'I've loved being with you and sharing thoughts and responses, learning so much myself not just from our guest speakers but from all of you, all of us.'

She hadn't loved it; but now, in retrospect, now that it

had safely set in the mould of the past, her mind had composed the persons and their sayings into something lovable.

'I hope so much we may meet again and share our thoughts again.'

And so she translated her valediction into renewed invitation and for a moment half believed her own lullaby; but, correcting herself, went on, 'I myself am leaving the academic world, I don't like the way it is going with the cuts and "reforms" and so on' (murmurs of approval) 'and I want to have time to read — not read to teach, or examine, or write learned articles — but just to read, for its own sake, read and think.'

Chapter 13

King Julius left the south country
His banners all bravely flying;
His followers went out with Jubilee
But they shall return with sighing.

'I shot him down in flames,' reported Idris Price to his colleagues. 'Shot – him – down – in – flames. I thought to myself, "I've got you there, young man." Of course, the fellow didn't know what to do with himself. Squirmed. Too clever by half, too clever by . . . what did you think of him, Hugh?' He crammed half a Garibaldi biscuit in his mouth and chewed excitedly, thrilled by recollection of his feats.

'Too clever by half,' repeated Hugh, po-faced.

'There you are, you see. There you are. You've got it exactly right: my own thoughts, to the letter.' He spoke these words with a mouth full of half-masticated biscuit, unpleasing to his colleagues, who looked away. 'But what did you think – what did you *think*, Hugh – of the point I was making about stylistics and so forth? Be honest, man.' He sat forward eagerly; his jaws stopped working.

'Well, obviously – you shot him down in flames. He hadn't a chance when you took over. Obviously.'

'I have to confess,' said Idris modestly, as if pushed by

popular opinion to the very edge of propriety, 'I bowled him a googly. And he couldn't reply. Of course, he's young,' he conceded, 'and brash, and cocksure – and he may in time develop into an example of excellence.'

Idris gobbled another Garibaldi. His fellow examples of excellence sat with cups of tea in postures of strain or resignation. They had just interviewed a batch of applicants for a full-time and a part-time job to replace Marianne Pendlebury and Charlie Braine. The applicants, all new blood from Oxbridge, London and Edinburgh, had frightened Idris by their effortless mastery of a discourse he found impenetrable; and he had felt called upon to bring to bear upon them what he called his 'big guns'. Some had, as was natural, been thrown when this smiling, avuncular Welshman turned so snarlingly nasty. Others had faced him out with polish and equilibrium.

Hugh Brenner had felt sorry for the young people, especially the delicious girls, but he too was conscious of fighting for his skin, being one year over fifty and the recipient of a second annual birthday card from the Institute pointing out that he was now eligible for early retirement, if he would care to discuss it with the Registrar. Nevertheless, he had sought to atone for the pathological spite of his professor's manner by opening up his own question so that the victim was free to say more or less anything about anything.

One shapely young person had used this opportunity to tell them all about a holiday she had spent on the island of Crete.

'I believe it's very nice to go in October or November,' Hugh had observed. 'Not too many people and weather very tolerable.'

She had thought so too.

She was devoted to ruins, she had breathlessly added.

You'd do very well here then, thought Hugh; but she wasn't going to get the job, despite her bronzed skin, blond hair, interest in minotaurs and three precocious scholarly articles on Bakhtin.

For Idris, despite his dedication to the principles of equal opportunities, had let it be known that he wasn't interested in employing another woman after Marianne Pendlebury. They came with too many built-in drawbacks. They were liable, as his experience of his wife, Amy, confirmed, to irregular behaviour caused by premenstrual tension; as soon as you employed them, they had babies and exercised their right to maternity leave; and then they had child-care problems and became unreliable, refusing to take on evening classes – or failing all that, they became bolshy bra-burners, entering into covens with their fellow feminists to demand crèches and courses devoted to the study of the interminable history of their sex's wrongs.

Kate Sanderson had only the other day told him hesitantly of her pregnancy; and that she was expecting twins. He'd thought, he'd really thought, she'd have had more sense.

'And when is the happy event?' he had enquired, with a solicitous smile.

'In November,' she said, pulling herself together. 'So I'll need to take that term off.'

'And who, if I may ask,' he continued, 'is the lucky progenitor of this blest pair of sirens?'

'I don't have to answer that question, and you've no right to ask it,' said Kate, and stomped off fuming, all five foot two of her.

No, no more females.

Not this time round at any rate. He searched the applications for a handy black to employ instead, to raise the

Institute's profile on employing ethnic minorities. But the sole black applicant turned out to be female and he was forced to detect holes in her impeccable curriculum vitae.

Idris, having finished his tea, signalled to the waitress by clicking his fingers at her.

Sharon, who didn't take kindly to people clicking their fingers at her, pretended not to hear or see, and continued to transport her rattling tray of pots to the counter.

'Hoi! Waitress!' cried Idris, leaning back in his chair and waving his hand.

Sharon advanced slowly, sloppily, a wet cloth in her hand. It dripped on to the carpet and made a wet patch there.

'More tea,' stated Idris.

'I'll make it, you collect it,' stated Sharon.

'I beg your pardon?'

'It's not in our contract that we have to serve you, *you* come for *it* – sir,' Sharon explained.

Since becoming a manager, Idris had grown to expect to manage. When he snapped his fingers, people scurried about. A weak, nervous and at heart rather shy man who had spent an oily lifetime currying favour and seeking to please, he had entered into the race for power late in life. It had been painful to sacrifice the genial, hail-fellow compensations of the lickspittle to the fixes of the powerful; to know that people feared and disliked you behind your back, and laughed at you in corners. But he had adjusted, with the help of doses of alcohol. And rarely was his authority questioned.

Now that this waitress refused to wait, Idris unpredictably reverted to type.

'Oh right – of course – apologise for . . . forgetfulness.'

The big girl marched stolidly ahead of him and re-entered her station. Boiling jets of water spouted into four steel teapots; she flipped the lids closed, blap, blap, blap, blap. The old fart had blushed fiery red; his full lips quivered with a silly little smile. He and David Villiers conveyed the laden trays back to the group.

Shot him down in flames, he thought.

He switched on ignition and revved up.

The engine roared.

He taxied slowly, then faster, down the runway.

David Villiers poured the tea and ladled sugar lumps. Hugh Brenner handed cups.

Idris' plane left the tarmac; he retracted the wheels into the undercarriage; he mounted to cloud level. Sighted the enemy. Trained his sights on Fritz. Saw the whites of his eyes. Sprayed him with bullets. Fritz plunged, spiralled, belched black smoke, went down amongst the trees, a charred wreck. Idris pulled away in nonchalant triumph.

'That young Jack-my-lad,' he observed, '*he* didn't last long under fire. These Oxbridge graduates – got the manner and the lingo – but fatally superficial.'

Hugh stirred his tea and sipped. He had grown used to Biggles commemorating his triumphs; his own were more in the Don Juan line, and vastly more entertaining. Idris' vanity embarrassed while it fascinated Hugh. He resembled a man walking round with his pants round his ankles, unknowingly exposing his pathetic flabby nether parts to public view.

'I hear poor Marianne is leaving Thomas,' he said. 'Taking the kids off to – somewhere or other in the Peak.'

'That so? Another man, is it?'

'Couldn't say. Danny Lesser says he wonders if she's having some kind of nervous breakdown.'

'Poor old Marianne.'

'Poor Marianne indeed.'

Sharon, wiping down the surfaces of the ash-sprinkled, coffee-smeared tables, heard the chorus of pity and resented it. She wiped round and round in unnecessary circles.

'Mind you – not wishing to be uncharitable – having a nervous breakdown has always seemed to me a fairly normal state for Marianne.'

'She is a perfect example,' observed Idris compassionately, 'of the kind of person (I may say "woman" without being labelled sexist by present company) who is a thoroughly nice, decent sort who cracks under pressure. No staying-power. Bit of a dreamer. Thought she could have it all. Not got the temperament for the modern world. My wife saw her in Green Lane Park pushing an empty push-chair round, crying her eyes out. Well, Amy, you know, is a sympathetic woman, other women tend to confide in her – she said, "Marianne, dear, are you all right?" and Marianne apparently said, "I'm probably better than I have been for a long time but it just isn't showing yet." Amy asked why the empty push-chair and she said the child was at playgroup. I went into her office to counsel her on Monday, she was clearing her books into boxes. I said, "Marianne I'm old enough to be your father, well, perhaps not, but let's say your uncle, so if you feel you'd like to confide in me . . ." But she said no, she was making a new life for herself, uncles need not apply. *Uncles need not apply!* Quite, well, you know – *off,* she was.'

Marianne had changed Sharon's entire life. Sharon knew she could not repay the debt. Not for the reasons Marianne imagined, of the awakening of her soul to Literature (though she had not the heart to put her right) but because without Marianne's taking notice of her she'd never have met Mark; and without Mark she'd never have known true love. Her life had changed out of all recognition.

She'd tried to tell Marianne something of this. Marianne

took both her hands and said, 'This is one of the things I've *not* failed in, Sharon, and therefore incredibly precious to me. If you'd ever like to phone me after I've left and have a chat about the books you're reading, I'd like that so much.'

Sharon said, 'Me and Mark are always up on the moors, Marianne. We love it there. Home from home.'

Marianne said, 'That's so good.'

Now, goaded by indignation at those old wankers pulling her friend to pieces, Sharon bull-charged the table round which the fraternity was gossiping, and emptied a pot of cold tea over the dandruff-speckled suit jacket of Professor Idris Price, just as he was articulating the phrase, 'Dead wood'.

Chapter 14

Fall, leaves, fall; die, flowers, away;
Lengthen night and shorten day;
Every leaf speaks bliss to me
Fluttering from the autumn tree.
I shall smile when wreaths of snow
Blossom where the rose should grow;
I shall sing when night's decay
Ushers in a drearier day.

Marianne, sawing logs on the paved area behind the cottage, found a rhythm after much snagging of the blade and loss of angle. The saw glided easily back and forth in its groove, until, about two-thirds through, the wood began to give, and she could stamp off the log with the heel of her boot. She piled the logs in a rough pyramid, liking the sawdust tang and the burn of her arm muscle as she worked. Over her head, the iron sky loured; and sometimes she would straighten up and stare its eyeless blankness in the face. Turning away, she carried on with her sawing, sweating and, despite the rawness of the wintry day, stripped to her shirt sleeves. Her tiny garden sloped steeply beyond the paving-stones within a high wooden fence which protected her from the less than cordial glances of her neighbours. The tortoise teetered around this perimeter looking for an escape route, so far without success. Sometimes the gradient tumbled it over and it lay on its back, waving its clawed feet in the air; and when Charlie or Andrew righted it, the creature hissed angrily and shot back into its shell. Opinions were divided about whether it was a he or a she.

The tortoise was nothing but a rock on legs. And, like the hills, you could not love it. In coming here, Marianne had expected the beauty of a fresh-air outing, extended to a lifetime. She had found harshness and dearth. The hill that rose behind her house seemed to loom at her each morning; the cold was intense and drove in icy gusts all winter through cracks and under doors. Washing froze on the line. By the time she had taken Emlyn, Andrew and Charlie down to the school and nursery in the morning and climbed back up again, she felt utterly fatigued. So exhausted had she been throughout that winter that she conjectured she might be ill. Perhaps she had cancer. The more she brooded upon it, the more likely this seemed.

But she must have known it was merely a metaphorical form of cancer, for she made no attempt to seek medical help. Instead she found herself making monthly trips to the doctor carrying a screaming Charlie, whose endless colds had led to chronic infection of the middle ear and deafness on one side. The local doctor was gruff and costive with antibiotics. He intimated that Marianne was a fussy mother. One night Charlie had to be rushed to Stockport Infirmary for an emergency grommets operation. All the muck was drained out of her ear. Marianne sat by her hospital bed all night.

The next day Charlie had been miraculously recovered, lavish with kisses, eager for snowballs. She knelt up with glowing eyes in her bunkbed at home, discussing matters with her furry animals. Marianne, cross-legged at the end of the bed, smiled at Charlie through tears. The cold sun set in harrowing beauty at the edge of the world.

Marianne had never known a loneliness so absolute. The loneliness travelled along beside her, a spectral companion. It turned up on the doorstep when she brought in the morning milk, shouldered in and stared from the mirror as she brushed her teeth. The uncanny presence mocked Marianne's pretensions to high-spirited independence. Dead-eyed, it read her beloved books over her shoulder and turned the words to meaningless type on faded blank sheets which her mind failed to vivify. The lifeless book slid from her lap and lay spread-eagled on the floor.

Yet she was not supine. She fought back with every scrap of her energy, thrusting the loneliness away; and, when she could not prevail against it, having the wisdom to wait for new buds to shoot. Her pain, she insisted to herself, would and must be seasonal only. She restored the books to the shelves, to await calmer days.

The children could not mitigate this loneliness; indeed they terrifyingly increased it. Marianne felt that she would certainly have become accustomed to carrying the burden of her self through life, but how could she alone be equal to their needs? So many props to identity had fallen away – not only Thomas, whose promotion had not mitigated his grief-stricken rancour at the proceedings of his unstable wife, but the whole world of work, which conferred identity and importance. She stood at the school gate with the other mothers. There were two dovetailing groups, the Derbyshire people born and bred, and the wives of Manchester academics and civil servants to whom Hayfield was a pastoral dormitory of the city. Both groups discussed jam and measles but with different accents.

Marianne's neighbours, especially the children, were hostile to the outcomers; she was sure she wasn't imagining it. They were telling her to go back where she'd come from. Bricks were lobbed over her wall. At Hallowe'en all the windows of her house were pelted with soot and flour.

'What they dood that for?' asked Charlie.

'Just for a joke,' Marianne soothed.

Emlyn was silent. He stared gravely at the soot-stained windows, fingering his glasses, which had just been prescribed. He was teased at school. Marianne, putting her arm round his narrow shoulders, registered his quivering stress. She bent to kiss him. He flinched away; then his control collapsed, his face worked and he thrust himself against the comfort of her body, howling, 'I – want – to – go – back – to – my – dad.'

'We *will* settle down; we *will*. It's bound to take time.'

On the morning of Guy Fawkes Night, a lighted banger came through the letter-box. Marianne called the police. The policewoman took down details and advised her to seal the flap next year. An immense bonfire roared down in the valley by the river; rockets burst in flakes of green fire in the basin of the hills. Charlie, Andrew, Emlyn and Marianne had a prime view from their upstairs window. They knelt in their pyjamas on Marianne's bed, licking toffee-apples, looking out; it was ten thirty, which fact alone excited carnivalesque Charlie to a peak of joy. The fire roared and blazed tree-high. The faces of the three children glowed orange. Their teeth crunched through the flesh of the apples. Dark hooded figures danced before the fire: something ancient, primitive and tribal seemed enacted.

Snows fell; snows on snows. The greengrocer warned Marianne to expect the odd freak snowstorm even in June. Through the black and white world Marianne ploughed, dragging her feet high, sinking them down nearly to the rim of her boot. Against the gunmetal skies, rooks and crows cruised in their black, hoarse hunger. The white landscape shouldered in through the gaps between the black houses, foreshortening all perspectives; and black lines of hedge, farms and single trees stood in graphic silhouette as though the world were a pen and ink sketch. Once Marianne would have been stricken to the heart with such beauty; now she laboured up the slope loaded with potatoes, unmindful.

Yet amongst all this, there were satisfactions, even joys. Sawing the wood was one – or rather, the whole process of collecting, sorting, sawing the fallen timber; laying, lighting and fostering the fire. They walked down by the sawmill and over the river, and filled their sacks with the abundant windfall wood. As they ran about, their voices rang from tree to tree. Marianne was proud of her fires: real fires, living fires, she called them. When she held the sheet of newspaper to help the fire draw, it took her back to her childhood, her father's dare-devil conjuring of flame. She felt she took the means of life from his hands and said, 'Let me do this; I'll take over now.' The flames rushed behind the paper; sucked it in as if fighting for possession. At the last moment, just as the text was being singed, she bundled the paper in and let it consume. Building the fire made Marianne feel able.

'Come and warm your hands – you're perished,' she said to the visiting Sharon – unrecognisable Sharon, who had lost, she boasted, two stone all but a pound. She'd ridden pillion behind her boyfriend.

'Well, he must come in too,' insisted Marianne.

The shy boyfriend was coaxed in. The two sat perched on the sofa holding hands. Still a big woman but in no way obese, Sharon shone with a new assurance. She explained how she'd been given her marching orders by the Institute.

'I accidentally emptied a pot of tea over your old Prof,' she said. 'Couldn't help it, could I? Spoilt his naff suit and they made me pay for dry-cleaning. He were roaring, "You damn slovenly careless girl!", tea-leaves all down his front. I still see him around but he doesn't recognise me.'

Sharon was now doing an access course at the Institute, leading to a diploma in Catering Skills. She'd grown her fine, glossy hair below her shoulders; it swung when she moved her head. She had a fresh, handsome look, and sat with an erect posture.

'It's Weight-Watchers what done it,' said Sharon. 'Potatoes I can eat but don't offer me a doughnut.'

'What about biscuits?' Marianne handed the plate.

'*One*,' said Sharon. 'You've got to discipline yourself like, and then you don't miss it.'

'I've read *Tess of the D'Urbevilles*,' she mentioned to Marianne in the kitchen, in a voice as casual as she could make it. 'Well, some of it.'

'What did you think of it?'

'It were good.'

'Is Mark a reader too, like you?'

'He's more into computers . . . So this is Timothy's house?'

She gestured round the small, wood-panelled kitchen, with its crowded pictures and carvings, its racks of spices and herbs, the corn dolly over the door, everything as he left it except for the pile of red and yellow wellington boots at the back door, a scatter of toys, papers and felt-tip pens, all the junk and chaos of childhood which Marianne was never successful in sorting away. In Timothy's day the house had been orderly and neat. His spinning-wheel still stood in a corner of the sitting-room: Charlie would twirl the wheel, spinning imaginary garments out of air.

'Joanna's and Timothy's house – now mine and the children's.' She wanted to express the continuity.

'I were sad he went. It were a year ago this weekend, the conference. Our anniversary, Mark and me. We're going to walk up to Withens to celebrate.'

Sharon and the mute boyfriend got up to leave.

'Give me a big hug, Sharon, before you go.'

She watched the scooter out of sight, down the cobbled street. This weekend the children were with their father, a time to which she theoretically looked forward, until its silence hit her. Looking back from this high perspective, she could scarcely recognise the woman she had been a year ago at the conference, a woman in the public world, respected and listened to. Now she was a private person, almost perfectly invisible.

She was no one.

How peculiar endings and beginnings were. For, as she latched the door behind her, she found it necessary to correct herself. She was no one in particular *yet.* This transition was her chance to rebuild a self, more firmly grounded in real values.

Everything here was Timothy's. She had got rid of nothing but his clothes, which had gone to the British Heart Foundation. The sister would have nothing to do with her, though Marianne had offered her the pick of his personal belongings.

'To think, after all I've done for him,' she had fumed. 'Who cleaned the house on a twice-weekly basis, I'd like to know? Who saw to his needs? Who put up with his mystical airy-fairy nonsense?'

Margaret Whitty, normally a placid, sensible type uncompromised by covetousness, had spoken of disputing the will when she learned he'd left everything to the privileged Marianne. She could see no reason why her brother should have violated the loyalty due to blood-kin save manipulation of his senility by the younger woman.

'I won't say he was out of his mind – but he was not far off. Most decent people would consider themselves honour-bound to hand back that property to his next of kin. Timothy was not in a fit state to will it away; and if I'd had my own wits about me I'd have secured an Enduring Power of Attorney . . .'

'But you didn't,' Marianne pointed out quietly. She did not allow herself to sympathise, though the sister's indignation was entirely understandable. Timothy had freely wished to offer her this chance of a new life, which she meant to seize with both hands. 'Timothy knew perfectly well what he was doing.'

The woman paused: there was no hint of a budge on this grabbing individual's part. Hard as nails.

'Well, you *are* a ruthless madam. You *are* though, aren't you just?'

'No. No, I don't think so. Just being practical.'

'Taking advantage of a poor old man who could hardly walk – and who *claimed the ghost of Emily Brontë visited him at night.*' She folded her arms.

'I'm really sorry. I didn't put pressure on Timothy. I'm going to accept his gift though, for myself and the children. We need a home. But any of his personal belongings – please do feel free to take them.'

'I wouldn't – sully – my feet – on the doormat. You'll be hearing from my solicitor.'

But no lawyer had intervened when the will was proved.

Marianne now slept not only in the room but in the very

bed where the ghost of Emily had visited the now dead dreamer.

Nothing spectral vexed Marianne's slumbers. Only a child somnambulist – Emlyn – calling out for his father; the dismally familiar howling of an insomniac Charlie.

She stood at Timothy's front window, looking out. The fields beyond the village were tenderest green; sheep were lambing. Last spring Timothy must have looked out through the same glass, and received the identical hopeful message of a new spring. He'd been at the end and bequeathed her a beginning; and a vestige of him somehow lingered to participate in that new cycle of life.

Opening the desk drawer, she drew out two packets of letters, the first being those she had written to him. 'My dear Timothy – ' in her decisive italic hand. Some of what she'd written seemed, as she read it over, so false and affected that it made her cringe; they had constructed versions of their characters for one another to read. The Marianne she had offered him was distinguished, vivacious, a touch condescending. Even when he had recognised the fiction, he had loved her, warming to the weaker human revealed face to face at Haworth. To that needy person he had reached out with his own need and his own abundance.

On the packet of letters, he had written, 'From Marianne: never destroy', and beside this text a picture of a lighted candle. Of course he'd had some weird and wonderful beliefs, enough to make the most tolerant sister groan. Throughout the house hung pictures of mysterious Egyptian subjects painted or fashioned by his wife, Joanna. The jackal god and the hawk goddess; a great metal ankh over the fireplace; Isis diligently searching out the crucial missing portion of her brother Osiris. And because the space in the terraced cottage was so small, these objects were squeezed in close together, competing for the beholder's eye with stone earth-maidens in cabinets and figurines on tiny tables. In his bedroom was a little shrine: pictures of Jojo above a candle surrounded on three sides by mirrors. Here Timothy had told her he'd sat meditating in the dark, and systems of candle-flames multiplied themselves to infinity. She had carefully put away the pictures of Jojo but left the candle. For Jojo and Timothy were truly together now – in and with one another, where images need not reproduce them at second-hand. Deeply asleep, she imagined. Perfectly awake, he had believed, or desired to believe.

The second packet of letters was, to Marianne's eye, the more singular and revelatory. These were signed 'Eileen'. At first Marianne had not guessed the identity of this Eileen; then it dawned that this was Mrs Passion, the scourge of Brontë lecturers, who'd gone for Laurie Morgan so memorably. (Laurie had landed a prestigious chair at Cambridge, the first Trotskyite ever to do so, and had her hair close-shaven in token of the wrongs of the working classes, whose cause she proposed to further from her new eminence in a blast of articles and lectures denouncing the bourgeois liberalism of the university authorities who had elected her.) Mrs Passion, who had spent the night locked in the Parsonage with Timothy. What exactly had happened between them that night? Something, evidently, for the letters alluded to some great but cryptic experience which both Eileen's affirmation and Timothy's initially reluctant responses seemed to confirm.

My dear Timothy – Thank you for telephoning last night. – I was beginning to think that perhaps you *wouldn't* & believe me it was beneficial to hear your voice and words of kind concern. It helped me to have a bit of a cry. I had not cried. But when I put the receiver down I cried. It hit me for the first time that she was really gone. Gone and and I shall not see her again. Gone and I am after sixteen years free. How terrifying is freedom. I find I cannot as yet face it. I have busied myself today doing all the necessary things – registering the death, making a start on probate proceedings, etc.

I keep looking round for her, wondering, Where have you got to now, mother? She would fairly frequently disappear. Melt away. Once I went running out after her: there she comes hobbling up the road with her stick in one hand and *a leg of lamb in the other*. What are you doing with that leg of lamb, mother? She was so pleased with herself. We hadn't one in the house, she said.

We shall bury her on Friday a.m. next to Dad. The sight of her support stockings hanging over a chair-back is dreadfully painful. Her black cardigan covered in ginger cat hairs. However, I have told *all* the neighbours I am glad for her, when they come in with their provoking long faces. Good God, I say, the woman was ninety-two. Yes, but if she'd hung on she'd have qualified for a telegram from the Queen, said the old chap from Number 7.

– Well, naturally my mother was a royalist, fervently so. Many an evening she took tea with the Queen Mother & all the Ladies of the Bedchamber, also equerries, footmen, etc., & Prince Charles occasionally stopped by to see Granny – so the telegram from the Queen may well have proved an anticlimax.

I am the sort to take a bracing attitude, as you must have gathered.

But I cannot at present restrain the tears. I am a daughter no more. She protected me – which is odd considering that I looked after her & had to fend for her in every conceivable way which I thought it my place to do, but still – she did protect me. I am an old woman, my mirror tells me so. The day before yesterday it told me no such thing.

Forgive these bletherings – I can tell them to none but you for there is between us I am so sure a *bond* (?) affinity may be too strong a word (?). Can our Parsonage night be only three nights ago?

Take care of that cough & do not forget to expectorate as regularly & often as poss., using the method I described.

Ever,
Eileen J.

Dear Timothy, I was most glad to her from you and of course I perfectly understand that you will not be able to write *often*. I had no wish to presume on an acquaintance so slight. As you remind me, the night in the Parsonage was a rather peculiar affair and hard to know how to assess. I for one shall not mention it again.

I buried my mother yesterday & I must say I was relieved to see her safely underground. – I was inwardly fretting somewhat as I had been used to do when she would not for some unknown reason be put to bed but insisted on rambling round the house in search of some non-existent article. Now I know she is tucked up. This must sound strange. She was a very *kind* woman. – Gentle. And she thought the world of me. It is most important either to have someone or to have had someone who thinks the world of one. Well, I have been blessed in this regard. There are people, I know, who think me rather an odd fish. Well, perhaps indeed I am an odd fish. I have never married.

My mother did not hit it off with my father. I could not help but consider, as they lowered her into the hole, how the two of them would get on down there. It poured with rain and the cemetery was a quagmire. I went back later. The men had just finished spading the earth in. They were stamping it flat with their big boots. I want her to have a turfed mound on the model of Catherine Earnshaw's but I am told black or grey marble is compulsory. I shall certainly complain about this in the strongest possible terms.

Do not trouble to reply until you feel up to it. I am managing very well. Take care of yourself.

      Yours,
        Eileen.

My dear Timothy, Thank you with all my heart for your comforting letter, which I shall treasure. – Yes, dear friend, I know only too well how frail is your health & do not imagine for one moment that I expect any (what shall I say?) 'passionate commitment' from you. How could that be? We are both old codgers. But friendship – genuine solid friendship between people, even if they happen to be codgers on their last legs is not to be sniffed at!! I shall write to you & think of you & wish you strength for the road. I have ditched a number of encumbrances both physical and spiritual in the last week whilst clearing the house. There is so much one *doesn't need*, when it comes down to it. There have been dizzying & dismaying moments when my whole past seems to boil down to trumpery of make-believe.

You say M. Pendlebury is giving up her academic position – you do surprise me. She was one of those privileged women I felt who had it all. I wish now I'd pursued a Career but in my day of course opportunities were scarce and encouragement for girls nil. Do you correspond regularly with M? Give her my best wishes for the future.

I dreamed of you last night. – Couldn't tell you precisely what happened but the gist of it was you were standing at the window of E's room. – But were you on the *outside* looking *in* or on the *inside* looking *out*? – I couldn't sort that out & of course I was always seeing you from the other side of the pane. –

I am reading a book on Emily Brontë now by a woman called Stevie Davies, do you know it? She seems a very wrong-headed individual. I shall almost certainly write to her and point out her errors.

Bubbles of happiness float up in my heart and catch me unawares. I do not feel my mother's absence *as* an absence, I sense she is somewhere else, not too far away – (They are going to let me turf her over by the way: *shows the value of making your voice heard.*) I begin to enjoy my freedom – going & coming as I wish – staying out late at night like a rebellious teenager – not cooking if I don't feel like it. I am meditating an educational cruise round the Greek Islands. And also I have your friendship for the road.

I send you my love.
　　Eileen.

My dear – Your most kind & welcome letter received yesterday a.m. It has bucked me up no end to know that you think of me with such concern & remember our extraordinary time together. I don't believe I had ever really looked at the stars before, I mean *really looked*. I intend to fill myself in on knowledge of the names of the constellations, etc., of which I remain (as on so many subjects) woefully ignorant – with the help of the book by that lady astronomer at Greenwich, unfortunately I forget her name but the librarian, Ms Workman, will know. – The world of knowledge is before me now, I just hope it is not too late to fill in some of my shameful blanks & gaps. Yr description of the full moon over Hayfield was so vivid & beautiful that I felt I had been there & seen it with you.

Reading between the lines, I sense that you are far from well – this shakiness and extreme weakness of yours worries me more than a little. I am so glad you are getting the mini-word processor since handwriting is so difficult & uses so much energy – the keyboard, as you say, is light of touch, you can have it on your lap, & it should not get you out of puff. – No, I imagine even an electric wheelchair would be no earthly use on a road as steep as yours. I should have thought you would qualify now for Attendance Allowance which would cover taxis. – My mother did not need to go out much as she was always visiting in imagination exotic spots such as the Arizona Desert & Jamaica – so much cheaper than British Airways and I only had to send imaginary postcards to all our friends.

Nevertheless, I do feel the need of a real change & to seize LIFE while there's time – and have booked for the Greek cruise – shall be away 3 weeks. By the time I return I hope this new treatment your doctor has mooted will be underway & that you will feel more chirpy –

COURAGE COURAGE, as Emily said to Anne –

and love,
Eileen

My dear Timothy – Warm sun – glowing sunsets – fascinating lectures on Minoan Civilisation by a most able young man – thirty aged ladies and four ancient crumbling gents – thinking of you, my friend – Eileen

Dearest Timothy – I am greatly concerned about your health. It was nothing less than a bombshell to get back and hear from your sister that you were so poorly. This is to let you know I shall visit the Infirmary the day after tomorrow & meanwhile have sent some flowers, which I trust will reach you safely. I hope the nurses are kind to you & that you will kick this wretched pneumonia before too long.

　Your loving
　　Eileen

Marianne, reading the letters, had felt intrigued and touched, the voyeur's guilty relish mingling with a more complex remorse. So that was Mrs Passion: the woman she had inwardly laughed at and avoided in public was in no way ridiculous – but stoical, dignified, tender.

On an impulse, she flicked through the pages of her address book and dialled Eileen's number. No reply.

Later she got through. Then, hearing the rather shrill, off-putting voice, she got cold feet and nearly put down the phone.

'Miss James . . . it's, er, Marianne Pendlebury.'

'Ah . . . yes . . . yes . . . hello. What can I do for you?'

'Miss James, I hope it's not a bad time to call – I was thinking, you see, that you were such a . . .'

'Eileen, for goodness' sake,' she rapped out.

'Pardon?'

'*Eileen* – not "Miss James". Call me Eileen.'

'Yes, oh, well, of course – Eileen – I was thinking, have been thinking for such a long while, that you were so close to Timothy – and that you may like to have some of his things, to, well, remember him by. I called earlier but . . .'

'Oh, I was out. I'm nearly always out nowadays. Today I was in point of fact down a disused mineshaft.' She paused, as if to insist on response.

'Oh really? How . . . interesting,' said Marianne faintly. 'What were you . . .?'

'Doing? Studying it. I have enrolled on a History of Industry course. We go down the mines, along canals, through mills and (those of us with a head for heights) up chimneys under the guidance of a trained steeplejack. I shall be in the vanguard of volunteers. You see, I am the only woman in the group and it is a matter of principle with me to show no sign of feminine weakness or hesitation. When I go up that chimney, the whole Female Sex goes up there with me. *I* shan't let them down.'

'Wonderful!' Marianne broke into a peal of laughter. 'That's really wonderful. And how Emily Brontë would approve.'

'Thank you, my dear. That is the best thing you could have said,' replied the steeplejack-to-be in softened tones. 'But you were saying, about Timothy . . . that I might like some memento?'

'Well, yes, it occurred to me. You might care to come and take some of his books — or anything that . . .'

'I used to be one for souvenirs,' Eileen reflected, 'a very much cluttered person. I had rocks from Tintagel and lockets with dead people's hair. Keepsakes. House like a reliquary full of holy bones. Then it suddenly dawned on me they were not only supernumerary, they were rather horrid, beastly things. When the life is gone, I found, the things go stale.'

'Yes, of course — I'm sorry I . . .'

'Marianne Pendlebury, stop apologising. You are like an apologising-machine. It was a *very* kind thought and one I greatly appreciate. But how are you, my dear? How is your new life outside the academic world suiting you?'

Marianne, who didn't like the word 'outside', which gave her a bleak, subdued feeling, did not at first reply. She had begun to realise that she found it more and more difficult to look people in the face; communicate with them freely.

'Oh,' she said finally. 'It's hard. It will get better.'

'The children must be a handful. How old are they now?'

'Seven, five and three,' Marianne recited. All the life had gone out of her voice, and she registered that the woman the other end was aware of this draining. 'But they are thriving – and we are coping,' she insisted.

'You will have need of all your pluck – all your grit – for a rather lonely road.'

Marianne wept aloud. The old-fashioned words were all the more touching in that they came out of the heart of the stoical experience of the older woman.

'I tell you what,' said Eileen. 'I'll come over and see you. I could come this very minute if you wished? I'm quite free now, you see, that mother's gone. Or tomorrow. I'll be on my bike and be with you by noon.'

'On your . . .?'

'Motorbike. It's a godsend. And environmentally most friendly – does ninety to the gallon. I call it Ariel. Putting a girdle round the earth. Only problem is *noise*. Ariel is, I regret to say, a noise pollutant. I await the invention of a silent engine.'

Eileen dismounted from Ariel after her Sabbath journey earlier than she had predicted. The roads being empty, she had swept past Shrewsbury and up the dual carriageway, encountering the occasional roadworks. The motorbike affected her like a drug: she found herself tempted by speed. With a sense of power and elation, she sped into lanes, through avenues, past fields and hills. Whereas her upbringing told her she ought to resist these demonic promptings, her new-found liberation advised her to take full enjoyment in what she would not possess for ever. Eileen had fleetingly attended the Stratford Bike Bash and ridden round in the common thunder of 5,000 leather-clad swaggering males and their molls. The burghers and cultured visitors of Stratford stared, laughed, pointed, gaped, clicked their cameras as the head of an old woman with flattened hair-do emerged from her helmet. She ate hake and chips from newspaper, leaning against a lamppost opposite the theatre while a silver automaton of Queen Elizabeth I rolled on castors round the inside of a circle of onlookers and ended by pulling a potato out of a jewel-box. A young woman automaton-impersonator peeled off a silver wig from her silver face to reveal a bush of ginger hair. She grinned at the applause and passed round a hat. Finishing her meal, Eileen had crumpled the papers and put them away tidily in the bin provided. She roared away over the bridge, beneath which punts and boats pottered and swans glided in gangs which landed and charged visitors, to rifle with their rude bills the crisp-bags in the children's hands.

The bike was her pride and joy. She polished it relentlessly, and took it to bits for the pleasure of putting it back together again. Few ladies had as much idea as Eileen of how to maintain their vehicles, the garage owner intimated, knowing how to flatter her. 'I took a course,' she explained modestly. She dreamed of the bike even now, and always with the sensation of flying.

Marianne from her sitting-room window saw a species of moonman alight from one of the most swanky motorcycles she had ever seen. The moonman wore white leather, with matching white and blue helmet and gauntlets. Unpeeling the Velcro fastening, Eileen balanced her helmet on the seat while she removed the gauntlets and fetched her handbag from the storage compartment. Marianne ran out to embrace the space-visitor. Holding her handbag in one hand, Eileen made her way to the house with a certain stiffness, caused, she explained, by all the leather padding and holding the same posture for so long. It took a while to unzip her from the gear. Marianne crouched to heave off her boots.

'Bit of a . . . hassle . . . getting it all on and off,' explained Eileen. 'And, at my age, of course, there is the problem of the aggravation of one's piles.'

A year ago, she'd have said 'haemorrhoids', or refrained from allusion to such intimate matters.

'I've had awful piles since Charlie was born,' said Marianne. She deposited Eileen's leather gear on a chair by the door. The suit seemed to sit there stiffly like a ghostly white chaperon.

'So this is Timothy's house,' said Eileen looking round. 'Yes . . . yes . . . it's like him.'

'I've changed very little. I liked how he left it. And anyhow, I've no time or inclination for decorating and so on. Come up to the fire and warm yourself – do. Timothy's wife painted that picture. It's an ankh.'

'I know an ankh when I see one,' said Eileen with a tetchiness which had so long ago become ingrained as to be automatic. She stood astraddle before the fire, examining the picture. 'Joanna,' she mused, 'Timothy's Joanna. Well, well. He was a . . . searching person. A kind, decent man. You can't say that for everyone, can you, these days? It's everyone out for himself now, grab grab grab. Timothy was not such an one. Mind you,' she added, her hawkish eye turning swiftly on Marianne, who had brought in mugs of hot chocolate, 'precious little good the ankhs and all their Life Force did for him and his Joanna.'

'Well – I don't know.'

'I've made a bonfire of my superstitions,' said Eileen, and

went on fiercely, 'and I can tell you, there was plenty of junk to burn. In fact, of course, one does not know if the whole caboodle has been disposed of, or only the more obvious items. For instance, did you know that I was not really a relative, however distant, of Ellen Nussey? Did you realise that?'

'Well, no, I . . .'

'It was, in point of face, a mistake – a genealogical error.'

'Of course,' said Marianne. 'It's easily done.' She saw her companion's blush; tried hard not to let on that she had known all the time; never been fooled. No one had been fooled. In fact, Eileen had not even the kudos of being a unique fraud. Various Nussey claimants had flourished their credentials in the form of sepia photographs and cameos. Like provincial Anastasias, they popped up and manifested their claims in colour supplements; they raved a little of secret knowledge and fell back into the common shadow.

'I suggest,' said Eileen, 'an assault on Kinder Scout. No time like the present.'

Up there they stood in a trouncing wind, looking out over the Peaks. Intermittent blue sky and running cloud made a dappled rhythm of fast-moving light and shadow.

The shadow raced towards them, blackening hilltops and turning the glowing green of slopes and valleys into cold zones of transient darkness. The shadow headed uphill towards them and they watched it coming, flinching back as the winds slammed in.

Now they were in the shadow: dead cold lay all about them.

But already they could see the sunlight advance. It turned the rocks of the High Peak greyish yellow, and goldened the green turf on the slopes. The clouds fled before it and the sunlight rushed across-country to meet them.

The river silvered over.

Sun shone in Marianne's dark brown hair, turning it to auburn, lifting threads in the wind; the pale blue of Eileen's eyes became skyey and astonishing.

Now again the shape of a shadow poured out across the floor of the valley and the two women braced themselves to meet it.

And then again the sunlight.

And the shadow again.

Author's Note

The epigraphs to the chapters of this novel are extracts from poems by Emily Brontë, as edited by C. W. Hatfield in *The Complete Poems of Emily Jane Brontë* (Columbia University Press, New York, 1941).

Prelude: 'A. G. A.': 'For him who struck thy foreign string' (1838), 9–12

Chapter 1: 'A. G. A.': 'Sleep brings no joy to me' (1837), 5–8

Chapter 2: 'If grief for grief can touch thee' (1840), 9–12

Chapter 3: 'Woods, you need not frown on me' (fragment of 1836)

Chapter 4: 'Aye, there it is! It wakes to-night' (1841), 5–8

Chapter 5: 'No coward soul is mine' (1846), 9–12

Chapter 6: 'Will the day be bright or cloudy?' (1836), 1–4

Chapter 7: 'A Day Dream' (1844), 45–8

Chapter 8: 'My Comforter' (1844), 11–15

Chapter 9: 'Julian M. and A. G. Rochelle' (1845), 69–72

Chapter 10: 'The Philosopher's conclusion' (1845), 15–18

Chapter 11: 'The linnet in the rocky dells' (1844), 25–8

Chapter 12: 'A. E. and R. C.': 'Heavy hangs the raindrop' (1845), 1–4

Chapter 13: 'Song: King Julius left the south country' (1839), 1–4

Chapter 14: 'Fall, leaves, fall; die, flowers, away' (fragment of 1838)